MW01137129

THOMAS WALKER PAGE is the author of four novels: *The Hephaestus Plague*, *Skyfire*, *The Man Who Would Not Die* and *The Spirit*. *The Hephaestus Plague* was made into the movie *Bug* by William Castle. Page also has extensive work in advertising and technical writing. He resides in Santa Monica.

GRADY HENDRIX is a novelist and screenwriter whose books include *Horrorstör*, *My Best Friend's Exorcism*, and *We Sold Our Souls*. His history of the paperback horror boom of the Seventies and Eighties, *Paperbacks from Hell*, won the Stoker Award. You can stalk him at www.gradyhendrix.com.

Cover: The cover painting is by Tom Hallman, who painted some of the most memorable paperback horror covers of the '80s. A selection of his horror book covers can be seen on his website at hallmanstudio.com.

THE
SPIRIT

THOMAS PAGE

With a new introduction by
GRADY HENDRIX

VALANCOURT BOOKS

The Spirit by Thomas Page
Originally published by Rawson in 1977
First Valancourt Books edition 2019

Published by Valancourt Books, Richmond, Virginia
http://www.valancourtbooks.com

ISBN 978-1-948405-33-1 (*trade paperback*)

Also available as an electronic book.

All Valancourt Books publications are printed on acid free paper
that meets all ANSI standards for archival quality paper.

Cover painting by Tom Hallman
Cover design by M. S. Corley

Set in Dante MT

INTRODUCTION

Starting in 1976 with the novelization of the *Six Million Dollar Man* episode "The Secret of Bigfoot Pass" by Mike Jahn, Bigfoot books were booming. And, Steve Austin aside, everyone wanted to have sex with Sasquatch. It seemed to start with John Cotter and Judith Frankel's "It's all true!" shock memoir, *Nights with Sasquatch* (1977), in which Bigfoot abducts Frankel, a lady scientist, for sex purposes before she's rescued by Cotter. The theme continued in Walter J. Sheldon's *The Beast* (1980) where another lady scientist gets abducted by Bigfoot:

> It can't be, thought Zia. No, really, it can't be. It was plain enough what the beast meant to do . . . she wondered if he would injure her seriously when he penetrated her . . .

J. N. Williamson took Abominable Snowsex to the stars in *Brotherkind* (1982), his tale of a Yeti riding shotgun in a UFO full of Grays who abduct human females for extraterrestrial gangbangs, employing the Abominable Snowman as a finisher. John Tigges may have come late to the party with *Monster* (1995) but he gets right with the program, his abducted human female cowering from the missing link's penis as it "jerked alive and swelled until it stood erect in front of him, massive, six inches around, 14 inches long."

So it's not surprising that the first thing you notice about Thomas Page's bigfoot novel, *The Spirit* (1977), is that absolutely no one has any sex at all with Bigfoot. In fact, we don't even get a single glimpse of his dong. This isn't the only reason—but it's certainly one of them—why *The Spirit* is the best Bigfoot book out there.

Sure, its Bigfoot smells "detestable" and enjoys decapitating people, just like he does in every other Bigfoot book. And there's a Native American character named John Moon on a spirit quest, a sure symptom of stereotype-itis, an affliction plaguing numerous horror paperbacks. But this Native American's analysis of Bigfoot, after seeing him raid a trailer park's garbage, is "Fuck him! He's stupid!"

Convenience store clerks gossip about Bigfoot ("Some folks say it tried to rape a woman down on Route Nine"), John Moon covets a fiberglass bow but isn't allowed to use one because he's told his wooden bow is "more authentic," an anthropologist reels off page after page of ridiculously useless Bigfoot information while claiming the manimal doesn't exist, a ski lodge owner plans to offer his guests a real live "Bigfoot Hunt" with plenty of condoms on hand since the thrill of the chase is bound to make everyone horny, and the survivor of a Bigfoot attack stands amongst the corpses and crushed skulls, marveling, "Bigfoot! . . . Ain't that something?" It's not *Catch-22* but it's the closest thing Bigfoot fiction has to an epic comedy.

Before he wrote *The Spirit*, author Thomas Page worked for the New York City-based advertising agency Diener Hauser Greenthal writing ad slogans for movies like *The Godfather* and *Vanishing Point*. Deciding to cure his phobic fear of spiders, he researched them to death, and the overexposure made him fall in love with insects (yes, spiders are technically arachnids), which gave him the idea for a book. Writing in his spare time, he delivered *The Hephaestus Plague*, about an infestation of beetles that set fires when agitated. It landed him an agent, who sold it to Putnam, who published it in 1973. It moved a few million copies and got turned into a movie by William Castle called *Bug*. Released in 1975 it made a tidy $3 million at the box office.

With that success under his belt, another book on his contract, and his editor asking for a follow-up as soon as possible, Page quit his job at the advertising agency and delivered *The Spirit*. In the Seventies, everyone was looking for Atlantis, hunting for Bigfoot, and searching for UFOs so it made sense that Sasquatch would catch the author's eye, but the book was, as he said in an interview, "the worst book anybody ever wrote." It was about a ski lodge under attack by a band of Bigfeet. He hated it. His editor hated it. His agent hated it. So Page broke his contract, trashed the book, and wondered if quitting his day job had been a mistake.

But the idea kept niggling at him. He flew to his mother's home town in Montana for a family event and while there remembered that his mother, an artist, had told him that out of all the Native American tribes the greatest artisans were the Blackfeet. Page drove to the Blackfeet Heritage Center and Art Gallery in Browning where the sculpture blew him away. And then it hit him: if anyone knew about Bigfoot it would be Indians, and probably tribes located in Montana or in states with lots of forests.

He rented a car and drove through Montana, Oregon, and Washington State, interviewing people from every tribe he met. The result? Zippo. It was only in Montana that he finally stumbled across any aboriginal lore about evil giants, and that was from the Flathead Tribe. He also ran across a lot of Bigfoot hunters. As he says of one, "He was a very rational man, but also batshit crazy." Which sounds like *The Spirit*'s thesis statement about the entire human race.

Page's father, a mining engineer, had a book about the Plateau Indian tribes and while reading it Page got the idea to make a Flathead Indian the central character and to send him after Bigfoot on a spirit quest. After all, the Flatheads were enormously spiritual (they were the only tribe that invited Catholic priests to preach to them) and Page also realized that Bigfoot hunters were on a spirit quest of their own, going out into the world and searching for an elusive creature whose discovery would give their life meaning.

Since there have never been any prehuman hominids found in the Americas, Page figured Bigfoot must have come over the land bridge from Eastern Mongolia, and there was folklore about a giant ape briefly living in Eastern Mongolia. The pieces started falling into place. This version of *The Spirit* came together fast and he took it to Rawson Associates, a small division of Macmillan where a young female editor had responded well to *The Hephaestus Plague*. She fell in love with *The Spirit* and on September 23, 1977 it hit stands in hardcover.

As Page says, "It was a huge flop."

There wasn't enough money for promotion, and even blurbs proclaiming it "By the author of *The Hephaestus Plague*" didn't help. The few trade reviews were snarky. Kirkus called it "grade B sci-why". A successful soap opera writer optioned it for film, but Hollywood didn't come calling. As a friend told Page, "No one is going to be real keen on a movie about a guy in a gorilla suit."

The editor who'd picked up *The Hephaestus Plague* was now at New York Times Books, an imprint associated with the paper, and she bought Page's next book, *Sigmet Active*, and published it in 1978. Inspired by James Lovelock's Gaia Hypothesis that was just starting to gain traction, it proposed that the planet Earth was not only a self-regulating, synergistic system that could essentially be thought of as a single lifeform, but it had antibodies. Connected to lightning, these antibodies existed in the upper atmosphere and when an experimental Navy weapon punches a hole in the ozone layer these intelligent lightning bolts enter our atmosphere and hunt down everyone at the testing range. Page describes it as, "A bunch of people being chased around the world by a living thunderstorm."

It did okay, selling to the United Kingdom and Italy, and recently being optioned for a miniseries, but his next book did great business. Published in 1981 by Seaview Books, then picked up for paperback by New American Library, *The Man Who Would Not Die* hit the ground running. Optioned by Herbert *"Footloose"* Ross, the director paid famed British scriptwriter, Dennis Potter, to turn it into a feature film. At the time, Potter and Ross were collaborating on the American adaptation of Potter's British television hit, *Pennies from Heaven*, but Page described the script as "a dud." He and Ross would keep trying to adapt it for years to come, with no success.

Page had moved to California to research the book, taking a day job writing trailers for Kaleidoscope Films, one of L.A.'s biggest trailer houses. An updated twist on *The Ghost and Mrs. Muir*, the book is a love story about a dead medical equipment salesman who haunts a woman after their one-night stand, his comatose body kept alive by an experimental, computerized hospital bed. Inspired by California's flipped-out psychic claimants and parapsychologists mixing ghost-hunting with quantum physics, it jerks between jargon-heavy scientific lectures, metaphysical rom com, and straight-up angry ghost action.

Line by line, Page's writing delivers brisk dialogue and colorful details, but *The Spirit* is his book that blends action, scientific speculation, humor, and spirituality so smoothly you can't see the seams. But what really elevates it above the rest of the pack (besides the lack of 'Squatch Sex) is its surprisingly moving spiritual side.

Page grew up in North Carolina but moved to New York City because he was "desperate to get out of the South." After he published *The Man Who Would Not Die* and Kaleidoscope went out of business, he moved back to Durham, N.C. where he'd work in public radio and as a country music DJ. He eventually moved back to Santa Monica and on the way he stopped off in Denver, where he lived in a nunnery while hosting a radio tarot show. In Santa Monica he became a technical writer for the Jet Propulsion Laboratory and Raytheon, and developed two massive, thousand-page proposals for Boeing dealing with both ground communication and the mission vehicle for their proposed mission to Mars. He also wrote and shopped around several screenplays. He recently married the poet, Nancy Shiffrin.

To Page, the spirit quest wasn't just for Indians, it was something that all of humanity, no matter what their ethnicity, shared. In *The Spirit*, it's John Moon's quest to find Bigfoot, who will reveal to him his true name. But it's also the book's Bigfoot hunter, Raymond Jason's, quest to bag Bigfoot because claiming the ultimate hunting trophy will finally, he hopes, give him peace. It's the mythic quest for the golden fleece, the searching spirit of the Sixties and Seventies, pseudoscientists looking for the God Particle, for Lost Atlantis, for UFOs, for Sasquatch, all of us wandering in the dark woods, both literal and figurative, looking for our holy grail, our true name, our place in the world where we finally belong.

"I met plenty of Bigfoot hunters while writing *The Spirit*," Page says. "They're on a spirit quest. In fact, anyone in the world who has any kind of faith in anything is on one. You go out into the world to find out who you are. Bigfoot hunters, Indians, everyone, we're enraptured by this mystery of something in the woods, and we spend years looking for it. It's something baked into the human soul and it's very powerful, and kind of beautiful."

GRADY HENDRIX

THE
SPIRIT

OBSESSION

On a late-spring afternoon in the Mission Range mountains of Montana, a solitary Indian trudged up a grassy slope to a rocky pocket of dark boulders that overlooked the valley sloping away below. In the waving bear grass far below he saw a spirit sidewinding through the stems. The spirit was a snake made of air, and it writhed up the slope to where he stood. Just before it reached him, the Indian closed his eyes. Wind touched his straight black hair and rustled the flap of the leather sack tied to his waist.

The Indian lay down among the rocks, his face turned to the sky. Only his eyes moved. It had been seventy years since the Plains Indians sent their young to sacred places such as this rock aerie for fasting and self-torture. The Indian had come up here to learn his name. This name would be given him by a spirit, a sort of guardian angel, who would leave a talisman. If the spirit were a bird, it would leave a feather, which he would tuck into the fringed leather medicine bundle tied to his waist. If it were a bear, it would leave a claw. In the old days humans and animals were the same. They talked freely to each other and helped in times of battle and famine. Sometimes the spirit was a human, the ghost of an ancestor or a great chief.

And sometimes the spirit never came. The Indian would not learn his name and he would wither away and die young, bereft of the taproot of his existence.

On the second day, thirst became a constant discomfort for the Indian. There was a puddle of muddy water by his head.

He did not drink. In his medicine bundle was some corn fried in brown sugar. He did not eat. The nearness of food and water was mental torture, which was good. Only through suffering would he gain a vision. Pain would scrape away the walls of mortality that kept him from his spirit.

The medicine bundle belonged to his dead grandfather, who had left it for him. The old man had come up here many years before and stayed three days. On the third day a man had stepped out of a lodge-pole pine tree and the two of them had a long conversation about crops, weather, and the bad game of that year. The ghost had given him a piece of wood, telling him he should be a carpenter. The Indian's grandfather worked with wood for the rest of his life in a pleasant, moderately successful way, building his own home and raising his family. The Indian was the only one left of that family now. A fire had swept the house one night, and he was shifted to the Catholic mission school. The Black Robes had said their medicine was more powerful than his grandfather's. Just to be safe, he had slipped a crucifix into the medicine bundle, along with his grandfather's clay pipe, the piece of wood, and the cartridge with which he had killed his first deer.

The Indian had tried for weeks to remember his grandfather. His memory had been shattered by certain events the previous year, events which doctors in white robes in an Army hospital had tried to neutralize. The events themselves lived under his mind as dreams. Down there somewhere was his grandfather, too, and the stories he had told the boy during long winter afternoons.

Under the twin attacks of discomfort and sun, the Indian tried as he had tried so many times to put his memory chains together. But they lay apart, separated by bloody gaps. Here he saw a piece of hospital sheet, there a fragment of a troop carrier. And further over there was his grandfather sitting before an orange fire, rocking in his chair and talking to him. He was trying to say something, but no words came out of his mouth.

The sun climbed higher.

The Indian wondered if he was out of his own time. Perhaps the spirits had been chased away by automobiles and machinery. But he did not really believe that. He knew they lived. He knew they had lived long before the white man came into the land. They had lived long before that man was nailed to a cross. They still lived.

On the third day, flies circled the Indian's head, attracted by the possibility of death. The Indian did not swat them. He had been drenched by a passing thunderstorm, and now it was a race between enlightenment and death by exhaustion. His mouth had dried and his tongue was swelling with thirst. The Montana valley folded upon itself and spun around. He was in a perpetual daze, in which time had slowed down and he was no longer bound to reality. His body had begun to assume the shape of the ground on which he lay. A hornet landed on his exposed skin and sank its stinger in without acknowledging him. Doomed by the loss of its single weapon, the hornet staggered back into flight.

The Indian wondered if his own existence were as futile as the hornet's. At the instant of defiance, it had killed itself.

In the woods above he heard the whistle of a marmot. He waited for it to come and speak to him. He waited as the sun slid over the sky and darkened the valley. The Indian knew he would not see it come up again unless his spirit came. He was too weak to wave at the flies now.

A velvet shroud settled over his eyes, blocking the sky. He thought about the sun. He cried for it. But all he saw was the hot orange glow through his eyelids. The sun's heat was heavy, like earth being piled on top of him. Soon the Indian was unaware of even that.

Something seemed to crackle in the air over his chest. The Indian awoke to find it was night. Standing in the grass below the boulders was a small, mottled mongrel dog with a face like a cat's and patches of skin showing through its tattered coat.

The Indian and the dog regarded each other with alert, unfrightened eyes. The marmot sounded again in the trees. The dog glanced toward the sound.

The dog said, Follow me.

With the aid of his rifle, the Indian unhinged his body section by section and painfully stood upright. He leaned on the gun. Corn spilled from his medicine bundle. The flap was open. The dog must have been sniffing at it. Thoughtlessly the Indian raised corn to his lips.

Don't eat, said the dog. Your spirit is waiting.

The animal scampered up to the edge of the woods and paused until the Indian caught up. The trees closed around him like a warm coat. The woods were silent. All of the animals were gone except for the marmot, which whistled again, summoning the dog. The Indian tottered through the trees after it.

Seated on a log in a clearing bounded by Douglas firs was a man, his back to the Indian. He was digging with large, oddly shaped hands at a pile of rocks and stacking them, one on top of another, in a pyramid. The Indian saw a field mouse run from under one of the rocks. The man grabbed it and popped it into his mouth.

The dog barked at the man.

The man grabbed a rock in each hand. He stood up and faced the Indian. He was at least seven feet tall. He wore no clothes. A thick coat of black fur covered him from head to ankle and curtained his face. His chest was fat and massive, his legs were short, and he had almost no neck. Because of the gloom, the Indian could not see the man's face clearly.

He was not a man. Not really. Such men had never lived. He was somewhere between man and beast. He was a spirit.

The Indian put his rifle against a tree.

The spirit set down his rocks.

The Indian waited for his name.

The spirit did not speak it. Instead, he blended into the slanted grays and blacks of the woods, heading toward the northern peaks and leaving the Indian alone with the dog.

The dog said, He wants you to follow him.

The Indian had no family, no job, no place to go. Nobody would miss him. He checked his clothes. He wore a tough Army jacket and moccasins. His pants were heavy corduroy, and there was a scarf around his neck. He dug out a handful of corn and hungrily ate it. The pain in his wracked body lessened; his joints filled with rigidity and strength that brought color to his face.

"I will come," he said.

I

The Central States Wildlife Fund was a Kansas-based tax haven supported by numerous businessmen who claim to be conservationists. For four years straight they had sent out expeditions to Canada to check out the caribou and moose herds. These expeditions consisted of two men from Kansas City, George Nicolson and Roy Curtis, who geared up in Calgary with a Land Rover and supplies, tranquilizer guns, directional-antennae devices, and a helicopter. Dennis Hill was the owner and pilot of this helicopter.

This year things were different. A herd of musk oxen had been spotted far south of their Arctic habitat, and Nicolson and Curtis wanted to tag a couple of them to see where they would go. In addition, there was a new member of the group, an edgy forty-three-year-old man named Raymond Jason. Jason was a tall, powerfully built man, who demonstrated his strength in a Calgary bar by bending a quarter between his thumb and first two fingers. He unconsciously practiced isometric exercises over his entire body. His robustness was a product of will, he said, necessary for camping weeks on end. He was a wealthy man who had worked hard for his money. Too hard, in Hill's opinion.

Hill knew why Nicolson and Curtis came on these trips. Nicolson was a sometime big-game hunter and fisherman. Roy Curtis was a veterinarian.

Raymond Jason packaged and sold pet food. For the life of him, Dennis Hill could not understand why Raymond Jason came to Canada, or why he made him so nervous.

Raymond Jason stroked the stubble of his new beard and peered out the plexiglass bubble of the helicopter at the lakes far below. Between them were craggy forested hills, a part of the wrinkled, tormented West Canadian Rockies. As the copter turned, fire from the sun sheeted off the silver surfaces.

This was one of the comparatively flat areas of the Rockies, and Hill's main concern was that Jason not direct him to some goddamned peaks or something before they ran out of fuel.

"Go on up a little higher!" cried Jason. "I think the hills are blocking the signal." Jason adjusted a tuner on the radio before him. The Land Rover, with Nicolson and Curtis in it, was down there somewhere in that lacework of streams, concealed under the timbers that whiskered the heaving land.

The speaker crackled, and Hill answered. It was Nicolson with his complaining voice. "Hill, it's almost eight o'clock. Maybe we should think about camping. What does Jason think?"

In spite of this being his first trip, Jason had somehow taken over the group. Hill was amazed at how Nicolson deferred to him. It was Jason who darted the musk ox leader with a perfect shot from the helicopter, and Jason who guessed correctly where the animals were heading. Things had gone fine until the day before yesterday, when the leader cut off from the herd and headed for the lakes. Around his neck was a collar with a beacon that transmitted signals to both Land Rover and helicopter. They had not heard a peep from it until this morning. Jason had seen the huge, brown, shaggy animal for a split second under the tree cover, running as fast as it could. Now it was gone again.

"Fine with me," said Jason into the mike. "Find a place close to the woods where we can land the copter. We'll stay up for"—Jason checked his watch—"another half-hour. I really want to find out why the thing's behaving like this. Can you see us?"

"Yes, you're about two miles southwest."

They were down in that delta edged with woods. With binoculars Jason could probably see the Land Rover with its whiplash antennae.

Hill said, "You know, you never can tell how an animal will react to a tranquilizer. It's a drug, and look what drugs do to people."

"I don't think it's that," said Jason, flexing his arms. "I think it's frightened."

"By what?"

"Maybe the helicopter." Jason adjusted his sunglasses and leaned close to the bubble. After a moment he pointed north, toward a sandy plain. Hill wheeled the copter around. As they rose, the square silver box with the aerial mounted on it emitted a small squeal, as if a mouse were trapped inside.

Hill halted the copter in midair and faced it in various directions, trying to pinpoint the source. It was coming from the sandy plain. "We got the signal," Jason said into the radio. "I figure it's about seven miles south of you. It's in this clear area."

As the copter moved, the steady squeal became a whine, then began receding again. Jason leaned out, looking down at the speckled brown ground. Hill juggled the controls until the beacon peaked. The musk ox should be right under them.

Jason searched the ground with his binoculars. A large brown boulder resolved itself into the carcass of the animal, with an aerial gleaming in the late sun. "It's dead, Hill."

"How?"

Jason sat back in his seat, the binoculars hanging from his neck. "Well, among other things, its head is gone."

"*What!*"

"That's right. The aerial is lying on the ground."

Jason jumped from the copter while it was still a few feet off the ground, and ducked under the rotating blades. When Hill joined him he was kneeling in the soil, examining the body.

The musk ox's bulk had been diminished to an empty sack of fur-covered skin and bones. Bullet holes punctured its body, and its internal organs had been neatly eviscerated.

"That's as neat a job of butchering as I've ever seen," mused Jason. "How much do you figure this thing weighs?"

"Oh hell, a thousand pounds, I guess. Most of it's the head and bones. And blood. Now . . ." He looked dazedly over the remains. "I guess he's missing about a hundred pounds of meat."

"So I was right. It was being stalked. That's why it was frightened."

"For two *days?*"

"Yup."

Hill could not conceive of any animal that would frighten a musk ox. Next to a polar bear, it was the worst-tempered and most dangerous animal in the north. Its head was thick, massive bone fortifying short curved horns; its body was coated with thick fur tough enough to keep out the coldest wind and the longest claws. Hill could easily imagine a musk ox winning a battle against a bear, and no animal could have done such a neat butchering job. And while it would run from an armed man, it certainly would not do so for two days. In fact, the beast was inclined to take its chances and trample down any man close enough to shoot it, regardless of the risk.

"Why don't we look for prints?" Jason suggested. "I'd like to see who this lumberjack is."

Hill expected to find the smooth moccasin prints of an Indian band, maybe even the sealskin indentations of an Eskimo pursuing the animal. He could even envision the nailed boots of white men, but why they would go after a musk ox was beyond him. Maybe they wanted the head for a fireplace.

They found only one print, stamped onto the gravelly plain close to the woods like a slashing signature. It was human. More incredible, it was barefoot. Most incredible of all, Jason's tape measured it out as fourteen inches long and seven wide.

Hill could not bring himself to say the word, so Jason did it, with a satisfied smile. "Bigfoot."

Nicolson unhappily removed his glasses and tapped them in his hand. His friend, Curtis, photographed the print with various objects—a hatchet, the tape measure, his own foot—set next to it for scale. Nicolson said, "Jason, I know we don't have any plaster, but isn't there some way we can make a cast?"

"No," said Jason. "Nothing. Either we let it erode and forget it or we bring the real thing back. A real, live, tranquilized Bigfoot. Otherwise, no one will believe us."

Nicolson flinched at the word. Bigfoot was the Abominable Snowman of the Americas, the legendary ape who dwelled deep in the forests of the Northwest. His existence, so far as scientists were concerned, was about as likely as that of leprechauns.

Curtis closed his camera and wiped dirt from his hands before putting it in its case. "He's a long way from his stomping ground. We're a good thousand miles from the coast."

"And outside of baboons and man, I never heard of any gorillas eating meat," Nicolson added.

"I expect he eats everything," said Jason. "He'd be an omnivore. By this print he must weigh close to eight hundred pounds. You're right, though, Curtis. Even for an omnivore, it's pretty slim pickings around here. And apes don't hibernate like bears."

"Maybe he's migrating," said Hill, who should have known better.

"He wouldn't migrate north," Nicolson snorted. "He'd go south."

"And gorillas don't carry rifles," Hill chortled.

"Oh, that's easy enough," said Jason. "Some hunter brought down the ox and the Bigfoot stripped what was left later."

The pale sun was sinking, thickening the trees into luxurious blackness and draining warmth from the air. Nights were startlingly chilly up here, even in May.

"We'll camp here tonight and get after more prints in the morning," said Jason. "He might still be around, since he ate so much. I don't suppose the Wildlife Fund would object to changing our mission."

This was directed at Roy Curtis, who was the group's treasurer. "We're the only ones that have anything to do with the Fund, so I don't know why not."

"I don't like to sound like a great white hunter," said Nicolson. "But I'm wondering if we should load our guns with real bullets."

"What on earth for!" Curtis replied.

"He's a meat eater, isn't he? That's not your normal ape."

That stopped Curtis. "Maybe we can just load one of the guns."

"No," said Jason, knowing his word would be final. "We don't want to kill it. There's absolutely no report of this thing being dangerous to anybody. If we load a rifle we'll use it. No," he repeated with final indissoluble certainty. "We can keep watches if that will make you feel better."

"Yes," said Nicolson, holding his rifle. "It would."

They pitched camp under the trees, close by a gurgling stream. Curtis and Nicolson played three quick backgammon games on a portable board, as they had done nearly every night since meeting twelve years before in Kansas. Jason offered to take the first watch. He sat with his back against a tree, a little apart from the other three men, with his blanket over his legs and rifle across his lap.

By midnight Hill, Curtis, and Nicolson were lumps of nylon curled around the glowing campfire embers, which pulsed whenever a breeze crossed them. Except for a marmot whose whistle broke the block of quiet that settled over the forest, Raymond Jason might have been alone at the end of the world.

He clasped his hands together and tightened all the muscles of his arms. Wrists, forearms, biceps. A pleasurable tension in the shoulders. Then he relaxed and felt blood pump through the strained tissues.

Raymond Jason had spent the better part of his life being successful. Success was money, security, and physical comfort. He had waited until his first million, accumulated by the age of thirty-five, to cash in on physical comfort. He got married. He bought a house and several cars. Having done all that, he discovered something was wrong with him.

This thing that was wrong had driven him to a psychia-

23

trist, who had told him a human being is just a log of the past. Jason considered that, then rejected it. "Doc, I've got everything I want. I had a perfectly normal childhood and everything, you said it yourself. By any sensible standards I should be as happy as a clam, but I'm putting on weight, I get depressed, and my temper's getting worse when it should be getting better."

Jason had a vicious temper, which had been an asset in his business career. He was a man with a short fuse and a long memory, whose reserves of sheer anger had crashed him through all obstacles, commercial, personal, and social. This temper was damaging his marriage.

"Human beings are slates upon which experience writes the only words," said the psychiatrist. Then after a moment he said, "Do you believe in God, Mr. Jason?"

"No."

"*God* is one of the words on most humans' slates. *Mystery.* I hesitate to say *mysticism.* It is an essential part of life. It is a center, a magnetic core as necessary to a human as sex."

Being a supremely rational man, Jason simply did not understand what the psychiatrist was talking about.

"Do you know what material success is, Mr. Jason? It is an earthly substitute for going to heaven. It is a nonexistent place where rich people live cushioned by money, with no cares or worries forever. When you made your first million, you died in a way. Only heaven isn't where you went. Heaven does not necessarily come after success."

Jason was not paying a shrink forty dollars an hour for a religious lecture. He found himself getting mad.

"You are angry because you are fundamentally frustrated, Mr. Jason. You are searching for something to devote yourself to, something to lose yourself in. A purpose to your life. More money probably isn't the answer."

"You mean find a religion," Jason asked through clenched teeth.

"You are a hungry man, Mr. Jason. Hungry for something irrational. If this were the Middle Ages, yes, you'd be hungry for God. But this is the twentieth century, so let's say you're looking for something ... inexplicable. Something to challenge you. Some—" which was as far as the psychiatrist got, because Jason had lost his temper and thrown an ashtray at him.

Shortly after that, his marriage broke up. He had struck his wife with his fist after an argument about vacations. He threw his fiercest energies into dozens of projects, including the Wildlife Fund. He decided to go to Canada and look for oxen. His business expertise and a sense of organization had slipped control of the expedition into his hands, and he welcomed it.

A hand touched his shoulder. He jumped in shock, clutching his rifle. Hill's hand clamped over his mouth.

"Listen," whispered Hill.

Jason was embarrassed at being such a lousy watchman. All three men had awakened and dressed while his mind drifted.

Nicolson slid his rifle from its nylon sheath. From the Land Rover, parked on the gravelly plain, came the clink of metal. Something was poking about the tailgate.

"It's probably just a woodchuck," said Hill with a delighted smile. "But let's pretend it isn't."

Jason found some antenna wire in the signal package. He cut two lengths and tied flashlights to Curtis's and Nicolson's rifle barrels. "You and Nicolson dig in at the river about fifty yards apart," he whispered harshly. "Me and Hill will go for him at the Land Rover. If he starts running, we'll drive him between you. And be quiet!" he said as they crashed excitedly into the trees like Boy Scouts on a treasure hunt.

He turned to Hill. "You take the light. I'll take the rifle."

"Aye aye, sir."

"Do you have a better idea?"

Hill did not have a better idea. Jason was a better shot than he was.

The river was actually more of a creek. It rose and fell seasonally, leaving steeply carved banks tangled with tree roots. Nicolson and Curtis slipped down the bank. Nicolson wiped perspiration from his glasses. He glanced at Curtis. "You look like Frank Buck."

"Are you sure you don't mean Pearl Buck?" Curtis shot back.

"Better keep your voice down."

Curtis lit his pipe and settled onto the ground. "What for? Haven't you ever been on a snipe hunt before?"

"This isn't a snipe hunt," retorted Nicolson. Then added, "Is it?"

"Oh, of course it is. Jason and Hill are laughing their rocks off now. I bet Jason's been planning this ever since Calgary. Nice to know he has a sense of humor." Curtis drew on his pipe. "Just a game, my boy, just a game. I like games. I think hacking up that musk ox was going a bit too far, but you have to be convincing. What I'm waiting for is Jason running through the woods and growling. Maybe he'll swing from a tree." Curtis laughed dryly. "What do we do if he swings from a tree?"

Nicolson shrugged and pointed his rifle to a bend in the river. "Well, I'll make my way to the other side of that."

"Take your time," said Curtis, puffing his pipe.

The rush of the river drowned the sound of Nicolson's steps as he picked his way upriver. He flashed his light over the tortured ground, then found a cut in the river bank, between two birches, with a fairly clear field of fire.

He was settling down when his light crossed a birch from which a huge crescent of bark had been torn loose.

He found the fragments on the ground. The inner layers had been scraped away by huge teeth that left gouges in the wood.

This was too much for a joke. Nicolson was beginning to believe the Bigfoot idea. He wondered if he ought to tell Curtis, and decided not to. Jason was obviously right; the thing was primarily a vegetarian that forced itself to eat meat. Why else would it have gone to all that trouble with the tree?

The helicopter and Land Rover were parked together in the knee-high meadow grass. It was a moonless but not starless night. Jason and Hill advanced a little way out of the forest and lay down in the grass. Jason adjusted his sight and pointed his rifle toward the vehicles.

As his night vision cleared, Jason saw what appeared to be a large tumor on the side of the Land Rover. The tumor resolved itself into a person, whose head projected a foot above the roof.

Jason's throat felt dry. He heard a sharp intake of breath from Dennis Hill. Jason's head was just about level with the roof, and he was six foot one. That meant their visitor was at least seven feet tall. Jason strained his eyes until tears formed, trying to see details. It was fifty feet away.

"Christ almighty," breathed Hill. *"Look* at it!"

"I'm looking, I'm looking."

The intruder was roughly pear-shaped, with long cranelike arms reaching down to its calves. The shoulders sloped downward. Something was not quite right about its head. The hair was looser than Jason would have expected, and longer, too, almost shoulder-length.

Jason pushed the rifle to his shoulder and quietly cocked it. He sighted down the barrel, centering the notch on the beast's chest. A droplet of sweat stung his eye. He wiped it and aimed again.

The giant stepped back from the Land Rover and became very still. The head jerked. Then the wind bore down a detestable smell of sweat and excrement.

It knows we're here, Jason thought.

"Will you shoot, dammit?" snarled Hill.

The giant whistled. Like a marmot, Jason realized in astonishment.

Hill jumped to his feet. Jason squeezed the trigger. The flash split the night, and the explosion continued in the form of a snarling hound that burst out of the trees and clamped its fangs around Jason's arm. He saw the dart splash over the helicopter.

Jason shook the frenzied animal to the ground, and it promptly attacked Hill, giving Jason time to trigger off two more darts, but the giant was heading for the woods in a humped, loping stride that swallowed great chunks of ground. The dog turned back to Jason, jumping with glowing eyes and yellowed, saliva-ribboned fangs for his throat.

Jason shouted while beating off the animal, "Nicolson, it's headed for you!"

Hill smashed his light against the dog's head. It dropped to the ground, a small mutt with a Doberman's fury. The agile little body tore off toward the woods as Jason fired tranquilizer bursts that splashed on the ground around it.

To Curtis it sounded as if a tank battle had erupted into the field and spilled full-tilt into the timbers. It was the snarling of the dog that got him to his feet, pipe dropping from his mouth. It was headed for the upriver bend, to the thicket of broken branches where his friend Nicolson waited. Jason and Hill were shouting, in full pursuit.

Curtis cocked his rifle and switched on his flashlight. "George?" he cried.

A gunshot sounded from the bed. It was followed by a

short, choked-off scream, then the wild, turbulent thrashing of water fading upriver.

Curtis called out, "George?" again, and again got silence for an answer. He swept the woods with his light. Probably George had turned his ankle and cried out.

Curtis walked toward the river bend. He heard Jason and Hill's voices and he was relieved. Nicolson was all right; they wouldn't be talking so loudly if he were not. Tragedy always silences people.

By chance he flashed his light into the river. It crossed a whitish object bobbing like a melon around the bend. Dead eyes looked at Curtis from under strands of wet plastered hair. His friend Nicolson's head looked at him upside down.

Shattered into complete psychic numbness, Curtis sat heavily on the rocks, keeping his light on the grisly object until it disappeared downstream.

"Curtis!"

Jason slapped him hard a second time. Curtis weakly waved away the next blow.

"Easy on him, Jason," murmured Hill.

Jason and Hill wrestled Curtis to his feet, where he adjusted his glasses and lurched forward as if about to walk into the water.

"He's coming round," said Jason. "Let's get him up to the camp."

They drag-walked him to the dead fire and seated him on a bedroll. Jason gathered the rifles and levered out the tranquilizer darts, replacing them with bullets. He shoved one into Hill's hands. "Go start up the helicopter," he said.

Confused by the headless form of Nicolson, which refused to leave his mind, Hill said, "What for?"

"The copter has spotlights! We've got to catch that thing before he gets too far away. I'll stay on the ground. We can back each other up." Jason tore apart the packs, searching for walkie-talkies. He tossed one to Hill and kept the other for himself. "Understand? We're going to kill that thing! Understand?" he shouted into the pilot's face, as though he took Nicolson's death personally.

Curtis looked numbly from the rifle Jason had dropped into his lap to the trees. "George . . ." he began in an incoherent mutter.

"That's right, Curtis!" cried Jason. "For George. That thing's a man-killer, and we're going to get him. On your feet!"

The dog's distant mournful howl threaded through the sentinel trees, freezing them into a marbled tableau of watchfulness.

"Where'd that dog come from?" whispered Hill.

"Scavenger. He eats what the ape doesn't. They're moving south. If the copter scares the dog, I can follow the barking."

"No!" said Curtis, galvanized by the howl to full furious possession of himself. "Not south. He went up the river. I heard him! Follow the river!"

Jason did not look at Nicolson's body as he splashed up the river. He forced himself to forget that it had been his decision not to arm themselves with bullets.

His light picked up a print under three inches of water, pressed deep into the silt of the river bottom. The current was eroding it. The ape was running through water to cover his tracks.

Just ahead of him the copter's light frosted the trees. Hill flew so close to treetop level that his rotor downwash bowed the tips and showered pine needles, twigs, and chunks of bark to the ground, some of which lodged in Jason's collar. The splintered shadows cast by the spotlights moved with the copter's passage. Branches became clutching hands that reached for Jason's clothes.

He distanced himself from the river so the racketing roar of the machine did not fill his ears. He heard the dog barking in the trees. They had left the water for dry land. Jason shouted into the walkie-talkie, "Hill? Go on ahead about half a mile and swing back this way. Try herding them toward me."

"Will do."

The copter gained altitude; then the motor changed to a hum a mile or so ahead as it began swinging in wide arcs from left to right. Jason leaned against a fir and listened hard. The dog's howling had stopped. Without it Jason was not sure which direction they moved.

They quartered the woods for a careful half-hour, Jason moving slowly through the brush. *We've lost them.* He despaired and pounded his fist against bark. They had changed direction all right. They were headed for deeper woods.

In the copter, Hill could hardly recognize the gun nut with brush-fire eyes as Roy Curtis, the shy, short man too afraid of heights to venture from the Land Rover. Curtis leaned halfway out of the bubble, one hand gripping the rubber rail, the other pointing the cocked rifle downward.

"Get inside!" Hill cried over the roar of the rotors. Curtis answered with a laser glare from his bloodshot eyes, comically distended by thick glasses. He thought only of his friend, Nicolson.

Ground zero was the treetop level. Hill danced the controls so close that pine tips grazed the belly. He watched his landing lights skim the bristly branches.

Curtis screamed and thumped the bubble. He jabbed the gun at the ground. "Back!" he shouted. "Back!"

Hill backed the copter up. Down below was the dog, jumping up and down at the copter in a space between the trees. Curtis fired bullets which spurted pine needles up around the animal. Something stepped out of the trees but was driven back by an explosion of bark next to its hairy arm.

Hill rose a few feet to spread the light wider. "Jason, Curtis is shooting at it. Get your ass down here!"

Jason ran through the woods, ignoring the roots tearing at his feet and the branches that slashed across his face. The copter swayed in midair, seemingly supported by the hard-edged beams of the landing lights. He heard gunfire above the motor. The dog was barking again. By coming up from the rear, he would have both in his sights within minutes.

One of Hill's shots echoed from the east. Now that was peculiar. Jason did not remember any cliffs or mountains that way. After a moment he heard the echo again.

Curtis shouted, "I saw it! There's something wrong with its head."

"What?" bellowed Hill, shifting the engine pitch.

"I said there's something wrong with—" The motor drowned out Curtis's words. He leaned out farther and watched for it.

Something hit the rear stabilizer with a violence that sent a shudder through the fuselage. The stick jerked out of Hill's hand, and the foot controls came up of their own accord.

Trees whirled and tilted below as if they were on a carousel dislodged from its axis. He had lost control of the rear rotor, and without that a copter will rotate in the direction of its rotor spin with an accelerating force that whirls the pilot into unconsciousness. Hill gathered the flailing controls and tried to still them. He managed to keep the belly flat as the trees rushed up to embrace them.

Just before the crash he realized that Curtis had been

flung out of the bubble like a dust mote flicked from a window ledge.

The first shock threw him against the dashboard. Then came the endless bumpy, reverberating fall in a shower of wood, branches whipped to pieces by the rotors. Bough after bough, layer after layer as bark tumbled down on top of the machine.

What was left of the copter swayed ten feet above the ground. Benumbed at still being alive, Hill grasped his rifle, unhooked the seat belt, and dropped the remaining distance to his feet.

Jason had watched the crash from an outcropping of boulder in a clearing. First came a metallic snap, then the screeching rhythmic clatter of something caught in the rear blades. He screamed into the walkie-talkie, but knew Hill had his hands too full to speak.

The copter spiraled down to the trees half a mile away and disappeared when the lights went out. Then he heard it hit with a swishing crackle, as if a huge bird were settling into its nest. The crash seemed to go on forever before dribbling off in a rush of falling branches.

"Hill? Hill?" he said tensely into the walkie-talkie.

Horror seeped through Jason at the howl of canine triumph rising from the woods. It was running for the wreck, well ahead of him. The horror propelled Jason as he ran off the rocks into the trees again. It rose from his legs to form an ache in his chest where his breath tore out in deep gasps. The dog and his master would get to the copter before him, and, failing the sudden appearance of wings on his shoulders, there was absolutely nothing Jason could do about it.

Hill was on his hands and knees, trying to clear his head. Blood dripped to the ground from a gash in his scalp.

When he heard the dog coming, he poked around the bush for his rifle.

The ground was covered by chunks of clumsily chopped pine. Gasoline dripped in acrid streams from the copter into the springy loam. Hill was in a hollow lipped on all sides by trees.

The walkie-talkie was gone. No matter. He didn't need help for this one. He had a good rifle and a steady hand. Even better, he had a good position, with a maximum range of fifteen feet on all sides. He had drilled beer cans with a pistol at that range without even aiming.

With a final woof, the dog sprang over the hollow edge and growled at him between pants. Its tongue lolled over its jaws. Hill shot at it, just missing, and the dog's courage vanished. It scrambled out of the hollow again.

Hill waited for the larger shadow to appear, his rifle muzzle probing along the edge of the hollow.

With a screech of aluminum and crunch of foliage, the helicopter was pulled out of the trees behind him. Hill whirled around. He got off one shot as the rock caught him squarely in the forehead. His last thought was a hope that Jason would take the shot as a warning.

Jason was fast approaching the wreck when the shot brought him to a full stop. "Hill? Curtis?" he said tensely into the walkie-talkie.

The dog was whining. Jason heard the loam being thrashed around. The copter was only twenty yards ahead of him, but he was in a quandary. That single shot could have killed the thing. Hill was an experienced hunter who knew better than to waste ammunition. Nevertheless, wouldn't he have emptied his rifle into it?

Jason slipped under the thick protective foliage of a spruce. Quietly, so as not to crush any needles, he lay full length over the roots and inched outward until the drooping needles of the tree scratched his neck. He flexed the muscles of his body until the blood sang under his skin.

The dog emerged from a line of trees ahead, its nose buried in the brush, searching out a new, possibly threatening scent. There was no sign of Hill or Curtis anywhere.

Jason waited for the other creature, his front sight fixed squarely on the dog, which made irritated little yips. Then the spruce foliage was swept away like a curtain opening and a foot kicked the rifle out of his hands. Another kick, in the ribs, rolled Jason over onto his back.

In the second before the lazily swinging rifle butt connected with his head, Jason impacted every detail of the stranger into his memory. Above a thin, dirty, corduroy-trousered leg and a torn Army jacket was an expressionless Indian face with onyx eyes. A leather sack was tied to his waist beside a bowie knife in a handmade sheath. His clothes were torn by thousands of encounters with thorns, and his moccasins were unraveling at the seams. He was young, not past thirty, with black hair as thick as coiled cables tied in a knot in back.

Even after the rifle butt burst the night into falling galaxies, a small part of Jason's mind scuttled to a quiet haven, bearing that Indian with it. *I'll remember you,* Jason thought, *I'll remember you.*

The dog tore off a mouthful of the white man's jacket. The Indian drove it off with his rifle. Having just saved his spirit from some kind of disaster by shooting down the helicopter, he did not want the dog interfering.

He peered at the white man's motionless form. This could be a test sent by the gods. If so, the body would shimmer into nothingness as soon as he turned away.

He stirred the hand with his rifle barrel. It was limp. He had hit him solidly with the rifle. Unless the white man was exceptionally hard-headed, the Indian was sure he was dead. If he were real, that is. A bullet was the only way to be sure. The Indian stepped back, cocking his rifle. He pointed it at Jason's neck.

The giant loomed up between the trees and halted some distance away. The Indian's emotions boiled to a pitch of agonized expectancy. He had not seen it since the first night. Not this closely. Surely he would get his name now. Now . . . now . . .

Hands clenching and unclenching, the giant waited. Waves of fetidness poured forth from his body. The Indian's senses had been honed to a steely edge by weeks of living in the woods, but no eyesight except Owl's could discern the features of a spirit in woods this deep. His great shovel feet crushed the wood in his path.

Then, with a hurricane of thrashing branches, the giant slipped sideways between two spruces. The Indian felt the faintest tremor of his passing. Finally the disturbed boughs ceased shaking.

The Indian took a handful of corn from his medicine bundle and chewed it. "What did I do this time?" His voice was calm.

The dog's whimper changed to a growl as its yellow eyes went to the rifle butt. Understanding was a flashbulb that lit up the Indian's mind.

"He's afraid of guns!"

He set the rifle against a tree. The dog seated itself and wagged its tail. The Indian was amazed. It really was a hell of time to tell him that. "He's a spirit. Guns can't hurt spirits. Can they?" The Indian had gotten into the habit of talking to himself.

Now he recalled that back in the Mission Range the spirit had set down his rock after the Indian had laid the rifle against a tree. The dog spoke the truth. The spirit feared guns.

To realize after all this time that his rifle had kept his

spirit from him was a frustration that would have driven a less stable man to madness. After all, the Indian had been shooting meat for weeks. He sent the dog with portions of his kill to the spirit as offerings. Sometimes the spirit did his own hunting for hours on end before braining his prey with a rock and leaving a headless carcass behind for the dog and Indian. It was the Indian who had wounded that musk ox after a two-day stalk, and the spirit who had walked off with the lion's share.

He scratched the dog's ears. "We live and learn, eh." A small victory had been won. A barrier between himself and his spirit had been lifted. Small victories were treasured by the Indian, and this one pleased him so much that he lost interest in whether the white man was real or an apparition.

The Indian emptied his pockets of bullets, dispersing them into the grass. He swung the rifle into the middle of the river where its splash was swallowed by foam. Then he crouched over the black, running water. He stabbed his hand deep into the icy water and emerged with a wet, flopping trout, which he killed with a blow against a rock. He pressed the fish into the dog's mouth.

"Take this to him!"

The dog ran away, bearing the fish in its jaws. The Indian waited, his heart thudding, for the animal's return.

What would his grandfather have done in such a situation? The Indian's memory was treacherous; he could not retrieve things he wanted from it until too late. Those drugs the doctors had given him, the treatments, the sedatives, they had cured him up to a point but had left his memory dark. He could not remember his grandfather's words. His grandfather had told him about Chinook the warm wind, the Blue Jay feast in the spring, and endless tales about Coyote, the laughing god who taught humans

how to build tipis and use medicinal herbs. His grandfather had told him over and over about the night he went to
the sacred ridge for his own spirit, who had been a human.
The ghost had been his grandfather's protector all his life.
He had helped him through epidemics of flu and bitter-
cold winters. He had been with the old man during the
difficult transition to death, chatting with him, calming
him, cheering him up, reassuring him about what was to
come.

Of all the gifts a spirit bestowed, friendship and protec-
tion were the most valuable. His grandfather had never
been lonely, never been lost, never been fearful about the
world because of the closeness of his spirit. The Indian
enjoyed thinking about his grandfather. He wished his
memories were not so broken.

Not so enjoyable was the single, isolated memory of an
Army doctor sitting before a sunlit window, hair waving in
the draft of a small fan. "You are subject to hallucinations,"
the doctor had said.

The dog returned without the fish, cheerful but yawn-
ing. That meant the spirit was going to sleep soon. Sometimes he slept for a full day. The Indian would not dream
of intruding on the spirit at these periods. It would have
been scandalously disrespectful. When the sleep was over,
the dog would awaken the Indian with small wet licks on
the ear and tell him it was time to resume the journey.

"I'll have to make a bow and arrow," the Indian mused
to the dog. He could get ash wood from anywhere around
and carve the arrows at leisure. The bowstring was
another thing. He had nothing on his person that would
suffice. What was needed was dried gut, as his grandfather
had used.

The musk ox.

He found the carcass about a mile away, next to a Land

Rover. He poked with distasteful movements inside the carcass and came out with a string of gut. He sliced a length of it with his bowie knife. The sun would dry it out, making it tensile and waterproof.

He returned to the woods, following the dog. At the mission school the Black Robes had taught him one thing of real value. Faith was a guttering candle flame that had to be cupped in the hands of the conscious mind lest the cold winds of existence blow it out. Once faith was lost, the present, the future, and even the past were yanked out from under your feet.

The Indian had to get his name. He would follow the spirit through hell itself if necessary. Occupied by questions of faith and eternity, the Indian put the helicopter incident completely out of his mind, along with all the other memories he had lost.

2

Jason awoke lying on his back, looking up at a dull gray morning sky veined by tree branches. A bird twittered from a bough somewhere up there. Buried deep in Jason's skull was a hard sphere of pain that swelled whenever he opened his eyes to sunlight.

The morning was damp with dew that had soaked his clothes and pressed cold deep into his body. A thousand itches from the pine needles on the ground plagued his body. He rolled over onto his side and saw lying before his eyes the severed head of Dennis Hill. It had been carelessly thrown there like trash.

Jason closed his eyes, beating down the rising tide of nausea. Curtis. Where was Curtis? Jason sat up and searched for his rifle. It lay on the ground.

What else? What else?

The pictures! Curtis had photographed the prints!

Jason relaxed somewhat. The camera was at the camp, tucked away in a backpack. First he had to check the helicopter. He wanted to see what had caused the crash.

The rest of Hill was in the little hollow, with the rifle still clutched in one hand. The copter was a broken heap of aluminum plates mixed with the branches. It had literally torn itself up. The radio was dead. Jason picked the walkietalkie off the floor. Still no Curtis. Either he had gotten away or he had fallen out. Or his body lay elsewhere.

Jason studied the curled stabilizer. The rear rotor blade was sliced to half its original circumference by the piece of the stabilizer that protruded inward.

At the joint where the stabilizer joined the fuselage, Jason found a bullet hole. It had punctured the base, weakening the cables. Maybe a smaller piece had done the original damage, but Jason knew he was right. That was not an echo he had heard last night. The Indian was a murderer, and a damned fine shot with a .30.30.

At the camp, Jason rewound Curtis's film in his camera. He tucked the roll into a plastic sandwich bag and placed it in his zippered jacket pocket. While the gray morning melted to a golden brightness, he tramped through the woods, searching for some sign of Curtis.

It was an hour before his eyes chanced on the boot lying at the base of a tree. Curtis was upside down high up in the branches, his weight bending them. Jason wondered if Curtis's death had been more merciful than Hill's. He decided it had not.

The beast could still be around. Jason looked over his shoulder frequently as he walked back to the copter and from there to the camp. Had he not done that, he would have missed one final detail. A rock, its moist underside turned up, lay in the loam by Hill's body. There was blood on one side. The thing could not have sneaked up on the pilot, so it must have thrown this rock to kill him.

Jason drove the Land Rover clear of the trees. The map showed a Canadian Ranger station not far away. He called them on the emergency frequency and told them there had been an accident and three men were dead.

Only after the voice on the other end said help was on its way did Raymond Jason dare to explore the tight, hard face of the Indian and that murderous giant locked in his memory. A hard feeling grew in his guts. He knew that feeling only too well by now. No matter how he analyzed the night's events, he could not make the pieces fit, and he would not sleep well until he did. He worried at the cipher, he poked, prodded, and clawed at it with every rational method he could devise, but the mystery deepened, and within minutes Jason knew he would never rest until he had tracked both of them down.

Wind rustled the golden grass, splattered with brownish-red drops of his blood. Raymond Jason sat motionlessly in the Land Rover, his feet dangling outside the door, oblivious to throbbing pain and the constant trickle of blood on his clothes, his single-track mind fixed on a single project for the first time since he was young. Jason had found something to believe in.

He was flown to a hospital in Calgary and kept under treatment for two weeks. The Canadians were presented with two headless bodies, a helicopter with a hole in it, several expended cartridges, a sheaf of photos, and a baffling, disjointed tale of death and horror recited by Jason into a cassette recorder carried by a policeman who interviewed him while he was under sedation.

On the third week, Jason was released, and a policeman accompanied him to a plane for Kansas City. The policeman was polite but skeptical. "It's not that we don't believe your story, Mr. Jason. It's just that there's no proof these things exist. Besides, there are almost no reports of this kind of beast—Bigfoot, Yeti, whatever you call it—committing violence." His face darkened. "We should very much like to find this Indian, if you know what I mean."

"It was not the Indian," Jason said emphatically. "I told you that. He wasn't around when Nicolson was killed."

The policeman smoothed down his hair and checked his watch.

"And the hole in the copter was a bullet hole, not a branch, like you said. I heard the shot."

"Quite. You suggested the Indian was hunting the beast and you got in the way."

Jason touched the turbanlike bandage on his head. He had been warned about dizzy spells. "Yes."

"We must be especially critical of the incredible, Mr. Jason. We will keep an open file and all that. Do get your rest, and we will keep you informed of developments." The policeman looked carefully at Jason's pallid face. "And if I were you, sir, I would forget this business. Your friends are dead. It is over and done with."

When Jason boarded the plane, the policeman wondered if that faraway look in Jason's eyes was the result of his head injury or if he had always been like that.

The Kansas City Primate Research Center was located hundreds of miles away from any primate other than man. The director himself, a Mr. Kimberly, said he would be delighted to see Raymond Jason and examine his footprint photographs.

Kimberly's office was filled with shelves, on which were displayed skulls, bone fragments, teeth, and other oddments from his jungle work. He spread the photos out on his desk and studied them intently. "Quite impressive.

Not bad at all, Mr. Jason. Have you heard of the Bossburg prints of 1969?"

"No."

"Those were quite impressive too. There were one thousand eighty-nine of them going along a river, over a fence, through fields and all. The right foot was crippled. Whoever faked those really knew his business."

"Faked them?"

"That's what I said. How about the Patterson film? Have you seen the Patterson film?"

"Day before yesterday," Jason replied. It was the most famous piece of motion-picture film since Zapruder's strip of President Kennedy's assassination. Filmed in Bluff Creek, California, by a sometime rodeo man named Roger Patterson, the short movie depicted a six-and-a-half-foot-tall female Bigfoot walking across a dry riverbed with one enigmatic glance back at the camera. Whether it was authentic was debatable. Patterson had forgotten at which speed he filmed the beast, which was a crucial point. At twenty-four frames per second, the walk could have been human. At a lesser speed, the beast had a gait that was distinctly nonhuman. Patterson died vouching for the film's authenticity, a fact which did not seem to impress Kimberly.

"What a mess that was. A gorilla head on a more-or-less-human body? A bare pink heel? The Russians examined the print and thought it was a Neanderthal man. Now, whoever faked that didn't know anything." Kimberly sat in a swivel chair and blew out his cheeks. "All these so-called sightings. All these prints. It's really such an embarrassment, Mr. Jason."

Jason tapped the photos. "These are not fakes, Kimberly."

"Oh?"

"I see I've come to the wrong place."

"You say you saw this creature?"

"Yes. At night."

"Exactly what do you think it was?"

"Some kind of gorilla," said Jason. "A very strange one."

"There are no gorillas or chimpanzees or hominids of any kind in North America, Mr. Jason. Never have been. There's no fossil evidence of anything older than modern man, not even Neanderthals."

"You mean you haven't found any," Jason retorted. "Kimberly, I've knocked around a few museums in my time, and they're full of bones in cardboard boxes shipped in by every digger in the Western Hemisphere. Folsom Man's skull was kicked around for seventeen years before being identified. I wouldn't be surprised if a whole skeleton weren't rattling around some museum, waiting to be pieced together."

"Mr. Jason, really! Where are his bones? Surely Bigfoot dies occasionally, leaving bones!"

"There aren't any bones in the woods, Kimberly, what's the matter with you!" Jason's voice rose. "Birds eat them, insects, predators! They weather away after a week!" Jason reached for the pictures. Kimberly slid them a bit closer to himself. It began to dawn on Jason that Kimberly was using a dry kind of sarcasm to draw him out.

"But how does he eat? Really, when you come down to it, a beast this size has to eat tons! There are long winters up north, which kills off food for half a year, even for an omnivore. He can't migrate or we'd see them all over the place. And primates don't hibernate."

"Kimberly—" Jason began.

Kimberly continued talking, more to himself than to Jason. "And you may be sure it takes more than just a male and female to keep a population going. Ecologically speaking, there's a minimum population which must continue to exist for the species to survive. Life is too hard for just a male and female to continue the whole line. I've heard estimates that a minimal population of two hundred of these creatures is necessary for survival."

"They're not surviving, Kimberly," said Jason.

"Oh?"

"They're in the process of dying out now. The Indians say there were whole groups of them that fished the Columbia River. The white man's diseases wiped out most of them."

Kimberly clasped his hands and rested them on top of his head, rocking back and forth in his swivel chair. "You've done your homework."

"A bit."

"Then explain one last thing to me. Why is it that all the sightings of Bigfoot come together in the 1960s and 1970s? The Indians said they were all around in the early nineteenth century. The white man arrives, they begin to die off, then suddenly a hundred years later they seem to be popping up again. Does that make sense?"

It was one of the things that had bothered Jason in his preliminary researches. "Many people just feel more inclined to report sightings these days than they did a hundred years ago. I don't know, Kimberly. I do know it's real. I saw it."

"It appears I can't convince you otherwise."

"Not a chance."

"What did it look like, then?"

"It was a good seven feet tall. It was covered with black fur. It ran pretty fast on two legs. And it was mismatched, too, like the one in the Patterson film . . ."

"In what way?" Kimberly had become very still.

"I had the distinct feeling its head did not match the rest of it."

"How!"

"The hair was too long. And I think it had a more-pronounced neck than apes usually have. It . . . it . . ." Jason rubbed his bandage. "It's nocturnal."

"How do you know that?"

"I just realized it. He could have examined the Land Rover any time during the day while we were gone. And that musk ox was about ten hours dead, which means he was killed at night. I'm certain he's nocturnal."

Kimberly doodled on a memo pad. "Let's understand each other, Mr. Jason. I have a certain professional standing which necessarily excludes the existence of giant hairy apes in the great north woods. So long as we agree officially that Bigfoot is impossible and everyone who's ever seen one, including yourself, is a fool or a liar, we can safely proceed to a higher level of irrationality. Is that clear?" He smiled. "The academic world can be very incestuous when it comes to such creatures. Too many sword fights with hatpins, if you know what I mean."

"If I get him, I'll leave your name out of it."

"Thank you. What can I do for you specifically?"

"I want your professional opinion of those prints."

"You mean besides being fakes?" He peered at the black-and-white photographs, turning them about as if to shed sunlight on them. "Well, there's something that jumps right out at me, Mr. Jason. So far they've classified two separate and distinct types of Bigfoot prints, which clearly indicates this nonexistent creature exists as two entirely different species. And I do mean different, as different as trolls and unicorns." On his memo pad, Kimberly drew a rectangle with five circles on top. "This is the print left by Patterson's creature. It's called the hourglass print because of the shape of the shank. Hourglass prints have long toes lined up horizontally, like marbles in a rack. He walks from the outer side of his foot. It's a very clearly nonhuman stride with a nonhuman configuration." Then Kimberly sketched a more-or-less-human foot, with toes that slanted forward toward the big toe. "It's called the human print for obvious reasons. Not to imply it's made by a human, but he walks like one. He comes down on his heel and takes off using the big toe. There's an arch there, too."

Jason studied the two drawings. Something was wrong. Something was really haywire.

"Yes," said Kimberly. "It appears your ghost is a combination of both. You've got an hourglass foot with slanted toes. Yet according to the depth of the outline, he walks with his weight on the outer side. I bet his feet ache like hell."

"What do you make of it?"

"It appears you've found a third species of Sasquatch, Mr. Jason."

Jason remembered the word "Sasquatch." It was a Salish Indian word meaning "wild man of the woods." He knew he had been right. This ape was different, something that was not like the other primates—something that did not quite fit words like Bigfoot or Omah or the other legions of Indian terms.

Kimberly crumpled up the drawings and tossed them into his wastebasket. "Well, two species of a nonexistent gorilla are enough for me. Three is laying it on a bit thick. Whole groups of them, you said."

"That's right. Some Indian tribes say they were numerous right up to the 1850s."

"After which they die out. Then suddenly, nonsensically, reappear in the 1960s. They just sort of fade away while Indians and whites slaughter each other. You'd think the late nineteenth century, with the farms sprouting all over the place and all that grain around, is when they'd really show up."

Jason waited. Then he said, "Kimberly, I can't help feeling you've thought about this more than you're letting on."

Kimberly laughed and folded his arms tightly. "Of course I have. At three in the morning in my heart of hearts. Suddenly I get an attack of theories. It's sort of like hives."

"Can I get in on one or two?"

"Why not?" Kimberly straightened up and faced him. "I've been putting together a kind of idea that would explain why your beast would have a misshapen head and Patterson's beast would be such a mess. I think this hundred-year gap in sightings is the result of a behavior change caused by a certain type of . . . event."

"What kind of event?"

"A kind of disease. Nothing like a common cold or a pandemic that would leave carcasses all over the place. Something much more insidious, much slower, that would cause them to become less active for a long time." Kimberly lowered his voice. "A disorder, Mr. Jason. A genetic disorder."

"Genetic!" Kimberly was even further out than Jason was. "Like what?"

"Oh, something simple. Congenital arthritis. Bone degeneration, even a kind of primate Hodgkin's disease. It would explain the varieties of footprint you see. And why Patterson's would not match any other known animal."

"I thought animals killed off or abandoned deformed infants!"

"It might not be so obvious a deformity, Mr. Jason. It might be a very gradual process that appeared only every couple of generations. Their numbers could never really have been so big in the first place. If a species is limited in numbers to begin with, successive generations and interbreeding would concentrate it to a point after a hundred years where the whole species is threatened. A recessive gene would become a dominant one. Births would become fewer, infants would be more obviously deformed, and of course they would die right after birth. By the time the 1960s roll around, it is a continual menace and their behavior changes a second time."

"Why?"

"Desperation, Mr. Jason. They're like an endangered species. Their numbers are diminishing every year, so they have to take chances to get any kind of food." He tapped the photo envelope. "Maybe one of these prints belongs to the original species, and the others are arthritic variations of it."

Desperation. Maybe Kimberly was right. Maybe Jason's quarry was the sick or starving remnant of a band that had once been numerous in the deep forests of the Northwest. If it were one of the last of its kind, its behavior would be erratic. Dangerously, unpredictably erratic.

After some hesitation, Jason told Kimberly about the Indian.

Kimberly's face reflected absolute amazement. "Mr. Jason, I must say . . ." But Kimberly did not know what to say. He glanced at a shelf full of skulls. "But why would he attack you?"

"I don't know. It makes no sense. Is there any reason why a gorilla would steal heads?"

"It's the easiest way of making sure one's quarry is dead. Ancient man did it to neutralize the power of an enemy. It removes the danger from the spirit. You're sure it wasn't the Indian?"

"Indians weren't headhunters," said Jason, gathering up his envelope. "They took scalps a lot, but rarely heads. Thanks for your help, Kimberly."

Kimberly cleared his throat. "Mr. Jason, what do you do?"

"I run a pet-food company. Why?"

"What are your plans now?"

"That's obvious, I think."

"Don't do it."

Jason was surprised. "Why not? I've got nothing but time. I've got plenty of money, the company practically runs itself."

"Drop it, Mr. Jason. Forget it." Kimberly's face was solemn. As with most men of cheerful demeanor, his seriousness was almost comical. "It never appears to those who search for it. There are people who've tracked Bigfoot for twenty years and never laid eyes on it. One swings hourly between poles of elation and discouragement. It's a shortcut to manic-depression. It's not a healthy thing, Mr. Jason, really it isn't."

"It is for me."

"How so?"

But Jason could not explain that to Kimberly. How the quest made him feel young again, how his life had coalesced around something for the first time in years. He felt a bond to the beast, strong and tight, which he could not explain and could not sever. Kimberly would never understand. His psychiatrist might, but not Kimberly. "All I plan to do is run down sightings as they happen."

"It could be years."

Jason leaned closer to him, a hard, metallic, disturbing smile on his face. "You said it yourself. Food, Kimberly. They—or it—have to find food or die out. When autumn comes and the vegetation starts dying out, he'll become desperate. He's different, don't you see? He takes chances. He invades a campsite full of people, he attacked the pilot holding a gun. . . . Kimberly, in Oregon a bunch of kids reported shooting one of these beasts with a shotgun. What did he do? He ran away. What did mine do? He attacked. He's fighting for the survival of the species. He's as different from your normal Bigfoot as a tiger is from a house cat. Maybe he'll hit a farm or—"

"Decapitate somebody else. I see your point, Mr. Jason."

Kimberly shook his hand. "Keep in touch. In case you need any more technical advice on unicorns."

Nice fellow, Kimberly thought after Jason left the room. One of these driven businessmen, though. You could see it in his face.

Kimberly filled his pipe and sucked on cold tobacco. He looked up at the eye sockets of a gibbon skull on one of the shelves.

A very ferocious creature, the gibbon, especially when aroused by food. A very ferocious creature, the human being, Kimberly added to his thoughts, especially when aroused by food of another sort.

3

Summer passed.

After the Rockies, the Indian entered a horizonless plain of grass slashed with wildflowers in profuse rich colors. Days were long, nights were short. Many times their passage stirred a watchdog in some farmhouse to lonely whines. Then the Indian could imagine the people within stirring in their sleep.

The Indian was skin and bones, an engine whose entire purpose was placing one foot before the other and propelling himself forward. A long ash bow was slung lengthwise across his chest and back. From a deerskin he had made a quiver, in which he placed six arrows, also made from ash, their ends furred with feathers. He was so adept with this weapon now that he could bring down a quail at twenty yards.

The dog rested with the spirit during the day and led the Indian at night. Sometimes the Indian complained to the dog. "Where's he taking me? It don't make sense how he walks, he goes in circles! He drags me up some god-damned mountain and down again. Spirits are supposed to know everything, but I swear he's acting like he don't know where he is."

The dog agreed. The dog always agreed. The dog was a whore.

In the southwest a ragged line of mountains appeared. He watched them running southward. Some of them were strange mountains, with dry east slopes sliding down to wheat fields, and west slopes thickly jungled with vine maples and spruces of such density that sunlight barely penetrated their depths. Where the Rockies were sharp, these escarpments were smooth and slightly conical. Their heights were slit by fog layers and snow, which streamed into the wind like pennants.

Summer drained into fall. The wildflowers withered as the nights became cooler. Hot sun, cold air. The horizon climbed to the sky and fitted tightly under the curved bowl of the heavens. The spirit became bolder. He walked close to roads where campers scurried on their way to get berries, while the Indian and the dog hid in ditches. He paused at farms for dangerously long periods to steal fruit and potatoes.

The Indian was of two minds about this phantom who never ventured more than a mile from him yet whom he never saw. The rational half recognized him as a forager and hunter so shy of humans that he was apt to take the most tortuous route to avoid settlements. Before this thought could go on to a conclusion, the irrational half of his mind stopped it. The spirit was divine. The journey was a ceremony that he must complete. His name was locked in that great shaggy soul somewhere. The universe was a cipher which the Indian could never hope to fathom, but at least a name would place him firmly in his allotted place in that cipher.

But even the strongest faith requires encouragement. The Indian was all too human, and he knew he was losing ground. His sleeps became deeper and his body shrank. He expended more energy than he replaced with food. In the midst of farmlands and game he was in real danger of starving to death. Something had to happen soon. Winter would be on them. If the Indian did not receive his name before long, he would have to give up.

The gorge was filled with swarming mosquitoes. It was dim and greened by the sunlight passing through the trees on the top. Halfway up the cliff was a cave. The Indian knew his spirit slept within. It was hard to avoid climbing up and looking at the spirit as he slept.

The gorge was in the midst of thick cottonwoods just off a minor highway. The Indian followed the bottom of it into the trees again, with growing worry. He did not like where they were heading. Too many people were around.

At the other end of the gorge were more trees, and after that a gradual cleared slope leading downward and cupping a trailer park on three sides. The highway ran along the fourth side. Because of the electrical wiring and cinderblock mountings, the Indian knew this was a permanent establishment. The trailers huddled together like a nest of bugs, with propane tanks fixed to their sides. Brightly colored laundry flapped on ropes. The trailers were in two rows, separated by an alley of vegetable gardens.

To the dog, the Indian said, "Unless he backtracks, he's going to have to go right through them. He's taking a hell of a chance. Near as I can figure, he's going to make a dash through tonight."

The Indian squatted on his heels and sniffed the air There was an autumn tang to it. He was homesick. Back home the leaves had long since turned gold and fallen to the ground. Wind would sweep them around the meadows. Spring had been underway only a couple of weeks when he left. The mountain sharpness of the air cleared his head and lungs.

That night he lay on his back, waiting for the dog to summon him. He sat up as the animal padded through the leaves. The dog yawned and lay down.

"He's still sleeping?" the Indian asked.

That was a stupid question, the dog replied with a sardonic look.

The spirit slept all the following morning, as though storing up energy for some tremendous, exhausting undertaking.

The dog accompanied the Indian up the highway, where they found a small, tattered grocery store with a sign reading THE PICNIC PLACE. As the Indian closed the fly-specked door, a bell tinkled. Fluorescent light reflected off the polished steel-and-glass shelves, making him squint.

Behind the iron cash register sat a hefty middle-aged woman with red cheeks, silver-gray hair in a tight bun, and small eyes behind silvery steel-rimmed glasses. She looked at the Indian. Then she lowered her movie magazine and put one hand under the counter. The Indian guessed she had a gun there.

"Morning," she said cordially enough. "Didn't hear your car."

"Ain't got a car," said the Indian with a rusty, unused voice. He had spoken aloud to no one but the dog in a long time. The dog bristled in the unaccustomedly tight surroundings of the store as the Indian gathered some chocolate bars and a plastic-wrapped package of salami. "I'd like some of this stuff."

He poked through the medicine bundle until he found a greasy billfold. Dried corn clattered to the floor as he took it out. The woman stared at him as he counted out change.

She kept one hand under the counter and ran the cash register with the other. "One seventy-five. There we go."

"Thanks." The Indian watched her put the food in a small bag and staple it shut, with the register tape around the top.

"You from around here?"

"No, ma'am. Montana."

She became interested. "You from up around Browning?"

"No, ma'am. Stevensville."

"Oh yeah. Flathead country. You a Flathead?"

"Yes, ma'am."

Within the woman caution struggled against a human need to break her solitude. Even an Indian was better company than nobody. "Now my husband, Jack, was interested in Indians right up till he died. He collected arrowheads."

"Yes, ma'am." The Indian headed for the door.

"He was good with a bow and arrow. You any good with that one?"

"I'm getting better," he answered. "Thanks, ma'am."

"Watch out for the Bigfoot. Bunch of kids say they saw one around the Nooksack River."

The Indian's hand was on the door when the word detonated in his skull like a bombshell. Big Foot! The legendary chief of the Minneconjou Sioux who died at Wounded Knee with Sitting Bull.

Was that *his* spirit?

The woman saw his expression change. Her hand went back under the counter. "It's just a joke. Bunch of kids with more beer in their guts than brains in their heads."

The Indian searched her whitening face for some clue to her character. Was she lying? Trying to separate him from his spirit? His grandfather's spirit had been a human, after all. And when he had first seen the giant he had thought it was a man. The mission-school priests had solemnly warned him about the ways of the devil, who captured human souls and made them lie. He had had a bellyful of religion from them during all those years in school. But maybe they were right; maybe there was some truth to it.

Or maybe she was not lying. Maybe she spoke the truth and was giving him a clue of some kind. It was not the first time that he wondered exactly what his spirit was.

"Yes, ma'am," the Indian said, relaxing. "Kids are crazy, ain't they." He closed the door gently behind him.

Night.

It was ten o'clock by the stars when the Indian crumpled his last candy-bar wrapper, stuffed it into the sack, and threw the bag away. He watched the lights go off in the trailers. Somewhere a country-music station played loudly; the sound was punctuated by bursts of laughter.

The dog joined him at the top of the slope. The spirit was awake at last. He had summoned the dog an hour before, to issue instructions. The crickets were quiet, a sure sign that it was walking.

The Indian was still thinking about the encounter with the woman. "I wish he'd just let me close to him sometime," he murmured to the dog. "Just to see him good. He's big, you know. Maybe he was a chief or something. Maybe he was a man once after all."

The dog growled. The Indian was keyed up. Tonight would be the first time in a long while that he had seen the spirit at all.

The moon surged from behind a cloud, flooding thin, cold light over the woods. The dog woofed.

The spirit was already in the trailer park. He was pulling cucumbers, tomatoes, onions, carrots, lettuce heads out of the vegetable garden and shoving them, dripping with dirt, down his mouth, in full view of whoever cared to look out a window.

For a few seconds while the grunting spirit gobbled away, the Indian was paralyzed with shock and disgust. He rose to his feet with a trembling finger, pointing at the trailers. "He's—he's—" Words slithered between the interstices of the Indian's teeth. "God*damn* him! Get him out of there!"

The dog ran down the slope. A watchdog began barking in the trailer park. Lights came on in the trailer adjacent to the garden.

The spirit dropped the vegetables and blundered down the alley into laundry lines full of sheets. He had torn his way nearly to the woods when a door opened and a man in a bathrobe emblazoned ADVANCED INSTITUTE OF SEX, CLASS OF 69 came out with a shotgun.

The Indian dashed down the slope.

The man saw the giant and paused, then raised his rifle to his shoulder. The Indian chopped him in the neck with the edge of his hand. He saw the man's stunned face before he crumpled up like a sack of potatoes.

The Indian grabbed, too late, for the rifle. It went off close to his face, the concussion dazzling and deafening him, the barrel burning his fingers.

More lights came on. Several women screamed, and doors flew open. The Indian's dog added its sharp yelps to the other dogs' as it chased the spirit into the woods.

The Indian heard a rising chorus of voices as he sprinted past the trailers to the road. His feet slapped the hard asphalt with a pain that surprised him. His feet had adjusted to soft earth, not concrete.

He was clear of the trailer park before turning into the woods again. Pandemonium, shouts, screams, conflicting directions—"He's in the trees!" "Hell no, he hit the woods!" "No, I saw him on the road!"—added their uproar to the colliding bodies and flashlight beams. The Indian heard one more shot and a woman sobbing as the cottonwoods swallowed him up. The dog was waiting for him.

The Indian figured they had run three miles, following the spirit's stench, which hung in the air like vapor, when they burst into an apple orchard—so suddenly that he slipped on a piece of rotting fruit and went sprawling.

Gasping for breath, he climbed to his feet. He looked at the trees. Branches were stripped of fruit. He looked at the dog. It yipped and danced around him.

The spirit whistled from the other end of the orchard. The Indian heard branches rustle as apples were pulled from them. After his breathing stabilized, the Indian said to the dog, trotting off in response to the whistle, "Go on!" He grabbed an apple and threw it against a tree.

Shocked at the Indian's tone, the dog ignored a second whistle. The Indian stood up and, forgetting he wore only moccasins, kicked a tree and jumped in pain. "Go ahead! Let the scumbag take care of himself! Fuck him!" The Indian's voice rose to dangerously audible levels. "You know what's wrong with him? He's *stupid!* I didn't believe it till now. He is! His brains are in his belly. My name! He don't know my name, he's so stupid he don't even know his own name! I been feeding him, following him, taking care of him, and I still don't know what he wants or what he's doing!"

The Indian slumped to the ground again and dug, meaninglessly, furiously, at the earth with an arrow. Words continued sluicing out in a venomous despair that made the dog cringe.

"All he thinks about is food! I'm sick of this shit!"

Tail down, the dog snuggled up to the Indian's foot. That did it. The dog's bootlicking affection, its favor-currying streak, was the final insult. The flaming emotional force of the spirit quest was dissipated now. The Indian closed his eyes and reached for some noble memory, but all he saw was that man in the stupid bathrobe and the spirit tangled in laundry. The bond was broken, its snapped ends frayed by exhaustion, frustration, and garden fertilizer.

"I'm going home. Get away from me."

It was so abrupt a severing of this peculiar friendship that the dog whimpered around in circles, unable to actually leave. The Indian finally threw an apple at it, which sent the animal scampering down between the apple trees.

The Indian lay down and closed his eyes. He had just torn a bloody hole in his psyche. There was no pain. That would come later, when the numbness wore off. He would digest his despair piece by piece, lest the whole sudden weight of it overwhelm him. He would wake in the morning, go to the road, and hitchhike, rejoin the human race and this puzzling world.

After all, his memory was already a tattered garment. One more rip in it would make no difference. But he did not know what would happen now. His grandfather shook his head sorrowfully at him. He was more faded than ever, more shrouded behind darkness than the Indian had ever remembered.

Maybe the Indian would just dry up under the pitiless light reserved by the sun for the lost and useless, his skin and bones rendered into food for plants.

Ten hours after a humorous news dispatch reported that a twelve-foot-tall, fire-breathing ape had attacked the Happy Hunting Ground Trailer Park, Raymond Jason arrived in a rented car. He had spent the summer running down a dozen sightings that had panned out into nothing. He was always a day late at least, and the spontaneous trips, as well as his mounting frustration, were disrupting his life.

The trailer park was close to the border between Washington State and British Columbia, hundreds of miles southwest of where his experience had occurred.

Whatever footprints might have been left were long since stomped to mud by the campers as they blundered into one another the previous night, and the locals who were now photographing the vegetable garden. It looked as if a plane had crashed into it.

After some inquiries, Jason's spirits rose a trifle. This was not a fake. Something really had gone through the vegetable garden, and a man named Frank P. Stone had gotten a clear look at it.

Frank P. Stone opened a bourbon bottle and poured a shot for himself, his wife, and Jason. Around his neck was a collar bandage. His wife's stiff posture and drawn face were evidence of the tension caused by the event. Stone was politely wary of Jason's interest. "Can't really say folks have been very understanding about this business, Mr. Jason."

"I know the feeling. I saw one in Canada."

"No shit!"

Stone's wife's eyes lit with hope. "They all think it's funny. Funny!"

"It's not funny. And if I were you, I wouldn't talk about it any more than necessary. For your own good, you know?"

"Amen." Stone took a fervent gulp.

"I was wondering if there was anything you could tell me that you didn't tell anyone else. Just between us."

Stone and his wife exchanged looks. Then he poured out another shot. "Why not? Its head was wrong."

"Oh?" Jason became very still. "Deformed, maybe?"

"It didn't hit me till later, when I tried to describe it. I think its head was a different color from the rest of it. 'Course, I only saw it two seconds, so I can't say what color the rest of it was. The hair was different. Longer. I think." He looked at his wife, turning his whole body so he didn't have to turn his neck. "But that's not the big one. You heard the news saying the thing had thrown a tree at me?"

"No," said Jason.

"Well, it's a load of bull. Some snotty kid made that up for some snotty, crappy paper." He touched his bandage. "Somebody cold-cocked me just as I was about to shoot it, Mr. Jason. It wasn't that ape. How could I get the back of my head hit when he was in front of me?"

Jason's mind lurched. He glanced out the tiny curtained window to the slope and woods. "Cold-cocked by whom?"

"I don't know. He was real quiet about it. I didn't hear a thing."

Stone's wife said, "That's what's so bad about this business, Mr. Jason. Somebody must have been trying to break in here when the ruckus started and Frank and his gun and that ape scared him off. It all happened at once." Her lips trembled slightly. "Maybe that thing saved our lives."

"Oh, come on, Joyce . . ." Stone shook his head, the pain making his wince. *"Jesus,* what a night!"

"Did anybody see who hit you?"

"Nobody saw nothing!" grumbled Frank P. Stone. "Real good neighbors. Just me and Perkins's shepherd. I thought he'd bark himself into a cardiac. Dumb city dog, scared shitless of everything."

Jason found a squashed-up paper bag lying near the trailers, close to the woods. The top was stapled with a receipt from a store called "The Picnic Place." Someone had been up there.

He held the paper under the dog's mouth, keeping a good grip on the leash. The dog sniffed, then growled and tried to pull away. Obviously, the bag belonged to a stranger.

Within the woods was a rocky canyon, the floor littered with fallen leaves. Here they had more luck. The dog growled unhappily and tugged at his leash. Wedged in the rocks, next to a small pile of dog feces, was a plastic wrapper for sandwich meat.

The feces were not Buck's; the Perkinses did not allow the shepherd off his chain. Jason poked at the feces with a stick. The outside was a crust, the inside still moist. Very recent. No more than twelve hours old.

He looked around the cliffs and saw a cave high up near the top, accessible by a slanting ledge leading up from the floor. "Let's go, Buck."

The dog did not want to go onto the ledge. Jason dragged him, snapping and howling, up to the cave, then tied the leash to a boulder by the entrance. He slapped at mosquitoes swarming about the cave threshold.

It was small and empty of even insect life. The floor was silted with mud. Leaves had been piled into the back wall, then depressed downward by great weight. Jason scooped up a handful of these leaves and carried them to the dog.

He shoved them under Buck's nose. Buck went crazy with rage and almost bit Jason's arm. He soothed the animal with a silky, stroking rub behind the ears. "It's them, isn't it," he whispered to the animal. "And you've got the scent, haven't you."

That afternoon he bought the dog from Perkins. He paid exactly one thousand dollars for him, in hundred-dollar bills peeled from a roll he carried in his pocket.

He pulled the rented car up to The Picnic Place and let Buck out, still holding the leash.

The woman behind the counter looked up as the bell tinkled. "How do?" she said to Jason. "Come to find the Bigfoot?"

"Isn't everybody?" Jason looked over the counters, uncertain about how to get her to talk without sounding like a private eye.

"The real nuts all went home already," said the woman. "Some folks say it tried to rape some woman down on Route Nine."

"People are crazy," murmured Jason.

"Well, it *was* down at George Fraser's apple orchard," she protested. "George found his trees stripped about an hour ago. Good thing the nuts are gone, or they'd all be down there too."

Jason laughed politely. "Where's this orchard?"

"It's about four miles down that way." She pointed down the highway toward the trailer park. "He run through the woods after he got to the park and spent the night eating there. They say."

"How can anybody be scared of a gorilla that eats apples?" Jason laughed with an effort.

"The things that happen in this county. There was an Indian in here yesterday morning . . ."

It came down on Jason's head so fast that he could barely coordinate moving the mustard and the sandwich meat on the counter.

". . . scariest man I ever laid eyes on. He weighed about twenty pounds, and every ounce was plain meanness."

"No kidding."

"Had an Army jacket and a mangy little dog. Bet his pockets were full of razor blades. He was on the run, if you ask me."

"What from, I wonder." Jason opened a bag of potato chips and shoved several into his mouth. He had forgotten the dog until now. So it belonged to the Indian after all. He had wondered if it was wild or not.

"He said he was from Stevensville, Montana. That's up at the Flathead reservation, you know?" She counted up the food and rang the prices on the register. 'That's fifteen seventy-five with tax. Going camping?" Jason had bought a carton of food and sandwiches.

"I might. Your sign says you sell bullets. Do you have any three fifty-seven Magnum shells?"

"Nope. All the Bigfoot nuts bought them." The woman shuddered. "Try Springer's, in town."

4

The Indian had awakened before dawn that morning. He wanted to get clear of the orchard as quickly as possible. A pink line separated the night from the eastern horizon as he munched an apple from the trees.

The dog tried to follow him to the road, but he threw an apple at it. "Fuck you!" The dog barked furiously, trying to get him back to the orchard.

The Indian found a road sign pointing out directions to Spokane, Seattle, and a host of small towns unknown to him. He was vaguely interested to learn he was in Washington. Very vaguely. He had no friends out here, and had never been to Washington in his life. Glumly he trudged down the highway, watching sunlight fill the air.

The dog was extremely upset by this change in routine. It was not bold enough to approach the Indian and not smart enough to leave. It dogged the Indian's footsteps, yapping in outrage, dodging rocks thrown at it.

The Indian skewered a rabbit dashing across the road with an arrow, then took it into the trees to skin and roast it. The dog wagged its tail, expecting a piece for the spirit. Instead, the Indian ate the entire animal with deliberate thoroughness and threw bones at the dog. When he washed his hands in a stream and headed back for the road, the dog unleashed a thunderstorm of barks.

"I know he's sleeping!" the Indian roared. "I don't care if he don't wake up."

By seven the sun was high. The cold night was turning

into a reasonably warm day. The dog became hysterical, walking in circles, making little jumps in place, rolling on the ground. The spirit was being left far behind. The road was a twisty ribbon that crossed streams. Finally the Indian rained rocks at the animal, with such ferocity that the dog ran yelping into the woods.

And did not come out.

Good, the Indian thought to himself.

The Indian had hoped his disillusionment would give him a sense of freedom. Instead, he was more tired than he had been on the entire futile quest. He still felt the heavy presence of the spirit, and it was not pleasurable any more, rather like an unwelcome intruder watching him.

Produce trucks hurrying food to market appeared on the road. They sped up at sight of him.

By noon he had realized that no intelligent driver was going to endanger his life by picking up a skinny, filthy Indian with a bow and arrow, so he left the road and did some more hunting. He bagged three quail in a field, and another rabbit. For once he had the food all to himself, and it was a veritable feast that filled his belly and beyond. The heavy fatigue turned his limbs to iron.

He found a patch of firs where he could lie down. The sunlight hurt his night-sharpened eyes, causing a headache. He decided it was not a good idea to change his sleeping schedule so abruptly, so he decided to do some tramping that night.

A twig cracked. The Indian saw the dog settling down a discreet distance from him. "Fucking beast," he muttered at the persistent animal, but he was too tired to really chew it out. Let the beast sleep. He could always beat hell out of it later. He set his mental clock to awaken him around seven, when the coolness of late afternoon became the coldness of night.

In town, Jason bought a small tent, a bedroll, a kerosene stove, and a gas lantern. At the sporting-goods store he purchased a steel hatchet and a box of .357 Magnum shells for his Colt Python, a handgun so ludicrously deadly that six shots could sever a small tree. He was a better shot with this pistol than with a rifle, a skill gained by hours of practice at a Kansas City country club.

He found a U.S. Army survey map of the county, with markings for the trailer park, the apple orchard, and various small farms. This map revealed a group of five streams just beyond the apple orchard. Jason remembered that the ape had escaped down a stream after killing Nicolson in Canada.

He walked the dog through the photographers and curious gawkers swarming around the orchard, entered the cottonwoods, and tramped up to the first stream. It was like the one in Canada, with a shallow run of water leading to deeper depths overhung with willows.

Buck became nervous as he sniffed both banks for an hour. The scent was palpable, but there was no trail along the water's edge. Instead, the scent led to deeper woods.

"That's weird, Buck. I thought he liked rivers." Jason tried to ignore the small ring of alarm that went off in his mind.

The second stream was half a mile distant. This water was deep and slow-moving. Again the dog picked up faint traces of the ape's passage leading farther into the woods. Jason's alarm grew to a continual nagging itch.

The third stream was hardly a stream. It was more a series of rocky ponds, chained together by rivulets. The smell clinging to branches and bits of moss indicated that the ape had passed by this water, too. Jason was thoroughly puzzled. The beast had crossed all three rivers and gone deeper into the woods.

At the fourth stream, the shepherd howled mournfully,

little piteous cries of terror. Jason pushed his muzzle against the ground and noted that the ape at last was moving along water in a westward direction. This river was deep and slow-moving, gladed by spruce and moss. Deprived of the sunlight, the forest floor was clear of undergrowth, and the scent was embedded in the soft, wet gravel of the bank. Jason's worry abated somewhat. He was on to something, but he did not know what. At least it looked like the beast was moving somewhere.

He consulted the map. They were five miles from the orchard, in deep woods. "It almost makes sense, Buck. Almost. Except the logical thing to do is take the first river you come to, if you're on the run. There's something about this fourth one he liked." Jason felt that he had been given the key to some kind of very important lock, which he would have to find.

The soft, wet bank gravel did not hold footprints of either the ape, the Indian, or the dog. Jason noted how the scent always came from hard rocks or tight-packed gravel, where footprints did not take. The thing concealed its tracks perfectly. And Jason suspected the beast had an inordinate love, maybe even a need, for fruits. There was no other reason for it to stop running before it was well clear of the pandemonium of the trailer park.

He tied the shepherd to a tree and took out a ham sandwich. He laid the map on the ground and examined the squiggles of the rivers as if he could peel underneath the paper somehow and uncover secrets. The shepherd regarded him with sharp wolf's eyes. Already he was homesick for his old chain.

"Buck, old boy, here's the situation." Jason picked a piece of wax paper from the sandwich. "That scent's going to be dead cold in another day. Unless we trip over him, we won't get anywhere following him like this."

He gave half of the sandwich to the dog. It was easy

and comfortable talking to the animal. It was always easy talking to animals if you were a solitary man. "So we've got to put ourselves in that ape's mind and see if we can't get ahead of him somehow. Predict where he'll go. Right? What do we know about him so far? We know he moves at night. We know he sticks close to the water. Best of all, we know he eats constantly. Night, food, and water are three walls of a cage, if you look at it right. Especially food. *He always goes for food.*"

His finger hovered over the map. Bull's-eye!

He punched down on an oblong lake called the Little Harrington, about twenty miles west of where they were sitting. All five streams emptied into it. The Little Harrington was surrounded by ink bristles signifying swampland. Swampland meant thick vegetation, birds, beavers, rodents, and insects. Swampland meant food.

"Buck, I bet you anything he hits this lake! The way he eats, a swamp would be a feast for him! He hasn't got there yet! It's too far! But he'll get there tonight or tomorrow night, and we'll be waiting there." Elated, Jason rose to his feet, rolling up the map. The beast was his, he was sure of it. He could almost reach into the leaves and touch it. "We'll have him, boy! We'll have him by the short hairs. We'll nail him at the lake!" Jason burst out laughing as the dog's hackles rose. "You feel him, boy? So do I. So do I!"

Jason's elation was not total. The mysterious lock in his mind remained sealed. He looked at the map again with the irresistible feeling that it was trying to tell him something terribly important about his quarry.

The Little Harrington lake was a wetland basin with an indeterminate shore of reeds and vines, through which Jason and the dog waded in muck, searching for signs of the ape's passage. All five streams converged into its eastern end, forming a muddy delta. Frogs splashed through the water, and gnats dizzily circled one another in the dimming daylight.

"So far so good, Buck. There's plenty of gunk to eat, and he hasn't been through here yet."

Jason watched the small pips of nipping fish spreading outward on the water's surface into smooth symmetrical circles that interlocked with one another. For several moments he let the heavy peace of the lake massage him.

Then he took a metal ultrasonic dog whistle from his pocket. He threw a rotten stick into the water. Buck splashed into the lake, paddled out to the stick, and closed his jaws around it, snapping it to pieces.

Jason blew a short, soundless hiss on the whistle. Buck woofed, made a splashy starboard turn, and came back. He emerged trembling in the reeds, shaking off great halos of water that made Jason cringe. Although they were not friends yet, a working relationship was being forged between them.

They splashed around the muddy delta where it gradually separated into five component streams. "I'd like to know where I am in case I have to do some night running. He'll be here either tonight or tomorrow night."

Unless he was completely wrong about the lake and the beast did not show up at all. But Jason did not want to think about that.

After an hour of sweaty sloshing through mud, Jason returned to the car and let the dog inside, where it promptly soaked the floor and seat covers. He should have been feeling good. Instead, that lock in his mind, that tight question about why the beast took the fourth river instead of the first, remained closed.

"Buck, it has something to do with Montana. Ever since that woman told me the Indian was from Montana, a little bell went off."

He took another map from the glove compartment, a

large road map covering western Montana, Idaho, Washington, and Oregon. After searching for several moments, he found Stevensville, Montana. From there he drew a northwest line past the Rockies to Caribou, where the beast had attacked them. And from Caribou he brought the line down to their present location, on the border of Canada and Washington. Jason whistled. The two of them had traveled no less than a thousand miles on foot. It was a meaningless, meandering journey that began nowhere and ended nowhere.

Jason had heard of only one Bigfoot sighting in Montana. A Boy Scout troop had been visited in the Deer Lodge National Forest in 1964 by a giant who stirred up their camp gear. Generally that gigantic state did not figure in Bigfoot lore.

Where were they going?

They? Jason looked out the window, pondering the lake.

He just couldn't figure that Indian. He was not hunting it, or he would have killed it long ago. It was as though he was just tagging along with it, like . . . like . . .

Like Raymond Jason.

Jason had been petting the dog. Suddenly he snatched his hand away as though the fur were hot. He and that scroungy Indian?

For a terrifying split second Jason felt a dark empathy with the Indian. Both were moving alone in pursuit of this enigmatic ape. Both had traveled hundreds of miles . . .

"Nuts!" Jason said loudly.

Thinking like that would land him back on the shrink's couch. Jason could not begin to guess the Indian's thoughts, but he knew his own reasons were solid, down-to-earth, practical ones. He had lots of good reasons! There was science and all that stuff. He was avenging the deaths of Hill, Curtis, and Nicolson! Look at the spell Bigfoot and the Himalayan Yeti cast on the human configuration. Why, this was an enthralling adventure, except for the bugs and all that wading through water. You'd have to be made out of stone to resist a Bigfoot hunt.

Maybe Kimberly was right. Maybe Jason should forget it and go home before the Bigfoot possessed his mind so totally that he could think of nothing else.

He put the key in the ignition. And, just as easily, the lock in his mind snapped open, releasing glittering revelations.

The fourth river! Jason fumbled open the survey map and looked at the streams. All five rivers led to this lake, but the fourth one was different. The lake's oblong shape opened into a delta at the fourth river farther east than it did with the others.

The fourth river was the quickest way to the Little Harrington. The Bigfoot knew this! The Bigfoot knew these rivers!

"Buck, I ought to have my head candled. Montana fouled me up. Just because the Indian's from there doesn't mean the Bigfoot's from there too! Dammit! *Maybe he knows these rivers because he's from around here!* By God . . . by God!"

The Cascade Range began a few miles south of here, the gigantic mountains that ran all the way down to northern California. The Cascades were the traditional stomping ground of the Sasquatch.

Jason stepped out of the car and looked at the peaks on the horizon. The sun was setting, its slanting rays bronzing their slopes, as they marched rank after rank toward the south.

"He lives around here somewhere, boy!" said Jason in awe. "He's been running around the country for some reason, and the Indian picked him up in Montana." Fully eighty percent of all Bigfoot sightings occurred in the Pacific Northwest, in a fairly even area from where Jason stood. Jason could not begin to understand why a non-migratory beast would set out on such a journey, but he was certain to the depths of his soul that the ape was headed for home right now.

He slipped the maps into the glove compartment. He squealed the car back from the lake onto the road. He had to make one quick phone call, and after that Buck wasn't going to be a city dog much longer.

The Indian was dreaming about Vietnam.

He lay deep in the rice paddy, absolutely motionless, hearing the lazy slap of rifles. The firefight had gotten the communications people first, so the rescue copters would not come. Now the guerrillas were moving in and killing the wounded.

The Indian had no spirit to protect him from the Viet Cong. He lay perfectly still, prepared for a long death, even as a bayonet tickled his leg. But the guerrillas moved on, apparently thinking he was already dead.

When night came, the Indian cautiously raised his head above the rice plants. All of his squad had died, none of them easily. A hard red boil formed in the Indian's gut. He crawled out of the rice paddy, into the jungle. That night he slit the throat of a guerrilla and made a string for a bow from a length of his bowel. He carved twelve arrows and barbed the ends. Armed with this weapon, he tracked the enemy devils at night: the sentries, the gun bearers, and once an officer. He was a part of the jungle, a plains and forest dweller more at home in wilderness than the cleverest enemy devil. For the next ten days he ate nothing but tarantulas, lizards, and wild pigs. He gorged himself on stealthy death, stacking bodies in heaps in his mind and on trails causing major dislocation in the enemy's forces.

Later a helicopter found him half dead. His leg was swollen to the size of a tree trunk. They told him a captured guerrilla had surrendered out of fear of him.

The Indian had hunted them down without a spirit to help him. This fact burst on him in the Army hospital, sending him into paroxysms of sheer terror at his own frail mortality. From then on he knew he could not face life without a spirit or a name.

His fingers tore out chunks of earth. He sat upright violently, just short of screaming his lungs out. Silent feet dashed away from him, thrashing the leaves.

He was not in a dream after all, or a jungle. He was in the woods somewhere in America. The dog cringed, wide-eyed, at the Indian's obvious distress.

The Indian calmed down and oriented himself. He had overslept. It was evening. And he was completely alone.

"He's getting scared now, isn't he?" snarled the Indian. "His little momma isn't sending him his dinner no more. So he come by to watch me." He leaned closer to the dog, which quailed, one foot off the ground. "I'll trade. A nice salmon for my name."

He gave the dog the finger and ambled back to the road. The sleep had done him good. That and the food were reminders that there were some good things to say about mortality. He liked the goose bumps raised by cold air on his skin and the way his lungs carried this chilled air to the blood and thence all over his body.

The dog was not the only one shadowing him. The birds and crickets were quiet. A moving pool of silence alerted the Indian to the presence of the spirit just within the woods lining the road.

The tables were turned. The spirit was following *him* now.

The Indian stopped and looked into the trees. The harder he stared, the more the darkness danced.

"Hey!" he shouted.

The trees ticked under a breeze.

"What do you want from me! Come on out and tell me! Come on!"

The dog was seated on a white divider line, its ears cocked, its nostrils trembling at the trees. The Indian said, "He's worried, ain't he. He knows I mean it."

The whistle cracked out. The dog dashed into the trees without a glance at the Indian.

The Indian quickened his pace down the road, his hands holding the medicine bundle so it would not bounce against his waist.

"Ah, Mr. Jason!" Kimberly chuckled over the speaking phone line. It must be raining between here and Kansas City. "And where are you?"

"I'm in a pay phone in a gas station in Washington." "And how is the hunting season?"

"Never better. I've tracked my moose to northern Washington. He came through a trailer park last night not ten miles from here."

"No!"

Jason opened the folding door to kick out a beer can. "And get this, Kimberly. I think the Bigfoot's from around here. He knows these rivers too well." Jason explained about the five rivers leading to the Little Harrington.

"It doesn't sound like he knew about this trailer park."

"The hell he didn't! He went right for a vegetable garden. After that he made a beeline to an apple orchard. He takes chances, Kimberly, like he did at the farm in Canada."

Kimberly said dubiously, "Maybe you're right, maybe not. I can't poke any holes in it yet. What about this Indian?"

"Oh, he's still around. I found out he's a Flathead from Montana."

He heard the frantic scratching of Kimberly's pen on

paper. "Splendid, Mr. Jason! I'm off to the library first thing in the morning to see what I can dig up on Flathead Indian lore. Maybe I can find out why the Indian's following him."

"That still leaves me with the big one. This ape's traveled a good thousand miles on foot. And five hundred of those miles since July. Can you tell me why he would be running around like this?"

Kimberly mulled it over, then grunted. "You've got me there, Mr. Jason. It makes absolutely no sense. Has he killed any more animals?"

"I don't know. I imagine he has." Jason slipped more coins into the phone slot.

"I'm tempted to say he's been hunting. There's a very elaborate, time-consuming activity called persistence hunting. You walk your prey to death. The trouble is, you have to do it in a band. It does sound to me like he holds food to be very important, maybe more important than sex, shelter, and even his own safety. He did eat a musk ox, didn't he? Not many members of the ape family outside of baboons eat meat. It makes sense that he likes apples. Most primates adore fruit. I bet he likes it better than musk oxen."

Jason said, "Yeah, but a thousand miles? That's a long way to hunt. That can't be it."

Kimberly was silent.

"Kimberly? If I were to look for a Bigfoot's home, what exactly should I look for?"

"A cave," Kimberly replied promptly. "A cave system would be better. Best of all would be a cave system in a fairly isolated mountain valley where he could gather roots and tubers all day without being seen. Besides, caves are full of tasty little bugs and things they could nibble on."

It occurred to Jason that the cave above the trailer park had been empty of insect life. His quarry couldn't pass up a meal, no matter how small.

Kimberly sighed. "I don't mind telling you, Mr. Jason, I'm glad there's no such thing as a Bigfoot. It's October already, and I'm wondering where he plans to spend the winter. Maybe you're right, maybe he came home. Then again, maybe he has a place in Florida."

Jason parked the car off the road under some trees and moved his gear to the lake. He selected a campsite that was fairly dry and opened a can of his company's dog food for Buck. The dog took a sniff and disdained it. "Thanks for the unsolicited endorsement. What did they feed you there? Filet mignon?"

He pitched a tent, unfolded the kerosene stove, and heated up a can of chili. He polished and cleaned the pistol and reloaded it. Strapped to his belt was the steel hatchet he had bought that afternoon.

Night was a long time falling this far north. By seven the sun was gone, but the sky was still orange, making black spears of the trees around the lake. From the trunk of his car Jason unloaded a bushel of apples, which he had purchased at a road stand. In the fading light, he set out the apples in conical pyramids around the lake. Next to each pile he drove in a stake and chain and attached it to a bear trap, which he buried.

The swampy woods were alive with bullfrogs and insects. They were extremely loud, especially the frogs, whose diaphragmed croaks were like the thrum of plucked rubber bands. When night fell, Jason still labored by the light of a flashlight, sweating open the spring-held jaws of the traps and covering them with light brush. The shepherd watched him, his ears cocked and his body trembling at each sound.

He was finished by nine o'clock. He rubbed the dog's neck as they returned to the tent. He had forgotten how watery areas attracted mosquitoes. He slapped and cursed them as he primed and lit the lantern. He concealed the light with a tent flap, then turned it so low that its glow was barely visible. He wanted to sharpen his night vision.

Presently his eyes could see the faint sheen of the lake surface all the way to the other shore without the moonlight. All the apple piles were in full view of his tent. He held the pistol loosely in his hands. He spoke to the dog. "They're out there somewhere, old boy. They're out there."

As the Indian walked down the road, he lost his thoughts in the steady progression of white divider lines sliding under his feet. The trees pressed in, withdrew, and pressed in again.

Claws scrabbled on the tarmac from a turn ahead. The Indian slipped off his bow and fitted an arrow.

It was the dog, running toward him with something in its mouth. It dropped it at the Indian's feet and sat down with its tail wagging.

The Indian ruffled feathers with his arrow tip. Had he hackles on his back, they would have shot straight out. It was a dead chicken, its head removed. Other than that, not a single piece of meat was gone.

"It's for me? He sent it?"

The dog barked. It ran to the woods and stopped, waiting for him.

The Indian forced down a surge of happiness with the cork of common sense. It was not his name, but it *was* a message, the first his spirit had sent to him. The spirit was reaching out to the Indian, asking him to resume the journey, perhaps because of the help he had rendered at the trailer park.

The spirit needed *him*.

It was not a hard decision. In fact, it was not even a decision; it was a surrender. He was a prisoner of the spirit as surely as if he were caged. The Indian did not really mind. The fire of his faith was rekindled instantly, as bright as before.

"I will come," he said. The same three words had launched him on his search for his soul. He plucked the dead chicken as he reentered the woods and tied it to his belt after placing the foot in his medicine bundle.

They found the footprint on a river bank sometime after midnight.

The spirit was moving with extreme caution through a landscape of low, scrubby trees. Low mists decapitated these trees, and the dog, nervous and upset after its joy at the Indian's return had worn off, swam in and out of this fog like a heavy fish. It had been roaming farther ahead than usual, sniffing the air and checking out every piece of foliage as the Indian slipped through mucky, trailing vines and puddles of brackish water.

The footprint came from a brand-new hiking boot. There was nothing distinguished about it, other than newness, yet it made the dog's hair bristle. It arched its throat to howl.

"Sssh!" The Indian cut it off. "Don't worry. It's just a man."

No, said the dog. This one is different. You know him. So do I.

The Indian rummaged through his memory and came up with a disorienting vision of wiping blood from his fingertip on his pants. It must have happened in Vietnam.

No! Not Vietnam! Somewhere else!

The dog's fear was primeval in its totality. To the dog this was an enemy far more fearful than anything in the trailer park. The only time it had been this frightened was when they passed close to a cemetery.

A ghost? Who left this print!

Try as he might, the Indian could not pull his shredded memories together. It was no use.

"That's why he wanted me back, isn't it?" said the Indian. "He's afraid of this fellow. He's afraid of trouble ahead."

The marmot whistle sounded, summoning the dog. After a few minutes, during which the Indian assumed instructions were given, the dog returned and lay down on the ground.

The Indian watched the trees, arrow tightly strung, waiting for the whistle that meant they would walk again.

He continued waiting as night waned and morning appeared in the east. Only then was he certain they were not going to move for a while yet.

5

Jason awoke at six in the morning, sitting in an upright position with the pistol still in his hand. Buck, tied to a tree, was straining at his leash for some ducks that were skimming the surface of the lake.

Washout! Jason examined the apple piles through his binoculars. All of them were untouched. For several horrible seconds he wondered if his reasoning was wrong, if the beast would bypass the lake altogether.

He boiled some water on the stove and made coffee. He turned on his transistor radio and heard a newscast that evaporated his black mood. There had been a break-in at a chicken farm last night, not far from the trailer park. Jason found the farm on his map; it was next to the second of the streams flowing into the lake.

"That's him, old boy," said Jason, untying the dog. "They're headed this way all right. They can't be any more than four, five miles from us right now."

The beast would sleep in the daylight. Now might be the time for Jason and Buck to search the swamp and woods for any caves. No point in waiting for night, Jason thought, checking his ammunition, if I can surprise him now.

He and the dog walked the perimeter of the lake, observing stones, willow thickets, and mud flats, until Jason was sure he could find his way around at night.

Then he began an exploration of each of the streams for a distance of one mile from the Little Harrington. Although Buck was firmly leashed to his hand, he kept lunging off in chase of the occasional rabbit and even more occasional squirrel.

By noon the wet, dank trees had become steamy with the sunlight. Gnats whirled around Jason's perspiring face, and his feet were hot and blistered. His gun hung loose and accessible in its holster. He studied every clump of willow, every maple, every possible place where the giant might be sleeping.

They reached the fifth and final stream around two in the afternoon. Jason sat on the graveled bank and took out a sandwich. He was wet to his hips. As soon as he sat, the mosquitoes charged after him. In between bites he slapped at them. The more he butchered, the more came. He knew better than to get emotional about them.

Buck rumbled, splashed into the stream, and pointed.

"You're not a bird dog, you stupid mutt."

Buck's rumble toned up into a glottal growl.

Water splashed upstream; then an answering growl came. The stream turned to the right, and the view was blocked by clawed roots of a tree. Buck barked loudly, and the answering bark was higher in tone.

Jason dropped the sandwich and kneeled behind a muddy peninsula. He drew his gun as Buck splashed up to the bend. It had been a dark night in Canada, the darkest in his life, but Jason recognized the other dog's bark as an escaped prisoner never forgets the voice of his betrayer.

The two animals collided once, then faced each other in slow circles, spring-taut at the slightest lapse in protocol for an explosive, blinding, bloody fight.

Other feet were splashing down the stream. Jason felt as if a hollow had opened inside him and was about to swallow his innards. Two feet. It was running!

Now . . . now!

He cocked the pistol and gripped it with both hands. Then the Indian stepped into view, his chest neatly bisected by the sight on his gun.

Seconds after the snarls began filtering through the trees, the Indian was awake and running down the slimy stream. He fitted an arrow to his bow and pulled it taut. The enemy was a big dog, and the conversation between the animals was becoming heated, their rumbles dropping down to the dangerous level which indicates a crucial moment when one or the other decides to fight. The Indian was still plugged with sleep. His feet slipped on the mud, so he ran into the water.

The German shepherd was big enough to make hash of the pup. It backed away from the Indian, snout wrinkled over white fangs, and growled at him. The triangle of rage between man and animals held as the Indian calculated the risk of killing someone's obviously expensive pet with an arrow.

The Indian whistled the spirit noise. The shepherd broke and ran downstream toward a muddy delta, where he halted and roared at them again. The Indian raised the bow.

The shepherd barked at something concealed behind the mud bank. Probably a frog or a squirrel. His pride was wounded, so he had to prove his courage against some quaking little animal.

His own dog started in pursuit of the stranger with reckless courage. The Indian lowered the bow, grabbed it by the scruff, and cuffed it. "Calm down, you don't want to get killed over a chipmunk, do you?"

The dog could not calm down. It barked, nipped, and scrabbled furiously in his arms, trying to get down to the mud bank. The animal's fear was contagious. The Indian felt himself at the muzzle of some nameless danger. Tension braced the woods in invisible bonds. It was not just the shepherd. The Indian felt eyes watching him with keen, baleful intelligence at this very moment.

He carried the dog back upstream to the Sitka spruce against which he had been sleeping. The dog stood guard, nostrils flared. The Indian lay down to resume his sleep.

"Tell him I don't like this place. Tell him to get away from these rivers, I want to go somewhere else."

They were futile words. The spirit went exactly where he pleased and did not give a fart about what the Indian thought about it.

Had he seen that dog before? The Indian sensed he had. It must have happened sometime during one of the holes in his memory.

For a full minute Jason had the Army jacket squarely in his sight. One shot would have taken most of the Indian's chest away. He had circled the body with the muzzle, trying to talk himself into coldbloodedness as the mosquitoes swarmed over his clothes.

After the Indian left, he finally sat upright and uncocked his pistol. He clasped his hands and tensed his forearms while speaking almost apologetically to the shepherd. "Buck, old boy, for a minute there I thought you really did me in." He strapped the gun into his holster and continued speaking without looking at the wolf face. "Couldn't do it, old boy. Not like that."

The Indian was wanted for questioning in Canada. Assault and battery. Murder. Justice was useless unless the recipient was faced with it. A sniper shot from concealment was not a proper execution. Also, it was illegal.

The Indian had changed over the past months. He no longer had a rifle. One did not throw away a perfectly decent pump .30.30 (incredible how details seen for only a millisecond come back later), particularly if one was living in the woods. That was final confirmation for Jason that the Indian was uninterested in hunting the Bigfoot. He was thin—indeed, emaciated. The bow and arrows were handmade, by a careful, time-consuming process. Why had he thrown away the rifle and taken the time to make the bow and arrows?

For the next three hours, Jason and Buck carefully poked through the woods, looking for the resting place of the Bigfoot. Jason watched the dog to see if he picked up a scent but although he remained ferociously tense, there was no sign of a trail. If they found one, Buck might raise hell. He tied the dog to a tree and went into the woods alone.

After several futile hours in the woods, Jason returned to Buck, who was delighted to see him. "It'll have to be tonight, boy," said Jason, feeding him another sandwich. "The first lesson for a trapper is patience."

He replaced the apples with fresh ones. He parked his car deeper in the shrubbery and banked his tent with camouflage brush. By sunset anticipation of nightfall was jangling his nerves. He polished the pistol, oiled the parts, and reloaded again and again.

He had this landscape in the palm of his hand now. Come what may, Jason would know where he was even at night for a radius of a mile in each direction around the lake.

As darkness fell he took a caffeine pill and ate the last

of his sandwiches. He believed himself ready for anything with his traps, his night vision, his fierce dog, and his big cannon pistol.

A gentle lick from the dog woke the Indian that evening. He sat up, trying to clear his head. Sleep was nothing to look forward to any more. It did not rest him, it merely presaged more walking.

The woods were quiet, which meant that the spirit was up and about. The Indian was hungry. He had had no chance to hunt today after the dog fight. Unless the spirit found a deer or he caught a fish himself, both would be walking on empty stomachs tonight. He envied the dog's energy. It pranced around impatiently, trying to get him moving.

He gathered up his bow and arrows, then kneeled over the stream, splashing water over his face. He had overslept again. It must be sometime around nine o'clock. He said to the dog, "I want to find a fish or something first. Then I'll be ready when he is."

The dog dashed away. The Indian ate a handful of berries from a bush. The dog returned, woofing. The spirit was walking southeast.

As they trudged along the bank, the Indian watched the water. Moonlight rippled the stones on the bottom. A dark shape silvered under a spit of water weed swaying silkenly under the slow current. A small fin protruded like a flag.

The Indian squatted down, hand poised. His fingers tined into the water and clenched around a slimy fish. He threw it on the ground and stomped it. The fish swelled and grunted in death. It was a cruddy old tripe, which the Indian hated. He whistled for the dog.

The dog hesitated, listening to the running water. The Indian whistled again, louder.

From the woods came the high scream of a woman,

slicing the night into fragments. At its highest point of soprano pitch it was punctured by a gunshot and the thunderous barking of the German shepherd. The scream plunged downward into a man's baritone and kept going until bottoming out in a wolf's snarl of rage.

Jason had been nodding when the bullfrogs across the lake stopped thrumming. His head jerked upright. The silence spread like a wave, silencing the birds, the crickets, and finally the animals on his own side. He reached for Buck's neck. The dog was on his feet. He nipped at Jason's hand.

It could be nothing: a quick cold breeze, a truck on a highway, even a sudden awareness of him concealed in the reeds. Jason had heard such silences on previous camping trips. Humans frightened mammals into quiet, and they in turn frightened birds, which in turn passed the fear down the evolutionary chain to bacteria.

Jason stepped gingerly through the reeds, night binoculars in one hand, pistol in the other. Moonlight sparkled on the water.

Then he saw it. A hulk made shapeless by its posture. It was squatting over a pile of apples. Jason's breath hissed through his teeth.

The steel trap closed with a clink that floated across the water. The hulk elongated into a humanlike shape and screamed from lungs massive as drums. The sound was unbearable. Jason fired to stop its scream more than anything else.

The gunflash was a ball of orange, half as tall as Jason's body. The recoil lifted the gun over his head and clanged his ears into deafness.

A tower of water spouted up and disintegrated exhaustedly as the figure limped along the shore with a dreadful moaning. The beast had left a severed section of itself in the trap's jaws. Jason cursed and fired again. A branch dropped from a tree by the thing's head as it scooted through the reeds and into the woods.

While Buck surged through the water with hungry growls, Jason ran around the perimeter of the lake. Buck was well into the trees, his barks an echoing howl, by the time Jason got there.

From the other end of the lake, Jason heard the barking of the Indian's dog and feet surging through water.

Jason plunged into the woods, mindful of the roots clawing at his boots. The thing was injured—that was sure. And Buck would get to him first, cornering him until Jason arrived. Jason was going to have to kill the beast; he could not take on both it and the Indian.

Then he realized that something else had gone wrong. Buck's barking had ceased.

The Indian stumbled out of the woods into the marsh-land. He kicked at a pile of fruit. A steel trap slammed shut, flinging muck into the air and missing his foot by centimeters. Glinting in the moonlight were an attached stake and metal chain.

Close by was a trap already shut, surrounded by half-eaten apples. In the steel teeth was a plug of gristly bone with hair matted around a toenail.

"Oh God . . . oh God . . ." the Indian breathed, separating the jaws. He dropped the toe into his medicine bundle. There were other apple piles about. Somebody knew his spirit's fondness for apples.

His dog led him to the woods but adamantly refused to enter. The Indian stung it with curses and blows, but the animal cringed in the reeds, back arched in terror, and would not budge.

From deeper in the woods came more gunshots, clustered together. With a final kick at the dog, the Indian entered alone, walking cautiously in case any more traps awaited him.

Jason's run decelerated to a walk as the silence became oppressive. He flattened his hand over the flashlight lens, then opened two fingers a crack. The slenderest of light beams flew out to a face on the ground. The light collected around white teeth and white eyes.

That was all there was left of Buck. The rest of the body was gone. Deprived of his dog's eyes and ears, his road presumably closed off by the pursuing Indian, Jason realized he was in a nasty predicament. He cut off the flashlight.

A smell hung in the air—the same toilet stench he had sensed in Canada just before Nicolson died. Many Bigfoot sightings were accompanied by an odor mostly compared to muck dragged up from a river bottom. The predominant odor was sweat, Jason decided. Sweat and excrement, the fear smell. The beast was frightened of him.

The fourth river was just ahead. The gurgling waters swamped out into marsh farther toward the lake. To his right the ground creaked.

Jason whirled around, pistol ready, as something long and sinuous was thrown through the air. It draped warmly over his arm and hissed. The dangling rectangular head buried its fangs in his left forearm and pumped fire deep under his skin. Jason shouted, shaking the rattler to the ground, and blasted a crater in the mud midway down its squirmy body, the bullet sweeping away the tail section even as the head continued striking against his boot.

A rock sizzled out of the brush, scraping skin off Jason's scalp and scattering pieces of bark from the lodge-pole pine behind him. Jason fired into the trees. The flash framed a hairy arm with another rock, and fiery green eyes.

Jason fired again, blowing away a pinwheel of pine needles in the area where he imagined its face was. His next two shots came with machine-gun speed. One bullet exploded a chokecherry bush, one gouged wood from a tree. The hammer clicked on an empty chamber.

Silence. Reload?

The beast swelled out of the forest like a pall of smoke. Jason turned to run, and a rock caught him between the shoulder blades. He fell over roots, then sprang to his feet and headed for the river, the great shaggy shape howling behind him.

A profound ache spread from Jason's left arm to his shoulder. He had read somewhere that rattlesnake bites are overrated. The poison is a hemotoxin that attacks blood rather than nerves. He had a couple of hours to get help, if the running did not force the poison too deep into his body.

Jason dove into the river and stayed under water, letting the current carry him toward the lake, until his lungs swelled to an intolerable limit. He came up for air and dug his feet into the stony riverbed to brace himself against the sluggish current. He looked around for the Bigfoot.

What looked like a mountain detached itself from the river bank downstream and surged up against the current toward him, plowing great wings of water around its chest. The beast's arms opened wide to embrace Jason.

Jason struck for shore. The Bigfoot surged up between him and the river bank and kept coming. Jason splashed water at it. Ludicrous gesture. He threw the flashlight, still clutched in his hand, then the empty pistol. Both bounced thickly off bone.

Jason balled up and sank underwater in freezing pitch-blackness. He pushed against the riverbed, hoping his momentum and the current would carry him past the beast.

A snake of fur, sticky despite the water, closed around his chest. With the relentless force of a steam shovel, Jason was hauled out of the water, lifted high over the beast's head, and flung in again, with such force that he felt as though he were hitting a brick floor. For one brief instant before the water closed over him, Jason saw its face.

The Indian walked like a cat, wary of bulges signifying more traps. He found the shepherd's head on the ground. The dog bustled up, his courage restored, avoiding the dead snake. Both heard the furious splashing in the river.

He heard a loud shout of pain from the river, then the frantic slosh of a body surging toward the shore. The battle had ended.

The dog looked at him. The Indian stroked its fur. "He is well," he said. After this there was no question that the spirit would be hungry.

Dazed by the snake poison and the paralyzing vision of the thing's face, Jason lay limp as he was propelled downward head first. The water burst into bubbles and chunks of mud as his head was pushed into the muck at the bottom.

He kicked his legs into the thing's chest as it closed those clamping arms around them and pushed him deeper. Jason grabbed at the trunklike legs sunk deep in the muck by his chest, but they were like hardwood. His ears and nose filled with mud. If he opened his mouth he would choke.

The hatchet.

The thing had limped. The trap had injured its foot. Jason touched the steel hatchet strapped to his waist. The movement caused the thing to savagely rotate his body, sending up mud-streaked air bubbles.

How had it limped? Right? Left? Right! Jason's right hand fumbled the hatchet from its case. It nearly slid out of his hands. He fumbled his fingers over the thing's legs. Right leg, right leg! He found the knee.

Water resistance slowed his swing, but the blade was sharp; it had been sharpened yesterday, when he bought it. The blade struck the knee a harmless touch, and Jason slid it down the thing's leg toward the foot buried in muck.

The water exploded before the blade reached its mark. Simultaneously, Jason kicked and felt his boot toe strike its chest. The current gripped him and tore him out of the beast's grasp.

His head, slimy with mud, broke the surface, and he tore in great chunks of air. The arms reached for him. He dove under water again and caught its foot with his hatchet as it took a step. The blade missed, but the wide edge grazed the foot, and that was enough.

The thing shouted, the cry coming from behind the bangs of hair covering its face, and lunged again. Jason was swept by the current down toward the lake. His last view of the monster was of its arms held above water as it walked to the opposite shore. The devil was gone. Burning bright in the forest of the night.

The river shallowed over stones just before spreading into the delta of still water around the lake. The frigid water sent convulsive tremblings through Jason's body. He rolled clear into the reeds and lay still, shocked to the depths of his soul.

Deformed—Kimberly did not know how right he was! That face burned away everything else in Jason's memory. He had always believed such faces to be imaginary, the kind of silly debris to be swept from one's mind in order to build rational foundations.

The face was conical, as though funneling out through a delicate chin. The hair on its head was long and stringy, covering the thing's cheeks down to his jaws. The mouth was thin and narrow, but large teeth protruding forward pushed the outer edges of the lips into a perpetual grin.

The eyes were narrow and gloating. Just above them on the outer edge of the brow were two small horns. A perpetual grin and horns.

It was not a gorilla's face. It was the face of Satan, delicate and long, stamped onto an ape's skull. The picture of the devil as inscribed in hundreds of thousands of medieval paintings.

Jason did not remember getting to his feet. His body functioned even though his mind did not. His legs carried him past the lake, through more brush, and planted him firmly on the road. He realized too late that he was walking away from his car.

Gradually the animals came alive again. Hundreds, perhaps thousands, of frogs, beavers, and birds, but to Jason they coalesced into one night creature that swirled around, waiting to tear him to pieces and drag him underground.

Blazing eyes lit up the trees along the road. Another monster's breath shivered the land as it forged toward him. Jason feebly held up one hand to ward it off, but instead a horn blared, brakes screeched, and he sank to his knees on the pavement.

The footsteps were wary.

"Snakebite," he gasped.

"There's a Ranger station down the road. Can you walk?"

It was a young woman wearing a granny dress. She had thin, surprisingly strong hands that grasped him under the armpits and guided him to the car.

Damn his luck, it was a Volkswagen, barely big enough for his legs. He rolled down the window and threw up. "Sorry," he choked.

"How long since it happened?"

"Few minutes."

The girl was in her twenties, with a wide, spare, attractive face completely devoid of makeup. She shifted gears.

The car turned back the way it had come. "Don't worry. You've got time. But you're lucky I came by."

Jason squirmed on the seat, trying to find a comfortable position.

"It won't work." She smiled. "It happened to me once. You can't get comfortable."

"I think I'm in love with you."

She laughed.

"What's your name, for my will?"

"It's Martha Lucas. And you won't have to worry about your will. You'll be fine."

He should have used bigger traps, long rectangular ones that would have taken its foot off completely. Set up ultra-violet lights. Poisoned the apples. Something. *Something!* He had almost caught a legend out there. Poor Buck. Poor, poor dog. No second chances for him.

It was a long way to the Ranger station. The girl accelerated, glancing with concern at him.

Jason tried to disassemble that thing's face and put it back together more sensibly. He made it from the hair to the eyes before, retching, he passed out.

The Indian watched the slow-moving waters for some sign of the demon that had attacked his spirit. A porcupine rustled the foliage down the bank. The Indian killed it with an arrow and carefully plucked out the quills. He led the dog across the river, then handed the limp, denuded animal to him. "Take this to him. I'll find more."

When the dog returned, the Indian had two squirrels and a chipmunk ready. The spirit was walking steadily southward, toward the mountains. At sunrise they left the dark woods and moved into a meadow at the base of the foothills.

The spirit left blood everywhere, on boulder tops, mossy patches of ground, and green grass. He was no longer hiding his trail. Nor did he stop to rest as the sun continued rising. He walked with steady, sure steps, setting a grueling pace.

The Indian realized that the spirit was on familiar ground. It knew every trail, every log, every blade of grass. They were coming to the end of their journey. Their goal was somewhere in the mountains.

For two days and another night, the Indian lived only for his spirit. He butchered everything that walked, flew, or swam, shoveling bodies into the dog's mouth to be delivered to the spirit like sacrifices on a conveyor belt.

They crossed mountain foothills and climbed upward, the trees changing from lush thickness to lean, well-spaced suppleness suitable for resisting blizzard winds.

Patches of snow appeared on foggy trails and at night the wind, sharpened by mountain heights, was laden with icy grains. The Indian clutched his coat more tightly about him as they climbed, and wondered if they would climb so high they would step off the earth into ethereal transparency. The rational half of his mind realized the spirit was trying to get somewhere before his strength gave out entirely.

"He ain't a man," he gasped to the dog. "Where's his clothes? How come he don't talk? You seen him—what kind of man looks like that? Grandaddy's was a man. Grandaddy's was a carpenter. Big Foot was just a short little guy. He can't be Big Foot's ghost. What is he? *What is he?*"

The Indian gave out completely in a mountain meadow puddled with water and ringed by tall, mournful pines. With the dregs of his strength he managed to kill a rabbit. He skinned it, planning to give it to the dog. Instead, his hand delivered it to his own mouth. He sat on the ground, knowing it was a fatal mistake, because he would be unable to get up again. "I'm okay," he muttered to the dog. "But I got to sleep. I'm okay. Tell him I'm sorry . . ." He fell backward into a reclining position and dropped off, the rabbit carcass still in his hand.

The Indian did not know how long he had slept. The dog did not awaken him this time. He cracked his eyelids and saw moonlight gleaming off the glaciers of a mountain in the west. He sat slowly up. His blood seemed to have thickened to glue clogging his joints.

Much to his relief, the dog was not gone. It was sitting placidly on the ground, finishing off what was left of the rabbit. The Indian tottered to his feet and that got the blood moving. "Where is he?"

The dog yawned. The Indian whistled. His shriek broke up against many cliffs and returned to him in pieces.

An owl hooted in a tree, then glided away across the moon. The dog cheerfully followed him around the clearing as he searched for prints.

"I don't get it. Go find him. Tell him I'm awake."

You don't understand, the dog barked, wagging its tail. Listen.

The Indian realized that a song had been playing for some moments. It came out of the sky and through the trees and up from the ground. The song faded to a distant smattering of applause, punctuated by an amplified voice congratulating skiers.

The Indian pushed away foliage from bushes and caught his breath. The forest plunged downward to a valley, where it became flat meadow. A mile away, the land washed up again, like a frozen explosion, to another mountain. Midway up the mountain was a cluster of buildings with lighted windows and spotlights, like a luxurious ocean liner plunked down in the wilderness.

Two separate groups of flickering colored lights descended ski trails that flanked the large central building. They crossed and intertwined, red over yellow, blue over green, in intricate patterns, a coiling jeweled necklace writhing in the velvet night.

On the Indian's side of the valley, a river cut through a deep canyon. A high steel-braced bridge spanned a deep gorge that channeled the water into boiling foam. The road ribboned along the meadow, then ascended to the buildings.

The colored ski torches congealed at the bottom of the slope to another ripple of applause. The stentorian voice boomed, "Aren't they something, ladies and gentlemen?" His words were drowned out by whistles and shouted appreciation. ". . . back for the second show in one hour."

Journey's end. The Indian rubbed the dog's fur and played with its ears. "He has to let his foot get well. Will we spend the winter here?"

No, we will just rest. The spirit led you here. He cares about you. There are soft beds and lights and music in those buildings. You can rest here, too, and sleep. See how warm it is over there?

Again the Indian wondered how the dog spoke to him, as he had often wondered over the past months. His snout did not move, words did not come from his mouth, yet the Indian heard these replies in his own head. The voice sounded exactly like his own. "Hallucination," the Army doctors would have called it. The Indian wished he could forget the words of the doctors and remember his grandfather's instead.

Gently the Indian grasped the dog's muzzle in his hand. It was his friend, his bond to the spirit. He was not sick, as the doctors said; he was not imagining this. "Let's go down," he said to the dog.

He led it down the slope into the meadow. He talked aloud to himself, getting his voice back in shape and prac-

95

ticing words. He would need many more words than he had used with this animal to speak to human beings.

The valley road connected to the side of Colby Lodge, where passengers were unloaded. It widened into a parking lot behind the main building, where the service entrance was located.

Lester Cole, who was working overtime that night, finished his dishes at eleven, climbed into his pickup truck with the jackrabbit racing suspension and hood blister under which was housed a supercharger, tuned into a country-music station, and hurried down the road to his poker game.

He rattled over the bridge and honked at the Volkswagen van going up. The van was emblazoned with a cartoon of a bear on skis, wearing a peaked cap and scarf, under which were the words COLBY LODGE. Skis and luggage were tied to the roof rack. Lester thought it was high time Jack Helder, Colby's owner, bought a proper bus for the place.

The radio hissed when the woods closed around him. He watched the white road dividers slide from the headlight beams under his truck like thrown spears. He was changing stations when a man stepped out of an old logging road near the bridge, right in the middle of a white line.

"Jesus!"

Lester hit the horn and brake. The man was covered with hair from head to foot. He flung up an arm to ward off the light.

Lester swerved to a stop on the road shoulder in a shower of gravel. He slipped the rifle from the rack behind him and climbed out of the truck.

His ragged breath made crystalline little puffs in the frosty air. His father had told him about a Bigfoot that came up to his camp one night while he slept. His biggest mistake was in not shooting it and bringing home a hunk of the body to sell.

Lester heard leaves stir in the trees. He selected a black square of forest and fired four shots into it. The shot echoes rolled around the hills like billiard balls.

A rock flew out with such speed that its trajectory was perfectly flat for a hundred feet and punched a dent in the truck fender. The second and third rocks smashed respectively the side mirror and the windshield. The fourth rock nearly hit him in the head.

Lester's nerve broke, as it always did when he was challenged. He jumped into his truck and roared hell for leather down the road toward the Augusta County Ranger Station.

OBJECTIVE

6

Simon Helder's third and final heart attack occurred as he sat in the Denver office of his land-development firm eating an egg-salad sandwich in defiance of his doctor's orders. At the time of his death, his son Jack was skiing in Vail, Colorado. As per his father's instructions, Jack had packed a black suit in case Daddy croaked while the boy was out of town and had to fly to the funeral. "Daddy said he had no intention of lying around a house full of machinery to keep him going," said Jack to one of a number of women who passed through his bed that winter. "He said he's had it and I better take a long vacation because his probate is going to be expensive. Daddy always was a practical man."

After Daddy's death armies of lawyers clashed with the tax authorities over a piece of land—an entire valley, actually—the old man had bought in a secluded area of Washington State. The valley was called Colby, after the mountain that dominated it.

Jack Helder flew out to look at the place. He promptly fell in love with its isolation, its purity, its delicious shape. The whole area was too high in elevation for a planned community unless it was planned for Eskimos. Maybe his father had dreamed of retiring to a hunting lodge there. Maybe he liked to tell his friends he owned a gold mine, for the north face of the mountain was littered with the crumbled remains of a ghost town called Oharaville and a played-out mine. Whatever his reasons, the government would chew Jack to pieces over taxes unless something was done to prove that the valley was a business venture. Jack loved the valley so much that he would have gone to bed with it if possible. Failing that, he decided to ravish it with his supreme expression of love for the land: a ski lodge.

They cleared trees on Colby's east face. They built a giant central lodge with them and surrounded it with bungalows. Jack Helder put in plumbing, a modern kitchen and dining room, landscaped two ski trails out of the mountain, mounted artificial snow machines on the slopes, laid the foundation for a swimming pool, and ran out of money. Running out of money was a new and novel experience for Jack Helder.

He moved from Denver to the lodge. He opened months earlier than planned. His office had a smashing view of the area. His desk was polished, fitted pine trunks. He had booked forty percent of capacity for the next five months, and reservations were still coming in. Life was good. He enjoyed roughing it, so long as he had electricity.

Outside his office door came the jarring sounds of a waiter's angry voice. He looked up from his bills. His office door banged open, and in stepped the most bizarre human apparition he had ever seen. An Indian, accompanied by a dog which left tracks on the carpet, shook off restraining hands and loomed over Helder's desk with eyes so dark and deep that the lodge owner felt he could dive into them and swim downward forever without hitting bottom.

He slid his chair a respectful distance back from the desk. The Indian meant business, and he had all kinds of advantages, particularly surprise.

"Hello. May I help you?"

A waiter answered, "He sneaked in the service entrance, Jack."

Helder waved the waiters back. They hovered at the doorway.

"I want a job," said the Indian, in a surprisingly high and soft voice. "That's all. This is your place, ain't it?"

"Yes," said Helder, pleased, favoring the Indian with a glazed smile. "How did you guess?"

"I saw your office. I came in the back, and they jumped me." The Indian looked at the waiters.

Helder's eyes traveled from the Indian's clothes, which were so tattered they barely made it as drapery strips, to the knobby knuckles clutching a homemade bow, to the face, which was largely cheekbone. He took in his matted hair and odorous presence. "What kind of a job did you have in mind?"

"I don't give a shit. Clean the crappers. Sweep the floors."

"I see. And what kind of salary?"

"I don't want no money. I just want a job."

Now that was intriguing! "I don't get it. What do you want a job for if not money?"

"I'm going to be camping around here. I just thought I'd ask." Abruptly, the Indian walked to Helder's picture window. He stood so close to it that his breath fogged the glass. Helder saw his eyes, button-bright and black, spot the valley features still visible: the line of forest, the silver thread of the river, and the dark meadow. His eyes flicked like an animal's. For an instant Helder had the odd feeling the Indian was not quite human.

Helder shrugged at the waiters. Common sense notwithstanding, Helder was a gregarious man, and intrigued by the stranger. He was an honest-to-God schoolboy's Indian. He was all the distilled fantasies about Natural Man, the Wild West, and the Noble Savage in one. Thinking of Apache movies, Helder found himself blurting, "Can you ride a horse?"

"Sure."

"Don't know why I asked that. We don't have stables yet." He felt the full weight of the waiters' astonished attention on him. "That's about all I can think of. We're underfinanced right now, and pretty well full up. You can fill out a résumé, though. Sorry."

The Indian shrugged and walked to the door, where the waiters parted for him.

"Just a second! The bow and arrow."

"Yeah?"

"Are you any good with it?"

A gently mischievous smile illuminated the sharp face. The Indian's eyes rested on the long-stemmed wineglass from which Helder had just drunk his post-dinner port. The lodge owner wondered if he was not making the biggest mistake of his life. "I was just asking. Oh no . . ."

The Indian held the glass out to him. "I won't hurt you."

"Oh, I realize that, but I wasn't serious. I mean this kind of William Tell stuff . . ." Helder flapped his hands in embarrassment.

"Come on," the Indian coaxed. The smile grew wider.

"Oh hell." Helder took the glass because the waiters were watching. He should learn to keep his mouth shut.

The main lounge, onto which Helder's office opened, was approximately forty feet across. On the opposite wall was a fireplace of black Cascade lava. The floor was scattered with throw rugs, chairs, coffee tables, and sofas. The east wall was glass, opening onto the sun deck, where most of the guests were standing around, drinks in hand, brightly colored sweaters festooning their bodies. The west wall housed the reception desk, stuffed, antlered animal heads, and Charles Russell prints. Tucked into the corner was the Grizzly Bar, guarded by an enormous stuffed bear with his paws clutching an esthetically gnarled branch.

The last mile. Helder slouched across the floor to the fireplace, his evident dejection attracting the attention of the guests, who began filing in from the sun deck. When he reached the fireplace, he turned and faced the Indian, who remained at the office door, fitting an arrow to his bow.

Helder felt the fire heating his backside. Those were awfully crooked arrows. They were really twigs with some kind of dipshit pigeon feathers to stabilize them.

"Get it up higher," the Indian commanded.

Holding the glass upright by the base, Helder raised it so high that his coat buttons popped. If the arrow went through his eye, he'd fall backward, still conscious, and burn to death in the fire. If he were lucky, it might just drill a kneecap. He would be crippled but alive. Being shot in the stomach would be enormously annoying, and he would probably have to have liquid food the rest of his life.

The waiters formed a human cage around the Indian in case he tried to break away after the murder. All the guests were indoors, watching the unfolding drama. They should not drink at this altitude, Helder thought; there was at least ten cardiacs among them.

With three small movements, the Indian raised the bow, drew back the arrow, and let go.

Jesus! Aim!

One girl's scream underscored the collective gasp from the crowd. Helder heard the arrow thunk deep into the pine over his head. Severed from its slender stem, the goblet bounced onto his head and crashed into gleaming splinters on the floor. The musical impact was drowned out by the convulsive pandemonium of applause, shouts, and whistles from the guests. When Helder finally looked up at the glass base and stem, the arrow was still vibrating in the wood.

"Ladies and—" Helder squeaked. He cleared his throat.

"Ladies and gentlemen! If I may—*please*—have—your *attention!*" The last word was a scream, which dulled the roar and angered the Indian's dog. "Colby Lodge is pleased to announce its amateur, intermediate, and advanced archery courses, which will be held beginning tomorrow in the fields by the snowmobile shed . . ." The guests ignored him. Their voices rose back to high levels, drowning out his praise for the archery equipment in the souvenir shop.

In the office, he shut the door, silencing the noise of the guests to a muffled roar. He dropped his smile. He was an employer now. He sat at his desk and pulled out an employee form. "A hundred dollars a week. That's not much, but the lodging is free and so is the food long as you don't eat us alive. Besides, you didn't want any money in the first place. Okay with you?"

The Indian considered, then nodded impassively.

"Set it up any way you want. You'll work from noon to five in the afternoon. Mondays are off. Still okay?"

The Indian nodded again. Impatiently.

"Now that dog. He stays outside. You can feed him leftovers, but I don't want him running loose in here. Ah!"

The door opened and shut, letting in a fragment of laughter from the lounge as well as a slight girl with dusty blond hair drawn back with a ribbon, a loose sweater, a granny dress, and clear gray eyes.

"This is Martha Lucas. She runs the gift shop. She's the nearest thing we have to an authority on Indian . . . culture." Most Indians did not give a damn about such things. But this fellow was not typical of anybody. "Martha, this is . . . Good question. What's your name, anyway?"

The Indian's face flickered. He hesitated. "Moon. John Moon."

"Martha, Mr. Moon is going to be with us for at least a month, running an archery course."

Martha stood to one side, her eyes on Moon's leather bag. "Marvelous. Where are you from, Mr. Moon?"

"Stevensville, Montana."

Helder filled out the form. "I'll need some identification, Mr. Moon."

Moon dug out a wallet and hard leather case with a brass clasp and handed them to Helder. "All my stuff's in there."

Helder opened the billfold and found a Social Security card in the name of John Moon. There were no other papers and just a few crumpled dollar bills. "Don't you have a driver's license or anything?"

"No, sir."

"What's this?" Helder picked up the leather case and opened the clasp. The interior was lined with wrinkled velvet, on which was folded a red-white-and-blue ribbon with a medal showing a gleaming eagle.

While Helder stared at it, the silence could have crushed a ball bearing. Astonishment carved some character lines deep in his smooth face. "Is this for real, Moon?"

"Yeah."

"Martha, look at this. You'll never see another one again."

She had heard of the Congressional Medal of Honor and seen pictures of it draped around the necks of men ranging from lean Viking warriors to tubby middle-aged pensioners. Knowing nothing else but her first impressions about Moon, she thought it appropriate. *Appropriate*—that was the word.

"And he carries it around like a wooden nickel." Helder handed the case back to Moon, who dropped it into his medicine bundle.

"Vietnam, Mr. Moon?"

"Yeah."

"Okay, Mr. Moon. No contract, just a handshake, right?

Let's give it a whack for a month and see how it works out. Feel like a bite to eat?"

Mention of food drove everything out of the Indian's mind. His face lit up. "Yeah, I sure would."

"George will throw a sandwich together in the kitchen for you. Tell Jane at the reception desk you're in the fourth bungalow. She'll probably shift you around according to business."

Moon gathered his bow and arrows together. He and the dog left Helder's office like twin shadows.

Martha sat on Helder's sofa and tucked her legs under her dress. They spoke in low voices, as if Moon were listening at the door.

"I'd like to find out about that medal," Helder mused. "There's a record in the Defense Department somewhere."

"What's he doing here?"

"You've got me. He said he was camping. I wouldn't be surprised if he was running from something. I guess we'll know when he starts stealing us blind."

"You're taking a big chance."

"So what? He's the best archer I ever saw. You've got to take chances in life."

"If he's from Stevensville, he's probably a Flathead," Martha said, her eyes on the door.

"What's a flathead? I never heard of a flathead."

"They're really Salish, or that's what they called themselves. They were confused with a coastal tribe that flattened babies' heads with boards."

Helder envisioned white settlers being scalped and burned at the stake. Martha smiled.

"Interesting tribe. They never killed a white man. In fact, they protected them from Joseph and the Nez Perces, who were headed for Canada. They continued helping whites right up to when their land was taken from them."

"Why?"

"The Flatheads were philosophers of a sort. They invited Catholic missionaries from St. Louis to teach them the faith, which is kind of a twist. Missionaries usually invite themselves. They did it out of curiosity. At the same time, they were so skilled in war that neither Joseph nor the Blackfeet liked to tangle with them. They were very religious," she mused, looking back at the door. "Did you notice that handbag he wore?"

"The thing on his belt?"

"That's right. Either I'm crazy or that's a real medicine bundle. A sort of a fetish bag. The Indians believed in a personal spirit who brought them luck and everything. The spirit usually left a talisman like a rabbit foot that you'd carry in a bag like that."

Helder brought his pen point down on the desk. "It smelled."

"Really?"

"Yes. Like garbage. I was going to ask him to take it off. You can't get close to him." Helder doodled circles on the paper. He wanted things to be nice and uncomplicated for Colby's first winter. Martha was a sweet girl but a bit too intense for his tastes. "So he's a religious fanatic. Lots of people are. Jesus was."

"I wouldn't go that far. I was just thinking out loud," she said, getting up.

"Come on out and see the ski show. You can hear my melodious voice hitting every mountain in the hemisphere."

"I saw the first one. By the way, what did you think of Lester's Bigfoot?"

"Lester's *what?*"

"It was on the radio. Lester says he saw a Bigfoot on his way home tonight. Right down there past the bridge."

"Tonight!" Helder screeched. The boss was always the

last to know. Lester was a nose-picking dishwasher whom Helder had always thought pretty advanced for a cretin.

"Lester even claimed the thing threw rocks at him."

Helder was disinclined to believe that Lester could tell a Bigfoot from an empty sock. Bigfoot added another angle to the glittering array in his imagination. The wilderness equivalent of a haunted house. He wrote out notes for a Bigfoot hunt. Only the strong of heart need apply. He finished with a notation about discreetly stocking condoms in case girls on the Bigfoot hunt became so frightened that a strong, manly, protective arm was not diversion enough. Helder giggled at his wicked thoughts, and wondered if somewhere in that land development in the sky Daddy was not chortling with him.

"Kimberly? It's Jason!"

"Mr. Jason! I've been on pins and needles ever since talking to you. What's been happening? Where are you?"

"I'm in a hospital in the State of Washington."

"Again?"

"Yeah. You're not going to believe this. He threw a rattler at me."

Jason had been taken to the Ranger station two nights ago and then transferred to this ward, where a multitude of antibiotics was added to the antivenin. Bruises covered his body, more from the snake venom than the fight in the river. He was so full of needle holes that he leaked. A tight bandage constricted his arm where the snakebite was. He had successfully evaded the questions about where he was that night and what he was doing.

"I'd rather you didn't tell anybody about it." Jason could see his company's stock dropping into the basement. CANADA BIGFOOT HUNTER IN HOSPITAL AGAIN.

"That makes sense," Kimberly said.

"Listen, I found out some stuff on the Flatheads."

"Oh? Shoot."

"They had a very rich culture, all of it oral. And over half their stories are about giants. Giants! How about that? Giant tree men, giants living in the Flathead lake, giant everything. The story is Coyote killed them all off and turned them into black boulders. I guess he missed one, what?"

Jason filed away that bit of information. "Listen, I got a pretty good look at the thing."

"What was it like?"

"Well, it had a very peculiar face."

"Uh-huh."

"The skin was lighter-colored than the rest of it, and the hair was different, longer, with a widow's peak—"

"A what?"

"Widow's peak. A V in the middle of the forehead. Pointing down. And it had this narrow protuberant nose. The eyes were set deep. Now get this. You know how apes have this heavy eyebrow ridge over their eyes?"

"Oh yes. It's a shield of bone. The eyes are set well behind it."

"Well, he had two of these eyebrow ridges. And if the light was right they kind of looked like . . ." Jason gulped. "Horns."

The director of the Kansas Primate Center did not laugh out loud. His scratching pen was audible over the phone. "Anything else?"

What else do you need! "That's about it. Sounds pretty stupid, doesn't it?"

"Let me ask you this. Did it have a chin?"

Kimberly had hit it. A chin! Even more than the horns, that fragile, aristocratic, pointed chin was the single feature that transformed a simple gorilla in Jason's mind into something else. "Why?"

"And what about buttocks? Large protuberant buttocks? Oh, never mind. We know he walks upright, don't we? Buttocks anchor the back muscles. I believe you said he even runs upright?"

"Yes."

"We can identify your Sasquatch, Mr. Jason. Are you ready for this?"

Jason took a sip of water. "I'm ready for anything."

"The chin is what really does it. There's only one primate that has that feature. *Homo sapiens*, Mr. Jason. Your beast is a human of some kind. He's not an ape at all."

As Jason's equilibrium tilted, water spilled from his glass to the bed. He did not know whether to feel anger or disappointment. The face crowded back on him, that wicked, leering demon face curtained by shaggy hair . . .

Kimberly was still talking. "It's been growing on me ever since you said it was a headhunter. Neanderthal man was a headhunter, Mr. Jason. During an excavation in Italy they uncovered a skull cult in a sort of altar made by Neanderthals. They found a skull propped on a little stick. Now you're saying he's intelligent enough to throw a rattler at you to defend himself. Doesn't that sound pretty human to you?"

Impossible!

Jason furiously waved away a nurse who looked in, concerned about his white face and shaking hand. "A human being!" he grated into the phone. "Kimberly, he's seven feet tall! He eats bark! He's covered head to foot in hair and his arms reach to his knees! What the hell, do you think I'm crazy or something?"

"Certainly not, Mr. Jason. I fully realize it raises more questions than it answers. But a man is what it is, a man of some kind."

"*What kind, Kimberly?*"

"Remember what I said about genetic deformities?"

"Yes!"

"It sounds like this thing is deformed all right. Only I'm wondering if it's a deformed human instead of a deformed ape. Giantism is a well-known glandular disorder, and so is excessive body hair. And when you think about it, seven feet isn't all that tall. Basketball players reach that height all the time. So that *might* leave us not only with a human but a modern one, some poor, retarded wretch who escaped from an institution somewhere and has been running around the woods."

"Kimberly, he weighs a good eight hundred pounds! He's got to be smart enough to fuel all that weight!" Jason roared. "A human that messed up wouldn't survive an hour in the woods."

Kimberly was silent for a moment. A heavy professorial silence, during which Jason could almost hear him clambering through dusty mental detritus of his past learning.

"Well, Mr. Jason, that leaves us with Paranthropus or some other predecessor of *Homo sapiens*. I don't know. It doesn't fit any fossil I've ever heard of in the human line, but we have only scratched the surface of that study anyway. It does sound to me like it's deformed. And if he has a chin, he's a *Homo sapiens*. Period. I'm sorry, Mr. Jason, but that's the bottom line."

A man.

Some pitiful rejected soul wandering through the wilderness? Or an ancient manlike thing, part of a whole species, a primordial shape that walked the mists of prehistory, whose face stamped terror on man's memory for ages to come. He was a headhunter. He threw stones. Even his prints were manlike.

A prehistoric human would be a find indeed, something bigger than a dumb gorilla. A living relic of human evolution, an ape man. Or a man ape.

Did the Indian sense this somehow? Was it just curiosity like Jason's that kept the Indian on the thing's trail for hundreds of miles? Was there some kind of bond between them, some mutual—there was no other word for it—friendship? It would explain why the Indian had conked Jason with his rifle. The Indian had seemed to be protecting it.

"Protecting it," Jason muttered, looking out the window. That was exactly what the Indian was doing; that was why he had attacked Frank Stone at the trailer park, too.

That his quarry was deformed was inescapable, Jason realized. Man or ape, the head did not fit the body. Well, he would figure that out when the time came. More than ever the central enigma of the thing filled Jason's head, to the bursting point. He ate, slept, and drank that creature. Every moment in the hospital room, snakebite or not, meant the thing was getting away from him.

The nurse at the reception desk was astonished to see him walk down the hall fully dressed. "Mr. Jason, where do you think you're going!"

"I'm checking out, thank you." Jason unsteadily filled out a check for a thousand dollars. "That should cover expenses, time, ambulance service, plus contributions to a new wing or whatever you want, plus any mental anguish caused by my temper."

"You cannot leave until the doctor's seen you."

"I am leaving now, madam."

"You need at least four days of rest—"

"I never felt better in my life. I need fresh air and sunshine." Jason tore out the check and handed it to her. He sniffed his hand, realizing he still smelled of disinfectant.

"Mr. Jason . . ."

"No, madam."

"At least let someone change your bandage."

In a rack in the reception room were copies of a local newspaper called the *Garrison Tribune.* As a nurse angrily wrapped a new bandage around his forearm, Jason opened the paper to the second page and felt adrenaline rush through him.

The paper was a day old. On page two was a photo of a fat man pointing at a section of woods where he said a Bigfoot had thrown rocks at him. Next to it was a photo of James Drake, the chief of the Augusta County Ranger Station. He was propping up two plaster casts of footprints on his desk.

James Drake was the Ranger who had slit Jason's snakebite and drained poison from it.

"When did this happen?" He held up the paper.

"Night before last. And don't get any ideas of hunting for it like the rest of the county, Mr. Jason," said the nurse. "Unless you want to die of exhaustion."

"Didn't you hear me?" beamed Jason. "I never felt better in my life."

"Well, how do, Mr. Jason." Drake put down a sheaf of papers and extended his hand. "Thought you'd be in that place the rest of the week."

"I got tired of bedsores. I thought I'd drop by and thank you for saving my life." Jason declined a beer poured from Drake's thermos into a paper cup. James Drake looked like a slightly melted bear whose heavy strength was still formidable but had sloped a bit farther down his body. He worked hard at giving the impression that he liked outdoors work better than running a desk. He leaned back in his chair, scratching both elbows with his fingers as though he were hugging a pillow.

"I didn't do nothing but cut you up a little. Glad you stopped by. I was going to call on you."

"What for?"

"Oh, a bunch of paperwork. Stuff for reports."

"I'll do what I can."

"Mind showing me your camping permit?" Suddenly Drake did not seem like an easygoing woods lover. Suddenly he seemed like a cop.

"Camping permit?" Jason shifted uneasily in his chair.

"Now let me guess. You didn't fill one out, did you?"

"No."

"I sort of figured that. I figured that because your car wasn't parked near to any trailhead."

"Trailhead?" Jason said.

"We maintain little places in the woods for folks to park their cars, Mr. Jason. All these places have little boxes with papers in them. You fill these papers out and it tells us when you went in and when you plan to come out. It's sort of nice to know if anybody's running around in there."

"I see."

"Augusta County is officially classed as a wilderness area, you see. Why, there's places around these mountains I bet nobody but Indians've been."

Jason squirmed, trying to rest his weight on a different bruise. "I'll certainly be more careful in the future. One snakebite is enough for me."

"I reckon." Drake acted absolutely delighted to have Jason in his office. His delight increased whenever he said something that made Jason uncomfortable. "Let me show you something else."

He reached into a drawer and pulled out Jason's traps. They were all clotted with dirt. "You'll never guess where we found these. Right up there at the lake. And do you know what? Every one of them was buried next to a load of apples. Apples! What kind of pinhead would do something like that?" He made a clicking sound with his tongue and dropped them back in the drawer.

"Probably some dumbbell looking for animals."

"Do you think that's what it was? He must have forgot to clear it with us. If I find out who did it I'll slam him in the cooler for a few days. We can do that, you know." Drake smiled and folded his hands on the desk before him. "I've done it lots of times."

Jason shifted position again. "I hear you had another type of emergency the other night."

Drake's delight flared into absolute joy. "You mean Lester and his ape? Ain't that something?" He slapped the table with his hand. "I knew old Lester was going to pull something one of these days."

Jason swallowed hard. "You think it's a fake?"

"I *know* it's a fake. Of course it's a fake. Lester admitted it. He sat right there in your chair and told me how much money he was going to make on the Johnny Carson show. He told me he was going to write a book."

"What happened?"

"Search me. He called me yesterday afternoon and said he was sorry about it all. He said he didn't really see anything. You know, Mr. Jason, people do the damnedest things. Why, the University of Washington wanted casts of that print right away. Looky here."

Drake took out an eight-by-twelve blowup of the picture Jason had seen in the newspaper. The prints were square with horizontal toes, without the slightest resemblance to his own quarry.

"Lester, he cut himself a piece of wood and fitted it to his shoe. We found this one in river mud close by the bridge. Know what I thought for a while, Mr. Jason?"

"No. What?"

"That the fellow who set these here traps was looking for a Bigfoot."

"You don't say."

"'Course, that was before Lester called me and confessed. Where do you think he is now?"

"Who?" mumbled Jason, wishing he was gone.

"The fellow who set the *traps!*"

"Oh, him. I imagine he's long gone, Drake."

"He better be. If I ever catch him I'll put a boot up his rear." Drake stuck out his hand, dismissing Jason with a forceful courtesy. "You ought to run up to Colby Lodge and say hi to Martha Lucas on the way home. She's the one who saved your neck, not me."

"Where is it?"

Drake tried to describe the route, but Jason could not follow him. He pointed it out on a wall map as a dot floating amidst wrinkled elevation lines. Finally, he drew a route on a piece of stationery. "I don't blame you. Helder plunked it down right where it's hardest to get to. He says it's better for folks who really want to get away from it all." Drake obviously disapproved of ski lodges built in virgin wilderness. "They'll be getting some snow before too long. Maybe they'll go broke," he said hopefully.

Jason yawned pressure from his ears as his car ascended through a tunnel of trees past the thousand-foot level into the valley. The last stand of lodge-pole pines opened like a curtain on a stage set dominated by a squat fireplug-shaped mountain, with the lodge clinging to its east slope.

He stopped the car at the Silver River bridge and stepped out. The valley was startlingly isolated, and this natural loneliness besieged Colby Lodge. The lodge strung out a line of little bungalows like droplets separating from a blob of water. Twin, straight downhill ski runs flanked the buildings, topped by two snow guns, which looked like wrecking cranes.

No attempt had been made to blend the buildings into the setting. Colby had been chopped out of a thicket of pines, which, according to Drake, had been used to construct the buildings.

Jason looked up and down the gorge through which the Silver River tumbled. It seemed likely that the river would be the place for a cave system, but he could see none from where he stood. The river seemed to circle around the mountain at the north.

He arrived at the lodge as a van was unloading a bristle of skis, poles, handbags, and suitcases. The reception desk directed him to Martha Lucas's shop.

The shop was built into a gallery. It had a glassed front displaying postcards. Inside were souvenirs, mostly Indian beadwork, hammered belt buckles inset with turquoise stones, Navajo rugs, and carved-leather gear.

The shop was packed with people, most of whom seemed to be purchasing archery wrist and arm guards. The girl at the counter must be Martha Lucas. All he had seen in the glow of the dash lights had been a wide face.

"Mr. Jason!" She waved behind the glass.

Jason walked in and showed her his bandaged arm. "I guess I'll live, thanks to you."

"Don't be silly," she said, embarrassed.

"It's true. Good deeds are hard to come by." As she rang up a wrist guard, Jason looked curiously around the shop. The plaster was new. In fact, the whole place had a brittle, unsettled air about it. "How did you get stranded up here?"

"Jack Helder wanted somebody to run his shop. He figured I'd be good because I know about Indians. The guests are interested in them. Are you staying with us?"

"No. I'm on my way home. How do you know about Indians?"

She was unable to answer until she had disposed of four customers. During the interval, Jason saw little wooden Bigfoots with schmoo smiles and the name Melvin engraved on the base under a glass counter. The Melvin heads were pierced for key chains. "I'm an anthropologist," she said, slamming shut the cash drawer. "Half an anthropologist, anyway. I've been working on a thesis for the last year, on and off."

"Don't suppose you know anything about a tribe in Montana called the Flatheads, do you?"

She gave him a look. Immediately Jason's aches and pains retreated.

7

The Indian's new clothes were stiff and uncomfortable, rubbing his body in unfamiliar places. Helder had looked in on him eating breakfast in the kitchen that morning and sorrowfully shaken his head. "Moon, I hope you take this in the right way. You need a bath. Also, your clothes simply won't do. Get yourself some jeans, a nice shirt, some Indian gear, whatever, from the shop and charge it to me. Martha can fix you up. Okay? Okay."

Last night the Indian had wolfed down two cheeseburgers, potato salad, a quart of milk, and a handful of cookies. As he walked to his bungalow, the whole mess came up again and splashed over the ground. Sleep in the soft bed had erased him completely until columns of sunlight poured through the window and someone rapped on the door, crying, "Moon, Mr. Helder sent me. It's eleven thirty, and you're supposed to be ready at noon."

The Indian had realized that he was not a free agent any more. This Helder owned him body and soul. But it was only temporary, only until the spirit spoke to him. On the whole, food and shelter was not a bad deal. He was honing his skills under the eyes of people, who—particularly the women—seemed fascinated with him.

"Get it up higher, ma'am." The girl was struggling with the bow, trying to aim at a cottonwood trunk. She released the arrow, threading it through the grass. "That's okay. You see this here?" The Indian touched a peep sight on the fiberglass shaft. The sight was adjustable by a screw and worm gear. Balancing poles protruded from the bow shaft. "The higher this is, the lower your arrow goes. The lower it is, the higher your arrow goes. Do it again."

What they really enjoyed was seeing him shoot. The Indian slid the sight up and put an arrow in the base of the trunk. He lowered the sight and put the next one in halfway up.

Some of the women stood a little closer than necessary to him. They were exceptionally friendly and attractive. Abstinence from sex over the past months had built up an oppressive physical pressure in him that hampered his concentration. Whenever the distraction became too great, the dog emitted a startled bark. The beast could read his mind.

"Mr. Moon, can I talk to you a minute?"

"Sure."

Helder had been watching the demonstration for several minutes. He led him away from the crowd and spoke with his arm around the Indian's shoulder. "Moon, I can't help but notice you're using one of our fiberglass bows."

"Sorry. I'll put it back."

"No, no, no, it's not that. I don't mind if you tone yourself up with it or whatever it is you do. But I'd suggest you use your own while teaching these people." Helder leaned in closer, a teenager sharing a secret. "These people, Moon. It's a funny thing. They spend their lives in offices, dreaming about weekends when they can be pioneers and cowboys and getting back to nature and all that. It's a technological age, you see? Now, that fiberglass bow was probably stamped out by some machine in a factory that makes a thousand of them every hour. These people want to get away from all that. They've got the feeling no

machine can make a bow as well as an Indian using his own hands. By the way, that's true, isn't it?"

"Nope."

"It's not?" Helder was visibly disappointed.

The Indian could not imagine arguing about the manifold advantages of these machine-made fiberglass bows over even the finest Indian ones. They were more accurate, more powerful, and better balanced. They did not go limp when wet or break in the cold. The steel shafts with their plastic stabilizers flew truer and punched deeper than ash arrows with feathers. "You can take them down, too, Mr. Helder," he said, breaking the bow down into small pieces. "And these here balance things are just great. 'Course, it's all expensive, but it's great."

"Moon. Just use your own goddamned bow. As a favor to me. Okay? Okay," Helder stalked away, muttering something about craftsmanship.

The Indian released an arrow as his dog began a frenzied bark. The shot went wide. The Indian turned as the animal was about to attack a tall man with a bandaged arm. The Indian whistled, and the dog reluctantly backed away from the stranger, leaving its snarls coiling about in the air.

The man walked rapidly away from the group.

"Hey, that's okay, mister. He won't hurt you."

The man turned around and slowly walked back, eyes fixed on the Indian. The dog roared again, and the Indian smacked it with his bow, sending it with a yelp behind the legs of an outraged girl.

The man was tall and built square, with a head of thick brown hair and a face like a fist. Although of massive stature, his face was pallid and his skin was smooth. His muscles must have come from deliberate indoor exercise rather than physical labor.

Something about the man's face! He looked at you

from under, as if you were taller. Yet the Indian could not imagine where he could have seen him before, unless it was in the Army.

"The dog's crazy, mister. If he bothers you, kick him."

"Your name is Moon? John Moon?"

"Sure."

The man joined the line of guests, waiting his turn. The Indian went through four people with three arrows apiece before the man grasped the bow in his injured arm and fitted an arrow to it.

"Sir," said the Indian. "That's a fifty-pound pull on that thing. Go easy on your arm."

"Don't worry about my arm," the man said in a belligerent manner that started the dog barking again. Although his pain was evident, the man raised the bow, pulled it all the way back, and fired the arrow into the cottonwood.

"Not bad," said the Indian admiringly. It was the best shot of the morning.

"Do you ever use a rifle, Moon?"

"Not any more. Now, this time get the arrow up a little higher. That's it. That's it."

The man's face sweated with pain. A faint double stain of blood soaked through his bandage. Nevertheless, his second arrow landed just over the first. It took him a while to fit the third arrow. "Ever been to Canada, Moon?"

"I might have. I been lots of places."

"How about Caribou. Ever been to Caribou?"

"Is that in Canada?"

"Yeah. There was an accident up there a few months ago, a helicopter crash."

"You don't say."

"I do say. Some men were killed. It seems somebody shot the helicopter down and this rather nasty animal tore off their heads."

"That's terrible."

"They were friends of mine. I barely got away with my life. Remember that, Moon?"

"No, sir, can't say as I do. I don't read the papers very much."

The man stared at him.

"Sir," said the Indian with the respect he always accorded a good shot. "There's other folks waiting."

The man yanked back the arrow, tearing open his bandage. Blood flooded his arm. Despite his pain, he sent the arrow squarely between the other two. The Indian admired him even more. He was a proud man, one who showed how little pain affected him. He stalked away toward the lodge before the Indian could compliment him.

There was another ski show that night, so the guests cleared out of the dining room by eight o'clock and congregated on the sundeck. The Indian helped carry in cutlery, tablecloths, dirty plates and glasses. They scraped and stashed the dirty dishes in the washer and replaced the tablecloths for breakfast.

One of the men in the kitchen was a fat little fellow with pig eyes and a mouth dragged down in a perpetually resentful scowl. The others addressed him as Lester. Lester did not seem to like Indians.

At ten o'clock the Indian was leaning against the service entrance, watching the men climb onto motorcycles, into trucks or station wagons, and head for home. This parking apron had been leveled from solid white rock and surfaced with tarmac. At each corner was a spotlight mounted on a power pole. The back of the parking area was a wall of smooth-faced granite, with trees standing sturdily upright on top.

The Indian heard a roar of laughter from the window of the Grizzly Bar at the corner. It was open, and the color television was on.

He patted the dog's neck. "What do you say? Think he's hungry tonight?"

Faint steam indicating the cool air chuffed from the dog's snout. The Indian took out a plastic garbage bag he had taken from the kitchen and began a systematic raid on the odorous bagged piles lined up against the wall. It was a scavenger's heaven. Beef rind. Lettuce. Onions. Gravy. Half-eaten fruit. Bread crusts and rolls. He stuffed the small bag so full that the dog had difficulty dragging it.

They walked clear of the lodge, into the bungalow area and beyond that until the sentinel trees enfolded them. The Indian felt at home here, in his element. "Do you know where he is?"

The dog said it did not. It said it while scratching an ear. "You're lying to me."

The dog scratched some more, then grasped the sack in its jaws, anxious to be away.

"What is it? You don't want me to know where he is?"

The dog tugged the sack over the ground. It looked back once at the Indian. Don't follow me. Then it was gone.

The Indian was puzzled. Instead of turning right for the valley, where he expected the spirit to be, the dog followed the road which wound past the lodge around the mountain to the north face. There were no rivers there, to the best of the Indian's knowledge, only higher ground and more mountains. At this height, the vegetation would be skimpy and the water scarce.

A foundation shivered within the Indian's mind. Again, it was the spirit's animalness rather than its etherealness that bothered him. The spirit was behaving exactly like a wild animal deliberately hiding from the ski lodge. Animals avoided humans out of fear. But spirits?

The Indian sat on the ground and closed his eyes. He hummed a small tune taught to him by his grandfather. Bits of memory shook loose. The melody of the song

threaded clearly from the dark past, and he hummed it in exquisite precision, remembering every silky, colored tone just as the old man had taught him.

A jolt of terror coursed through the Indian's body. His grandfather was interrupting his song, grasping him by the shoulders and warning him about something. He spoke one word, but the Indian did not want to hear it.

He opened his eyes and listened to the forest. Instinctively his hand went to his medicine bundle. He was being watched.

The luminous dial on his watch told Jason he had been watching the Indian through binoculars for an hour. The lodge infirmary had rewrapped his bandage, but his arm still felt as if hot steel bars had been drilled through the fang marks. He had to prop the heavy binoculars on his good arm.

When he had followed the Indian out tonight, excitement had pumped blood through his body so hard his wound burned. He had kneeled in the bushes, fervently wishing he had a gun, for he was sure the beast would show up again. The last act of this drama was about to begin.

The dog ran off with a sack of food. The seconds ticked into minutes, then the minutes into an hour, and the last act fizzled into anticlimax. Whoever was writing this drama did not know how to end it sensibly. The Indian lay down on the ground and to all appearances fell asleep.

The Indian clearly shared some kind of relationship with the beast. Jason had seen him pack the food in the bag and give it to the dog. Kimberly's words came back to haunt him. Suppose it really was some poor deformed human, a friend of the Indian's whom he was caring for, and not the legendary Bigfoot?

No. Not with that face. Not with a face that could only

have been dreamed up by a witch doctor at his most concentrated moment of existential terror. Deformed faces were ugly but dulled the senses, the personality behind them, barricaded by their own features. That face was alive.

A pretty picture, Jason thought ruefully. The Indian shadowing the giant and him shadowing the Indian. Was somebody shadowing Jason? Again he felt that peculiar empathy, as though if he looked in the Indian's face he would see his own features.

Something hissed.

Half fainting, Jason hit the ground and flattened out, binoculars raised like a stubby club. But it was not a rattlesnake—it was Martha Lucas, with her finger to her mouth.

Martha Lucas lived in a bungalow so stuffed with piles of papers, books, and prints that little incidental room was left for such functions as walking and sitting. She knocked a mountain of stuffed file folders to the floor, revealing a chair for Jason. "I don't usually have guests in here," she apologized.

As she waited for water to boil on her hot plate, Jason picked up a stapled sheaf of pages. It was entitled "Trickster of the Winnebagos." Everything in the room was about Indians. Martha Lucas was an organism whose sole purpose was the gulping down of information about Indians. By the look of her kitchenette, she was a vegetarian, too.

She handed him a cup of herb tea, then kicked out a niche for herself from the papers on the bed. "Why are you following Moon?" she asked.

"Why are you?" Jason countered.

"We could always flip a coin to see who goes first. Fair enough?"

"Heads," said Jason, sending a quarter into the air. It came down tails.

"I think Moon's on a spirit quest," she said.

"What's that?"

She described it as she had to Helder.

Jason nodded, stroking his chin. "It fits. It fits. I always wondered why he carries that bag around. Medicine bundle, you called it."

"Yes. If I'm right, he's not going to have much luck."

"How come?"

"He's too old. He's in his twenties, and the vision is a rite of puberty. Besides, you're supposed to remain isolated during the quest. It'd be interesting to know if he was prepared by a shaman."

"How long does this quest take?"

"Three or four days at most."

"Did they ever follow their spirits around? I mean tag along after them?"

"There were all kinds of spirit quests, Mr. Jason. In some tribes it was how you got your name. You always had to go to a sacred place to find them."

"When I say follow them, I mean for hundreds of miles."

She thought over an answer while watching him, trying to pierce his face to the brain behind and see where he was leading.

"You would do what your spirit told you to do. Normally, however, you'd be in no shape to walk, unless . . ."

"What?"

"Unless it was a really special spirit. It's a religious experience, and you know what that can do to some people." She blew steam from her cup. "And before I go any further, I'd like to ask you some questions."

"I'll answer one now. Moon is wanted by the Canadian police in connection with the deaths of three men in British Columbia last summer."

"Are you a policeman?"

"No. I was with the men when it happened. Moon knocked me out with a rifle butt."

She played with the handle of her cup. "Did he do it?"

"The circumstances are suspicious. I think he shot down a helicopter in which two of them died. He definitely did not kill the third man."

"Were you looking for Moon at the Little Harrington that night?"

Jason hesitated only a moment. "Yes. I have been for several months."

"Are you going to turn him in to the police?"

Jason pressed the teacup to his bandage to see if it soothed the ache. He thought over an answer. He wasn't ready to tell anybody about the monster. "I suppose I should. But I don't think he's all there in the head. I tried to get a rise out of him by mentioning Canada, but he said he didn't remember. I don't think he was faking. Then again, he's got the original poker face."

She spoke over the teacup, her eyes wide. "Are you frightened of him, Mr. Jason?"

Jason took what he thought was a nut from a clay bowl. He bit into it and felt the shell crumple into tiny husk splinters. They were some kind of goddamned seeds. It was another tiny frustration to add to the considerable mass this business had brought him. The distant roar of amplified applause resounding across the valley reminded him that they were not as alone as they felt. "Yes," he admitted. "I think he's capable of killing people."

Martha settled herself deeper into her papers. "You're right about him not being all there. He was in a mental hospital for a year and a half."

"How do you know?"

"He's got a Medal of Honor in his medicine bundle. Jack Helder spent the morning on the phone running down his war record. Moon was a Green Beret."

Jason whistled. "Now that really fits."

"He was in Vietnam. His squad or platoon or whatever you call it was wiped out by the Viet Cong. Apparently it was pretty much of a massacre. Rather than let himself be rescued, Moon went into the jungle alone and spent a month killing guerrillas. And I mean killing them, Mr. Jason. He blew up ammunition dumps, he practically wiped out villages single-handed. There's no telling how many he got. The way the Army learned he was still alive was when guerrillas began surrendering in droves. Out of fear of him."

"Him personally? How did they know it was just him?"

"Because of the way he killed them. He used a bow and arrow."

Jason felt a thrill of disconnected terror. Capable of murder—the Indian was a master of it! He was as brutal as his spirit. Until now Jason had thought his own survival was evidence of some kind of restraint in the Indian's mind, but Martha had wiped out that possibility. He would never know how he had survived Canada. "What about the mental hospital?"

"He was under treatment in Los Angeles for combat fatigue. That's when they gave him a medal. Then he was released and went home to Stevensville, where he checked in with a psychiatrist once a month. Last spring he disappeared. The doctor in Stevensville was very worried about him."

"Why?"

She spoke into her teacup, hair shrouding her face. "He was being treated for schizophrenia."

"Ah! Which he probably had a long time before he went into the Army."

"That's right. You see, he doesn't have any family. His father left them, his mother died when he was young. Typical broken home. He was raised by priests in a

mission school and a grandfather whom he revered. His grandfather apparently was responsible for a lot of his mental problems. He told him all sorts of stories when he was young."

"What kind of stories?"

"Indian stories that they used to tell their young as they grew up. It's how the Indians passed on their culture, Mr. Jason. They had no writing, so they spent winters banked up in their lodges, talking about how the chipmunk got his stripes and how the world was made and all that. He revered his grandfather. He was the only family he had. He died just before Moon went into the Army." Her voice lowered, and her hair slowly covered her face. "You know, when they treated him in the hospital, they gave him all these drugs and shock therapy that wrecked his memory. He had spells of amnesia . . ."

"And still does, I'd venture to say."

". . . and couldn't remember his grandfather's words. To somebody like him that's death, Mr. Jason. Absolute death."

A war casualty like millions of other broken, blasted men through the ages. That was John Moon, Jason reflected. Every world he had lived in crumpled before his eyes. So, like others, he had found religion. A spirit. Something to live for, something to heal the split between his mind and the shambles of his life.

Some guardian angel!

"Could I have some more tea?" Jason held out his cup.

"Of course." Suddenly flustered, Martha Lucas knocked over papers as she took his cup into the kitchen.

For some moments Jason had been looking at a book cover on the couch next to her. He had wanted her out of the room in order to examine it more closely.

The book cover showed a wooden mask carved by a Northwest tribe called the Kwakiutls, who believed giant

cannibals lived in the mountains. The face was a skull with added details. Tendrils of hair formed a widow's peak, and eyeholes burned from beneath frowning brow bones.

Stretch those brows, Jason thought, and there were the horns. Narrow the nose and forehead, add a bit more hair, and there it was the face of the Bigfoot as he had seen it in the river. Probably the artist who carved this mask had worked from somebody's description.

He dropped the paper as Martha returned with a steaming cup of tea. Jason forced down a mouthful of the awful stuff. It sure woke him up, he could say that much about it. "That medicine bundle Moon wears. What's it for?"

"He's supposed to carry a talisman of his spirit in it."

"What kind of talisman!" In the dim light, his eyes gleamed.

"If your spirit was a bird, you'd carry one of his feathers. That kind of thing. A piece of its body, or if it was human some belonging, like a clay pipe."

"Not to change the subject, but how long has this lodge been here?"

She counted with her fingers. "Ten ... no, eleven months. That's when the foundation was laid. It wasn't habitable until last spring."

"Was anybody killed while working on it?"

"How did you know?" A certain suspicion clouded her face.

"I'm making brilliant deductions. There was somebody killed, wasn't there?"

"Yes. A plumber. His name was Jameson. Mr. Jason—"

"And it was at night, wasn't it?"

"Yes."

"And his head was missing, wasn't it?"

She swallowed hard. "Jameson came up one night with a rifle because something was messing around with his equipment. All the pipes and lumber piles were being

thrown around. Jameson wanted to surprise it, but it killed him and took his head away. The Rangers said it was a grizzly bear."

"And has this grizzly bear been back?"

Her voice became very small. "Mr. Jason, this lodge has been jinxed ever since it was finished. Practically every-day the phone lines go down. Sometimes the garbage is broken into—" Her mouth opened, and tea slopped over her thumb. "Moon's spirit! That's *it!* It's a grizzly bear!"

Jason found himself feeling protective toward Martha Lucas. He had not felt that stab of tenderness since his last sulfurous blast of temper ended in divorce. She had nice hands. He wondered how she kept them so nice. And she was logical in that maddening perfect way that made things come out wrong. He set down his teacup. "I have to be going. I want to get a room, if it isn't too late."

"Wait a minute." She ran into the kitchenette and returned with a bag of dried tea, telling him it was full of medicinal properties and could cure diseases that had not even been discovered, even snakebite. She told him how to prepare it. Eventually Jason managed to get out of her room without seeming too abrupt.

"I don't know nothing about no Bigfoots or nothing." Lester Cole tried to scurry past Jason to his pickup truck. "I didn't see nothing, I made it up."

Jason inserted himself between Lester and the kitchen door. He summed up Lester Cole as a man covered with little pressure points of fear subject to minute applications of force. "Why would you do that?"

"Cause I wanted to. I wanted to get in the papers."

Jason followed Lester out of the kitchen into the park-ing lot, then cut in front of him again before he could open the door to his truck.

"That's my truck, mister."

"What are you going to do, shoot me?"

Lester's jaw muscles bunched up. "Get away."

"Sure. Soon as you tell me the truth, Lester. I can tell when somebody isn't telling me the truth, you know."

"You can, huh?"

"I mean, if you really wanted your name in the papers you wouldn't have admitted a hoax. People would come here to interview you, reporters from television and everything. No, you're just not telling me the truth, Lester."

The parking-lot lights made Jason's face a cold series of slabs of the same texture as the granite walls of the lot. His arm bandage glittered whitely under the lights. Lester noticed that Jason was a big man and sprung tight.

"I never could keep my mouth shut." He laughed.

"Oh, that's okay, Lester. Look, I'm not going to bite you, I just want to know what it looked like."

"Fucker's long gone by now, so if you come here looking for it, you're wasting your time. You might as well go home. What's your name, anyhow?" Lester became jovial to hide his craftiness. His rifle was still in the truck cab.

"Jason."

"And you want to know what it looked like."

"There you go."

"And that's all you want."

Jason held up both hands, palms facing Lester Cole. "Swear to God, Lester, my friend. After tonight you'll never see me again."

Jason had big hands, Lester noted. "I only saw him for a minute, Mr. Jason. He didn't look like much. He was about six feet tall but real heavy. He had gray fur and a big belly and these long arms with hands turned in like this." Lester dangled his arms, palms turned facing his body. "And that's about it."

"What about his head, Lester?"

"Just a head. Just a lot of hair on it."

"Nothing unusual about its head?"

"I told you! It was just a head. Kind of like a monkey has, that's all."

By the way Jason's rocky face seemed to turn inward Lester realized he had said something important. Finally Jason took out his billfold and stuffed a five into Lester's shirt pocket.

"You've been a big help, Lester. Sorry to corner you like this." With a pat on the shoulder, Jason walked away toward the kitchen.

"If I remember anything else I'll let you know, Mr. Jason."

The kitchen door closed behind Jason as though dismissing Lester Cole from existence.

There were two of them in the valley!

Jason's feet seemed to float over Jack Helder's lounge carpet. Robotlike, he walked to the desk and reserved a room for three days, his mind in turmoil.

The one Lester had seen was not the one he had fought in the river. Every eyewitness had noticed a misshapen head except Lester. The footprint cast in Drake's office was of the hourglass type, not Moon's beast. And one had stayed here ever since the lodge was erected and had killed a plumber.

Kimberly had warned him that it took more than one to keep up a population. He had said a cave or cave system would be the ideal home. Somewhere around Mount Colby there had to be a cave. He would go to the Ranger office tomorrow and get a chart.

Dangling the key in his hand, Jason was walking across the lounge when a terrain map showing in relief the features of Mount Colby and the valley caught his attention. A road crossed the north face of the mountain to a town called Oharaville. The town buildings were small black squares.

On the mountain's base at the edge of town was a large black cross symbolizing an old mine.

A gold mine! In more ways than one.

The key fell from Jason's fingers to the carpet.

8

Guests at Colby Lodge were discouraged from going to Oharaville. The mine area was thin earth pocked with sinkholes. People had fallen into the ground at Oharaville and vanished. Children had been trapped there with broken limbs. The Forest Service would run you out if they caught you there.

The road around the north face had been built when muscle and dynamite smoothed the earth and transportation was by horsedrawn buckboard. It followed a rusted railroad line used for transferring ore from the Limerick mine to the town of Garrison.

Oharaville lay at the terminal of a creaky railroad trestle spanning a gully full of old tin cans, newspapers, broken beams, and bald tires. The town was laid out on a slope running upward away from Mount Colby's north face. Basically, it was a single rutted road called Bullion Avenue, which originated at a huge hole blasted out of Colby's side, from which a collection of rotted, decrepit buildings seemed to spill out. All the windows in the ghost town had been boarded up. The most distinctive edifice was an old wooden church with a leaning steeple at the end of Bullion Avenue, almost in the trees.

When Jason pulled into the town, he was twenty-five hundred feet above sea level. He wondered if that were some kind of record for a mine. He parked the car on Bullion Avenue.

A faint wind blew down the street, creaking a hanging

sign with the faded word SADDLERY on it. Of the two dozen or so structures, half were little houses around which long-dead housewives had tried to grow gardens which were now thickets of fungi and tight grass, enclosed by rotting fences.

Jason looked into the saloon. Shelves and counters with dusty glass jars lined the walls. The floor was full of jagged holes. Jason envisioned a winter in the Cascades when miners huddled blind drunk under a swaying lantern in here. The wind would sweep like a flash flood down Bullion Avenue as if draining into the mine shaft, rattling doors and shutters back and forth and tilting the church steeple. Up here skies were always gray and mountain peaks crowded your horizons.

Before the gaping hole of the mine was a string of twisted rail and some overturned ore cars. The mine supervisors' hut was a long-gone jumble of wood. Metal barrels were strewn about, and piles of earth were stacked against the cliff. These were tailings, heaps of dirt through which scavenger prospectors picked for small hunks of silver ore.

Jason opened the glove compartment and took out a brand new .38-caliber revolver, a heavy flashlight, and a ball of twine on a rotating spool. With his pocket knife he carved a notch into each of the soft-nosed lead bullets, then loaded them into the pistol.

As he walked toward the mine he searched the ground for any depressions or other weakness. He flashed the light inside the entrance. Water dripped. A small avalanche of wet gravel hissed down the wall.

He tied the twine to a wooden beam and spun it out as he continued downward. The blackness was almost liquid in its density. His light beam was a white bar gliding fish-like over shaley walls which were soft and cheesy, apt to crumble under his touch. His major worry was the beams. Some were just stacked railroad ties. All were at least thirty years old, and each step caused them to vibrate.

The tunnel junctioned, one trail leading to the right, the other to the left. Jason paused, remembering the old Robert Frost poem about roads diverging in the woods. The old pioneer method of choice was spitting into one's hand, slapping a fist into the spittle, and following wherever the largest gob went. Jason flipped a coin, thinking of Martha, and it came up tails. He went to the right.

The tunnel led straight down. Dust congealed into mud from overloaded ore cars parked on either side of the tracks. None of it had been disturbed, by either feet or rockfalls. There was no sign of recent activity.

Unless they walked on the ceiling, too.

The shaft curved again. This time Jason smelled something. An incongruous crowd of odors crushed together by the still, dank air tumbled over in a riot, as if to see which could reach his nose first. They were fresh and alive, more appropriate to spring sunlight and open ground.

The shaft ended in a wall of greenery, piled, spilled, crammed, and packed wall to wall, ceiling to ceiling, in a tight jungle barricade. It rested on a bed of seeds of every kind: acorns, pine nuts, oak and spruce, even peanuts. Every type of vegetation imaginable was represented. Huge strips of bark in layers on top of layers of berries, on top of apples, all resting on a bed of spruce tips. Jason stooped down and picked up a red berry. He bit off half of it, chewed, and spat it out.

Piled into a hollow in the wall by the vegetation was a stack of yellowing bones. Like the vegetation, they were a selection of all the wildlife that roamed the countryside. Bear. Woodchuck. Beaver. A horse skull nestled against that of a dog. The meat had been stripped from them, and Jason could see notches in the calcified surfaces where they had been gnawed.

Pulverize them into powder and add to the diet for

calcium and minerals. Pack the meat in a higher tunnel, where cold was a natural deep freeze.

Now Jason knew why he saw no prints. The vegetation was a plug many feet thick which blocked intruders coming in from the Oharaville side and them from going out that way.

Most of the vegetation was seeds, which made sense, too. The gelada baboon lived at mountain altitudes where the only food at all was seeds. Seeds could be dug, plucked, and gathered all year round without being missed. Ounce for ounce, they were second only to meat in protein. Barricaded by tons of rock, the mine would be even in temperature all year round.

Jason played his light over the bones. Shadows crawled behind the eye sockets with the light's passage, as though pupils were rolling. After a second, Jason decided that in the case of Jameson the plumber, ignorance was bliss.

After the mine's darkness, the gray cloud-scudded daylight made Jason's eyes water. A light drizzle drummed against the ore cars and dripped over the shingles and wood false fronts of Bullion Avenue.

A red Volkswagen with flowers pasted to the hood was parked beside his car. Behind the wheel was Martha Lucas, dozing in a maroon shawl. He rapped on her window, frightening her awake. "I saw you driving up here," she said, rubbing her eyes. "Really, Mr. Jason, this place isn't safe for humans, living or otherwise."

Jason sat down on the passenger seat next to her. He lit a cigarette.

"Moon's spirit is a Bigfoot, isn't it." It was asked in a very matter-of-fact way. She might have been speaking about an interesting bird that had just flown by.

"Moon's spirit is a type of man. Otherwise known as Bigfoot."

"What does that mean?"

"Seeing as you're an anthropologist, maybe you can tell me." He told her about his fight in the river and what Kimberly had said about the chin. And his theory about Bigfoot's resurfacing for food.

Normally she could believe the most peculiar things — disinfectant teas, the wonders of vegetarianism, probably even astrology. But face to face with Raymond Jason and his story, she faltered. "I don't believe it. A man?"

"What's more, that mine is packed with food for the winter."

"And you've seen it?"

"Twice. I'll never forget it. I figure Moon saw it in Montana and figured it was the Holy Grail. From Montana it moved to British Columbia and from there down to here."

"Why was it moving around?"

Jason cracked the window to let the cigarette smoke out. "I had a hell of a time figuring that out. This mine is their home. Or it was until Jack Helder moved in and started dynamiting foundations, laying in pipe, and bringing all kinds of people up here. So one of them left to find a new home. Since there aren't many isolated places left in the West, he had to run all over half the country. He returned here only a couple of days ago."

He had buried the hook in his words, but she caught it anyway. "One of them! There's more than one?"

Jason took a suicidally deep inhalation of smoke that almost certainly shortened his life by hours and exhaled luxuriously. "There's at least two. Not many more, I expect. Not any more. The whole county doesn't have enough food to sustain a population. One stayed behind, holding down the fort, so to speak, while Moon's spirit was wandering around. That's the one that killed Jameson and tore up your phone lines."

Martha seemed to become physically uncomfortable,

as Jason had been with her the night she picked him up. She sat upright in the seat, then slumped down again, then rolled down her window and rested her elbow on it. Then she looked at Jason for a long time as if trying to divine his intentions. "You've sure got this all worked out in your head, Mr. Jason."

"Not all. I won't have it all figured out till that thing is pinned down in a glass case with about fifty biologists looking it over. I wouldn't throw a seven-foot-tall hairy man at you if Kimberly hadn't thrown it at me."

"Mr. Jason, the ski season is just beginning. They've killed people . . ." Her face suffused with panic.

"Yeah, I know, but don't call out the Air Force just yet. They may very well be gone."

Jason walked over to his car and came back with his own map, the one with the line tracing the thing's travels. "Like I said, he was looking for a new home. If he found one, it seems to me, they'd want to get out of here before winter really comes down hard on them. If that's true, I've lost him for good and Moon's going to be very unhappy in spring."

"Would they have left already? It isn't very cold. They've got all that food."

"He sprang one of my traps and injured himself. How badly I don't know. It wasn't fatal, since he made it from the Little Harrington. He might want to recuperate for a few days. Get himself back in walking shape, kiss the bats and neighbors good-bye and all that. Then again, he's tough as leather, and may have split as soon as he could, food or not."

"And what if he didn't find a new home?"

Jason flicked his cigarette out the window and fanned away the smoke with his hand. "Then I'm still in luck. This mountain's served them well for God knows how long, maybe they'll just decide to stick to their side while

Helder sticks to his. There's a question of the territorial imperative here somewhere, too, but since we don't know anything about them, we don't know how strong it is."

"Jack Helder won't stick to his side if he hears there's a Bigfoot nest in that mine. Nobody will, Mr. Jason. And Jack says he's going to turn Oharaville into a Wild West town if it kills him."

Jason folded up his map. "I guess it's time we paid a call on Drake. But I'm going to ask a favor of you. Let me do all the talking, okay?"

She sat quietly as Jason told Drake about Canada, his trek down here, the Little Harrington, and the mine. Jason told him everything, that is, except about John Moon, and she knew he was dragging her into a lie against her will. She closed her clammy hands together and stared at the photo of the Secretary of the Interior behind Drake's desk. *Pray God please, Jason had a good reason.*

When Jason finished, Drake stirred his bulk and spoke to Martha. "Honey, is this guy kidding me?"

"I don't think so," she said softly.

"You sure that snake poison didn't get to your brain, Mr. Jason? Cause that's the damned silliest thing I ever heard. And I've lived in this county for five years!"

"You're welcome to go look in that mine if you don't believe me."

"And you telling me you fought this thing in the river."

"Yes. It nearly killed me."

Drake sucked on a tooth, his small eyes darting back and forth between Martha and Jason. "I never seen any Bigfeet or any signs of them up here, Mr. Jason."

"How many wildcats have you seen? How many deer antlers, which are supposed to litter the woods every fall, Drake? Where do you think they're hiding? Go look at that food."

Instead of responding, Drake hauled himself from his chair and poked his head through the glass door to the other offices. "Jimmy? You there, Wallace. Go on over and see what kind of chart we have on the Limerick mine." As he waited, Drake slipped his hands through the back of his belt and rotated his torso as if he had been sitting too long and had to work his spine around. A young man with a nametag reading WALLACE passed him two long rolls. Drake shut the door and spread the charts out on his desk. He sucked his teeth again and shook his head. "Spaghetti."

Martha leaned over Jason's shoulders. The charts were obviously based on old ones. The shafts were parallel lines with open corners. Some ended in dotted lines. "Those are dead holes," said Drake. "Some of the tunnels just fade out. The companies that dug up the mountain didn't give a shit about making good records of them a hundred years ago. If they smelled copper or iron, they went after it like moles."

"Is this chart complete?" asked Jason.

"Hell no, I don't think there's a single complete chart anywhere. The government's marked out every mine, but that don't mean they have every tunnel. That's a five-story mine, too. A real maze." Drake put his finger on a shaft whose end was turned outward. "This would be where you went in, Mr. Jason. How long was your string?"

"Five hundred feet. I used up about four hundred and fifty feet of it. I remember going right."

"Which would put you right here. The other branch is a dead end." He laid the other roll over this one. "And as you can see, there's a whole 'nother network above and below yours." He tapped a fat sausage finger on the paper. "Did you know they used to have gun battles down there?"

"No."

"It's true. Claim jumpers and all that. There's a lot of bones down there all right, and they don't have anything

140

to do with Bigfoot. You didn't happen to see any dynamite, did you?"

"Jesus no," Jason replied, involuntarily looking at Martha, who looked away.

Drake explained with relish, "The companies got careless sometimes and left whole boxes of equipment behind. Railings, pipes, pickaxes, lanterns, all that stuff. And sometimes dynamite, all packed up nice and neat. The old stuff is sawdust soaked in nitro. After a while the nitro leaks all over the floor. It's still got a kick to it."

"I think what you're trying to tell me, Drake, is that you don't intend to go in there."

"I didn't mean that, Mr. Jason. We're going in to look at this food you told me about. Yessir, I wouldn't miss that for anything. But I'm not about to tackle any of the real deep shafts till I get some better charts from the state bureau." Drake's voice hardened. "Until then, I don't want anyone near that mine."

"In other words," said Martha, "don't tell Jack Helder or he'll blab it all over the place."

"You got it, Miss Lucas. Right now every damned body with a gun is running through the woods looking for Bigfoot, ever since Lester got on the radio, and that I don't like. Mr. Jason, is there anything else you want to tell me?"

Moon is wanted! The Canadian police! Concealing a fugitive! Martha wiped her hands on her dress as Jason made a great show of thinking.

"No. That's about it. As you know, Mr. Drake, the lodge is on the east face of the mountain and the town's on the north face. They're just around the corner, so to speak."

Drake reached into his drawer and clanked Jason's traps onto the table. "I'm not about to forget that lodge. If this damn-fool story of yours gets out and I hear somebody's fallen into a sinkhole and he's carrying all sorts of guns and nets you hunt Bigfoot with, then somebody in this office right now is going into the slammer for setting traps without permission, smoking in the woods, malicious mischief, and packing a handgun without a license." Gun-metal eyes speared through Jason.

"You don't have to threaten me," said Jason, blood filling his face. "I can keep my mouth shut. And I have a license." He showed it to Drake.

"Issued in Kansas for a Colt Python. Is that a Colt Python on your hip, Mr. Jason? I know this isn't Kansas."

"It's a thirty-eight, and it didn't seem to bother the dealer this morning," Jason replied tightly through clenched teeth. "And I carry it because these animals are dangerous."

"I reckon he's even more dangerous since you shot at him. I reckon that went for Jameson, too. We'd all be a lot better off if folks didn't shoot at everything they saw."

Jason made a little choking noise.

Drake suddenly smiled and clapped him on the shoulder. "Now hows about a beer?"

Jason pushed open the glass door and stalked out of the office. Martha followed, leaving Drake with a flick of her shoulders and a grimace indicating that she thought Jason as peculiar as he did.

Jason paced around the car in an absolute fit of rage, kicking the tires, slamming his fist on the hood, and slugging the ventilator window so hard he dislodged it, jostling his wounded arm in the process.

"You sure get mad, Mr. Jason," said Martha as his anger fragmented away kick by kick, leaving him weak and frustrated, leaning against the door. "I hope you never get mad at me."

He pointed a finger at the Ranger station. Spittle was in the corners of his mouth. "That—that—talking to me like that!"

"Why shouldn't he? He knew you were lying about something."

"I did not lie to him!" Jason blazed.

"Of course you did. You didn't mention Moon once." She was sorry they had left her car at the lodge. She was not certain she wanted to ride with him. He exhaled and yanked the door open.

"I'm okay. Really I am. Get in."

She hesitated.

"Go on. I won't kill you."

She slipped in and sat as far from him as the front seat would allow. He punched on the radio, and they caught a weatherman cheerfully predicting catastrophe: ". . . low-pressure front moving down from Canada . . . snow flurries in Vancouver . . . This is breaking a few records, folks." Jason reached for the dial.

"No, listen a minute," said Martha.

In plain English, a storm was whiplashing down the spine of the Cascades, a storm of such proportions that the parts broken off by the mountains were blizzarding cyclones with a potent fury all their own. Jack Helder was going to get his slopes tested with real snow sometime this weekend.

Jason stopped at the Silver River bridge. He got out of the car, leaving Martha inside, and walked it from one end to the other, peering down at the water below.

He had not spoken on the way up. In a way she was grateful that he had not invited her into his thoughts. She tried to sort out her thoughts about Raymond Jason. He could be classed as forceful, organized, tenacious, and altogether admirable. Except that she sensed something missing from him, a little chasm in his character, a lack of something necessary to complete his personality as originally designed. The chasm had to be filled in somehow. With rage. Or habitual isometrics.

Or with a spirit. That was it! She caught her breath. Raymond Jason was a carbon copy of John Moon. Two jungle creatures, two acolytes on a thousand-mile pilgrimage in pursuit of God only knew what. Carry it one step further and Jason would be just as schizoid as John Moon.

He was leaning over the bridge, looking down to where the supports were sunk into rock. White water foamed through the gorge and down a terrace of rocks.

"I wish I knew what Lester's Bigfoot was doing down around here," said Jason, climbing back into the car. "It can't be fish. There isn't a calm spot on the river for miles. And there isn't much game in the woods." His anger was completely dissipated.

"Why didn't you tell Drake about John Moon?"

"Because he'd have shipped him off to Canada. I think Moon's innocent, essentially. I don't think he really knew what he was doing when he shot down that copter."

"He's still wanted, though."

"Yes," Jason admitted, a small vein swelling in his temple.

"A lawyer would get him off."

"No, they'd jail him, lawyer or not."

She watched the lodge grow bigger as the car began the final climb up the road. "That's not it. You're afraid of losing the Bigfoot."

Jason glanced at her and tightened his hands on the wheel. "I misjudged you. I thought you had a thing for Indians. I thought you'd be in favor of keeping him out of trouble."

"It's me I'm worried about now. If Drake finds out Moon is a felon, you've made me an accessory."

"He won't find out. Not from me, anyway."

"And I don't see why you need Moon any more anyway. You know where they live. It's just a matter of time now."

"It needs Moon," Jason said stubbornly. "It needs the food he sends."

"Oh bull," she said bluntly. "It got along fine without him all its life. Besides, it's still got the food in the mine."

"It's a psychological dependence, don't you see?" Jason flared. "The food's just part of it. Moon's protecting it."

"You figured all that out just by watching a dog run off with a sack?"

"Yes."

"Suppose they're gone, Raymond?" Her voice was gentler, sympathetic, not angry.

He dropped her off in the lot without answering that. After she left he just sat, hands on the wheel, staring fiercely at the lodge.

They're still in the valley, he thought over and over. If they were gone, Moon would be, too. He could convince himself of that if he tried hard enough.

9

For several minutes Jack Helder watched John Moon stand at the edge of the woods, whistling into them as though there were something in there to hear him. He had spent the morning trying to think up tactful ways to fire the Indian. Moon's war and medical record had shaken him up badly. He imagined the Indian turning on the guests as though they were Viet Cong.

Hesitantly Helder walked toward him. The Indian was covered with leaves and twigs. "Mr. Moon?" he said in a voice laced with steel.

The Indian looked slowly back at him. Helder's courage shrank. "Yes, sir."

"Unless my watch is fast, you should be at the archery range now."

"They're eating lunch, Mr. Helder. I told them I'd be ready in an hour."

"I'm a little confused, Moon. Why aren't *you* ready?"

"'Cause I can't find my dog."

Among Moon's weird talents was an ability to make Helder feel like an oaf. As if Moon was sane and everybody else in the world was crazy. "Where did he go?"

Moon answered sweetly, "If I knew that, Mr. Helder, I'd know where to find him."

"You don't need your dog to shoot bows and arrows."

"I need him. He didn't come back last night."

"Moon, I like dogs as much as anybody. But it's not a question of when we're ready for guests at Colby, it's a question of when they're ready for us. And they're ready now. I want you back at the range. Your dog can find his own way home."

Moon stirred a pebble with his shoe. "He ain't really my dog, when you come down to it. I should have remembered that." He was obviously talking to himself, not Helder.

Helder chose to ignore it. "And look at your clothes! They were brand-new yesterday. What happened?"

"Nothing. I slept in the woods last night."

Moon turned on his heel and walked toward the archery range. Helder decided he'd wait until he had help before firing Moon. Get a couple of brawny kitchen waiters, in case his temper went off.

Jack Helder mopped his head with a white handkerchief. He turned to see two Ranger trucks ascending the Oharaville road. Drake was in the lead one, next to another man. The second truck carried several sawhorses with blinker lights. They drove fast, leaving a thin trail of dust behind them.

Now what!

On the smooth ground before the mine entrance, the Rangers pounded in DANGER SINKHOLES signs and bounded the area with a wire fence. Drake sat in the truck, listening to the staticky blare of walkie-talkie voices. Wallace, Jones, and Taylor, who had been filled in on the whole bizarre story, were in the mine, and they were nervous as cats.

They found the food. Jones expostulated over the walkie-talkie, "Jesus, boss, he was right about that. There must be a ton of the stuff. And bones, too! It's full of bones!"

Drake paused while eating his sandwich. Score one for Raymond Jason. A breath of wind creaked a board in Oharaville, and he looked back at it. "Okay. Look for prints. And be careful."

They checked out the other junction and found that it branched off into ancillary shafts not noted on the charts. It was not a dead end after all. In one of the shafts Wallace found a second neat pile of bones next to a rockfall which blocked off the tunnel. It took them an hour to go carefully through the remaining tunnels. All were blocked.

At five o'clock they filed out, blinking at the sunlight, slimy up to their knees with mud. They had marked off the shafts on paper, which was crumpled by their nervous fingers. Jones wound up his rope and said, "A thousand feet is as far as you can go in there in any tunnel. The one with the leaves and stuff is the closest to an open one." He popped a ring tab off a can of beer and took three heavy gulps.

"Any prints?" asked Drake.

They all shook their heads.

"So it could have been anything. It could have been people."

They shifted weight from one foot to the other. Then Jones said, "If you ask me, those shafts were blocked off deliberately. Those rockfalls fill them up completely."

Taylor chimed in, "And I bet they're keeping meat in there and smoking it."

The other two groaned. Drake said, "What's he talking about?"

"Taylor says he smelled smoke inside," said Wallace. "We didn't smell anything."

"They'd put it in one of the higher shafts," said Taylor stubbornly. "So the smoke would escape through the tunnels. That way nobody would notice like they would if it came out of one hole."

Wallace squashed his empty beer can in his hand. "It's just nuts, if you ask me. Man or beast, it's so dark in there you'd go blind in an hour. The only thing that can see in there is a bat."

Which had occurred to Drake. Nocturnal or not, human or not, nobody could live forever in the mine in total darkness. Were it not for the vegetation, that would have been grounds for dismissing Jason's story. "What about the bones?"

"Just bones. Nothing." Jones did not elaborate, which meant that Jameson's bones were not in the pile. For that small grace, Wallace was grateful. "Them bones, them bones, them dry bones . . ." Jones beat time with his knees, trying to discharge his tension.

"Boss, all that vegetation is sea-level stuff. Whoever did it has been foraging all over the county."

Drake said, "Well, I'd like to know how they got it in there without leaving prints."

"It was packed in from the other side. Had to be. Which means . . ."

"Yeah," Drake retorted. "I know what it means." It meant there had to be another entrance to the mine somewhere on the mountain. He looked at the useless charts. He had asked the state bureau for more recent ones after Jason and Martha left that morning. Which meant they should be here between now and Judgment Day, depending on how good secretaries were at rummaging through filing cabinets.

Somebody must have seen them! To Drake it was simply

inconceivable that they could have been up here unnoticed all these years. Well, what would a Bigfoot look like from a distance anyway? A man in a fur coat. Maybe they'd been seen all along and no one had realized it. Living up here without leaving trails even, not even a speck of shit, not anything!

Drake stood up, stashing his chart in the truck. "I think we better start combing these mountains before the charts get here. I think we better find out where the food is coming from and how they got it in. We'll look for stripped bushes and trees and holes where seeds were dug up and everything like that. Jason said they may have left in the past couple of days. If we find any sign they're still here we mount a hunt of some kind. I don't want anybody talking about this—not even to your wives—and I don't want anybody running after them at night, okay?"

"Why don't we close the lodge down now?"

Which Drake could have done with no trouble, but it was not quite as easy as that. Much as he disliked Colby Lodge, jobs were scarce in Garrison. Augusta County was what is euphemistically called a depressed area, and that was why Helder had been allowed to build in the first place. Drake would not like being responsible for driving Helder out of business on the basis of Raymond Jason's story, especially if the Bigfoot were gone already. "We can always do that. Let's give it a couple of more days first and see where we're at when the storm gets here."

They were blocking the road with sawhorses when Helder's Cadillac drove up. Usually the sight of the huge machine bouncing over back roads like a yacht in a bird-bath amused Drake. Today he did not smile at anything.

"Hello, Drake," Jack Helder said pleasantly.

"Afternoon, Mr. Helder," Drake answered with equal pleasantness. "You just saved me a trip to your lodge. I'm afraid I'm going to have to ask you to stop your overnight camping trips."

"Might I ask why?"

Drake expectorated a thin stream of saliva between his two front teeth. "Little bear problem. Some folks spotted grizzlies up at the town. So we're closing off the road."

"Oh." Helder thought it over. Yes. Okay. Grizzlies. "Funny, it's the first I've heard about it. In fact, I haven't heard about bears since . . ." Helder's stomach rotated, and his hands made an involuntary movement to his mouth. He was the one who had found Walter Jameson that morning, lying on the fresh sand, his blood soaking a patch the size of a blanket. A man without a head. Helder had never seen anything like that in his life. "Where did you say they were?"

"Up at Oharaville. They live in the mine. We figure they're about ready to hibernate, so they'll be sleepy and pretty impatient with folks."

Helder's father had once built some substandard houses. Someone had opened a shower door which fell apart in a shatter of thousands of deadly pieces. Even though there were no injuries, the lawsuit was horrendous. He shuddered at the consequences of having one of his guests mauled by a grizzly bear.

Drake said, "You wouldn't have seen anything poking around your garbage or anything like that, would you?"

"No. Not since summer. In fact, there don't seem to be many animals of any kind this fall. Is it always like this?"

In the years Drake had been at the Augusta station, he had wondered about the scarcity of wildlife around Colby. Maybe he had his explanation now. Maybe not.

"Helder, I don't want any of your people up here. If they hear about bears wandering around, they're likely to come and feed them. Once you start feeding grizzlies, you never get rid of them."

"But there's a storm coming. Surely they wouldn't be out now."

"Grizzlies are funny animals. It depends whether they're hungry or not. If you feed them, they're likely to follow you around like little puppy dogs."

At that image, Helder's stomach rotated in the other direction. Bears coming into the kitchen, bears on the sun deck, bears in the lounge, and *Christ!* bears sniffing around the heated bungalows at night while the guests slept.

"Right. Bears. Okay. I'll post the lodge and everything. Thanks for telling me."

As they finished putting up the roadblock, Drake watched the sun sink, casting deep, pointed shadows over Colby's cliffs. Outlined with trees, its features blackened into silhouette, it resembled a gigantic head overlooking the valley.

10

Beginning tonight, Lester Cole was getting an extra day off. Combined with the weekend, that gave him three days in which to attend the funeral of his cousin Murphy, who had driven his motorcycle into a moving van night before last. After the accident, Helder had inquired solicitously if there was anything he could do to help. Lester considered hitting him for two or three hundred dollars, then blowing the country altogether. But he had read somewhere that if you're going to pull a swindle, pull a really big one. Big enough to get far away and have a lot of money left over.

He had almost blown this whole Bigfoot business. The sudden thrill of fame had impelled him to shoot off his mouth to everybody before realizing he was going about it the wrong way. He had realized this blunder while scraping lettuce from a plate. Now everybody was hunting the beast. It was his. After all, he had seen it first and could do whatever he wanted with it. Like prospectors when they found gold and staked a claim. There was some law about that. Lester was sure there was a law for him, too. He hated all those people with time to hunt while he dipped his hands in pork fat.

He had tried to correct his mistake as best he could. He told everybody now that he had made it up, hoping to drive all those hunters back into their homes, leaving him clear. It had worked, too. Everybody knew Lester was a liar, except that goddamned flatlander with an arm bandage. Lester hated people like Jason, who pushed around the Lester Coles of the world and had it made. It was not fair how he had tried to pump the truth out of Lester. He had been about to hit him. Lester wished he had.

It would be too bad if that flatlander got in Lester's way. Got in his way, that is, down there in the valley while Lester had his gun. Just the two of them. Had his gun and the drop on him. Don't push Lester around. Lester gets even. Later.

He banged a lot of crockery around that day. Everybody thought he was upset about his cousin Murphy. Lester never liked his cousin Murphy. Murphy was a wiseass. Helder had looked pityingly on as he dropped a glass and said, "You can go home now, Lester. We'll see you Tuesday."

Lester wore denims and a sweater to keep the night chill at bay. He drove down to the valley and passed the van on the bridge, on its way to the lodge. Delbert, the driver, waved at him from the driver's seat, but Lester did not wave back. He did not like Delbert. He hoped Delbert never found out how much he hated him, because Delbert was six feet tall and could make tossed salad out of him. Unless him and Delbert found themselves in the valley at night and Lester had the gun and the drop on him. Usually he was nice to Delbert, because of Delbert's size.

The stretch of road through the trees where Lester had seen the Bigfoot always gave him the heebies. These woods were not like your regular scraggly mountain trees. These woods were so tight they leaned clean over the road, breaking moonlight up into clutching fingers and teeth. Somebody once said on a late-night TV show that people were afraid of the full moon because thousands of years ago the earth was covered with different types of humans who came out then. These humans lived in the woods with saber-toothed tigers and snakes and dinosaurs and mastodons, and got along great with them because they all ate the same thing: other humans. This guy had said there were wars between these humans and the real humans. That was where all that stuff about giants in the Bible and Greece and Scandinavia came from.

Lester pulled his pickup off the road onto the grassy entrance of the logging trail where he had seen the thing. He cut off his engine. Lester figured the thing came out only late at night. *Really* late. That was why nobody had found it. Lester had come home late that night only because he needed the overtime to pay off Harry for the poker game.

Lester had plenty of time to get to Murphy's funeral. But for the rest of the night he was not even going to go home. He did not have to get up early in the morning, and he had his Remington pump on the rack over the rear window. He shut the radio and checked the rifle chamber. Then he settled back into his seat and waited.

Fucking cold.

Sometime around ten, Lester fell asleep.

From time to time the Indian blew hot breath into his hands to warm them. He paced the little clearing with restless steps, whistling into the trees.

The dog had deserted him. Even the plastic sack was gone. The Indian had looked for it, afraid he would find the animal whimpering and vomiting under some bush from the unusually heavy food he had given it to share with the spirit last night.

The Indian lay on the ground, head propped on a tree root, and tried to calm down. He kept pushing down the thought of betrayal which surfaced in his mind, keeping him from slumber. His spirit had left him alone at this place after leading him hundreds of miles from home.

The Indian turned over on the ground, pushing away that thought. It subsided, but its stirrings tilted the great weight of faith he had constructed particle by particle over the past months.

His grandfather tried to speak to him. The dry, cracked lips opened and whispered.

Something about his spirit.

The Indian's hand slid over the ground to where he wished the dog's warm body lay. There was nothing but dirt and pine needles.

Why did his spirit not give him a name or at least a sign? Had he taken the dog?

Steamy jungle heat drenched his body in sweat. Ah! His grandfather's voice. He heard it clearly as he lay in the Asian bush with an arrow drawn back. A Russian rifle clicked down the path somewhere. They knew he was here, but they couldn't see him. Good. They were frightened. The Indian smelled blood as he drew the arrow taut toward the chest. A quick, quiet exhalation, the hiss of air, then the strangled cry and he was running, stooped under the leaves, as rifle fire split the night . . .

A shudder whipcracked the Indian's body. He grunted in fear as icy wetness coated his chest, his fingers, and caressed his neck, soft as cotton. His chest was covered with snowflakes.

Snow whispered through the hissing trees, branch to branch, causing the timbers to groan, whitening the ground into a pale, ghostly hue.

Helder's voice boomed over the hills: "Ladies and gentlemen, one free drink on the house, courtesy of the great god Snow."

The Indian whistled desperately for his dog. Winter or not, he wanted to get out of this place. He wanted his spirit back.

"Mountain weather" was Martha Lucas's only comment about the falling snow dusting her hair. "Looks like it woke Moon up."

She passed the binoculars to Jason, who observed Moon whistling into the woods. They were sharp, piercing, sad whistles, like a marmot's. "That's what the Bigfoot sounds like, too. The same whistle. That's how they both summon the dog."

"What do you think will happen to Moon when he learns the truth?" The Indian's distress apparently affected Martha.

Jason pushed the glasses tight to his eyes. "Him? He'll never learn the truth, not him. People like him always find a truth they want. He'll make his spirit into a devil if he can't have it as a god."

Jason was depressed, and when he became depressed he became mad. If only he'd burned out that food in the mine and gone after them. If only he'd searched the slope instead of wasting time with Drake. If only this girl had not become entangled with everything. Dammit, dammit to hell and gone! Jason was so damned mad about this business that even his arm did not bother him any more, as if the poison had somehow moved from his body to his psyche.

When Lester awoke at midnight, he screeched in shock. He was surrounded by pitch-blackness as tight as a box-sized jail cell. Then he realized he was seated in his truck with the radio off and the windows coated with snow.

Snow.

"Shit," he said, opening the door. He stepped out of the truck and promptly slipped on the ground.

The snowfall had stopped, leaving a coating that edged over his shoes. The trees were frosted in bony white. Although moonlight was gone, the snow crystals glittered from some light source he could not fathom.

More to the point, snow covered the trail down to the road. How in hell was he going to get home? His snow tires were down in his trailer, and that was a seven percent grade all the way.

"Shit," he repeated.

He was answered by a snarl ahead of the truck.

The next three seconds were the bravest in Lester's life. He slowly looked around into the trees while reaching through the window to the light switch on the dashboard.

Moon's dog stood in the snow, growling at him, the light exploding in its eyes. A dead beaver's head was clutched in its teeth.

"Hey, pooch. Pooch, pooch, pooch! You sorry sack of fleas, what are you doing out here?"

The dog slipped into the woods, a burst of sparkling snow marking its departure. Lester followed with his rifle. The dog ran up to a thick spruce, halted, and faced Lester again. It dropped the head and yowled in anger at him. The closer Lester got, the meaner the howls became. Now that was damned weird. That dog was real quiet around the Indian. What was it doing with that head? Where was the rest of the thing?

"I'm not going to do anything to you, boy. I just—"

A blood-freezing screech sailed out from the branches

over Lester's head. Lester did not have brains, but his reflexes were a source of pride. He jumped backward as the thing dive-bombed straight down with a squeal like chalk on a blackboard and killed itself in a sickening crunch of bone. The small, misshapen body thrashed holes in the snow.

Lester stepped clear and put three bullets into its back.

The dog howled and rushed into the woods, its barks transmuted into howls of terror.

Lester knew he was rich. This little thing here was some kind of baboon with a tiny tail and small fingers. It was about four feet long. There was a pelt there, not much, and kind of ratty-looking with ugly scabs and bare patches, but a pelt.

Well, Bigfeet had babies too, and this was good enough. He rolled it over with his foot. And looked at its face.

It was some seconds before Lester gained sufficient control of himself to grab its ankles and drag it to the truck. He swung it into the bed, where it landed like a feather, then climbed behind the wheel. Oblivious to his tires and the dangerously slippery road, he roared out onto the highway. As he left the forest he could still hear the barking dog.

He was kind of worried that his trailer on Hulcher Road was so isolated. It was all backed up in the trees on Colby's south face. The Petrie family, next door, had gone off for the weekend.

He turned on the lights in his trailer and cleared dishes from a small Formica table that served as a dining area. His walls were papered with motorcycle photos in full color. His refrigerator was well stocked with beer and nothing but.

Only then did he return to the truck, clang down the tailgate, and look at the thing huddled on the metal.

Lester pulled it out by the ankles again. Its head bumped

over the ground and up the cinder-block steps. He dragged it into the kitchen, leaving a trail of blood on the linoleum, then hoisted it up to the table under the cold fluorescent light.

Well, that was not so bad. Nothing like that hellacious scare its face caused when dimly seen. Lester cracked open a beer and searched for a butcher knife in the drawer. He was uncertain about how or even whether to skin it.

He had shot a child. Except if Lester ever had a kid like that he would be tempted to shoot himself. It changed from human to gorilla depending on how you looked at it. The head was flat, with scraggly lank hair that peaked in the center of the forehead. One cheek had tufts of hair on it, the other was smooth as a baby's. The mouth was open, revealing half a set of yellow, crooked, pretty goddamned big teeth. The jaw was narrow and kind of pointed. The eyes were rolled back and white, with red laces in them, just like anybody's, only two heavy brows sat over them, the ends curled into horns.

Lester closed his eyes and opened them again. Still there. The fur was blistered and patchy, and the arms and legs didn't match. It looked to Lester as though the little bastard would have died on his own soon anyway.

Lester shook his head, the barking dog's voice reverberating in his ears. He opened another beer and drank it down. Then another. He sank into a leisurely stupor made sweet by the anticipation of the money he would get for the pelt. Maybe he'd better call some lawyer in the morning to do what was legal to get possession of it.

Lester socked away beer after beer, mooning over money. The outline of the thing shimmered with his doubling vision. Keep on drinking like this and it might just sit up and say hi.

He'd better get started now, before he was too smash-blinded to cut right. This was going to be nasty. He spread newspapers on the floor around the table and set to work on the carcass, trying to think it was just like dressing a deer.

Sometime later, as he labored over the table, Lester realized that the dog's barking was not in his head. Claws scraped on the screen door. Lester pondered that. The little prick must have followed him somehow.

The suspension springs creaked on his truck. Then, with a crunch of collapsing metal and a clash of glass, he heard the truck roll over. He must have left the brake on. Piece of junk anyhow; he'd buy himself a Peterbilt with his money and run his own truck. Nice CB on the dash, TV back there in the sleeping cube, and loads of road whores bouncing around in the trailer . . .

Brakes. Dog. *Shit!*

Lester finally caught on when the trailer began to rock. Simultaneously, a rock blew in his living-room window, rolled off the unmade bed, and thumped to the floor. He looked across the kitchen to the crank-handled window. A face was looking in.

Lester could not take his eyes off it. It was horned and hairy, with narrow eyes rimmed in red, and it swallowed up more window than any human's would.

The window behind his neck smashed to pieces, and the draft brought in a sudden stench. He looked into a second face not ten inches from his own.

It was a knowing face, like the other one. The red eyes looked into Lester's, then at the shapeless mess on the table.

The face writhed into a contorted mass as though snakes were jumping under the skin, all the features going against each other. Lester flung his beer at it.

An arm the size of a tree trunk rammed through the window frame, grabbed Lester's entire head in a hand so enormous it swallowed it up, and squeezed convulsively.

The last thing Lester heard was the howling dog and the wall caving in as the other beast hooted into the kitchen to the child's body. Lester did not blame them. Lester did not blame them one damned bit.

NEMESIS

11

On Saturday morning, Jack Helder joyfully shut off the snow guns and serviced the five snowmobiles in the shed. The place was packed for the weekend. He told his staff Colby would stand or fall on the weekend business, so he was releasing half of them during the weekdays. They'd make more money on Saturday and Sunday. The worse the weather, the better for him. Naturally, the airport would be closed for the storm, but he could send the van to Clayton, where the diverted planes would be landing.

Saturday afternoon, he shivered on his sun deck, watching the sun lance feeble rays over the valley. Tomorrow the sun deck would be shielded behind heavy metal shutters. The storm would seize the valley as a dog seizes prey in its teeth and yanks it about. They would all move to the game room at night, where there were pinball machines and billiard tables. The colder it was, the more liquor he would sell. He could make it on the bar alone.

On Saturday afternoon, Martha Lucas and Raymond Jason visited a weary James Drake at Ranger headquarters.

"No, no, we haven't found anything. We did the north face most of the morning and found a lot of stripped foliage, but nothing recent."

Nor had they found any more entrances to the Limerick, but it could be a cave hidden somewhere. "Those charts will be here by Thursday, and we should really be cracking then."

Martha asked if she could tell Jack Helder yet. Drake yawned. "If you ask me, they've cleared out of here. Go ahead and tell him, but also make damned certain he doesn't let anyone run around that mine."

And she would have if it were not for John Moon. Helder would land on the Indian like the Gestapo, pumping him for every bit of information, wheedling, cajoling, demanding, offering more pay, perhaps driving that fragile sensibility beyond endurance. Judging by Moon's dark-ringed eyes and recent poor performance on the archery field, he was not far from there now.

"Cool it," Jason told her. "If they're really gone, he'll catch on before long."

That night Raymond Jason lay on his bungalow bed in a state of profound melancholy, watching cigarette smoke curl up to the ceiling. He dwelled on that medicine bundle at Moon's waist. The bag smelled like the beast, no doubt about it. There could very well be a piece of it in there, probably taken from the trap it had sprung. If so, Jason was going to take it.

It was either that or get out of this impasse the way he had come in. With nothing. For Jason was convinced that the beasts were gone for good, leaving him and Moon in the lurch.

Him and Moon.

Jason was a hair's-breadth away from hating that laconic redskin, that weirdo with his silly, savage superstitions. His psychiatrist would have said it was because Moon reminded him of himself. But Jason's hatred for Moon was tinged with contempt. Put a Raggedy Ann doll before him and he'd follow you anywhere.

And so would Jason. Two peas in a pod.

Jason angrily squashed out the cigarette and lit another one. Think about something else. Think about what they both had missed.

So far Kimberly had called the shots beautifully. He had suggested that some kind of genetic damage had decimated the population of Bigfeet over the past hundred years. And it had been confirmed when Jason saw its face in the river. A damaged mismatched face with a human chin on the superstructure of a monstrous primate. Parts that did not mesh. Kimberly had stated that the chin was irrefutable proof that it was human.

Jason believed that.

Almost.

The trouble was, primitive humans were small, not giants. Twinkletoes, not Bigfeet. Kimberly had suggested that giantism, some glandular disorder, accounted for its size and hair. Yet giantism was a crippling disease that weakened bones. This thing was *built* huge. He could walk and run for distances of up to a thousand miles. Nature had designed it that way, using the basic superstructure of the ape.

Dammit, it was a missing link. It was both ape and human. Had to be! Even Paranthropus had not been that big a hominid. This was a gorilla-scaled apparition no matter what kind of face it had.

Genetic damage.

Jason watched the smoke curl. Genetic *damage?* Now just a bloody minute here, there's a third possibility. It was so far out of imagination, he even had trouble pinning it down.

Jason slowly sat upright on the bed. Until now his plight paralleled the Indian's, in that he was not quite sure what he was chasing. To Moon it was a spirit, to Jason an equally unlikely creature.

A third possibility. A third Sasquatch. Kimberly had

neglected to speculate what could have caused a genetic upset in the animals. Bad water, air pollution, all that stuff was the assumption.

The trouble was, genetic damage was fatal too. Oh, you could make it through two or three generations, but still, the timing was off. They'd be extinct by the mid-sixties.

So maybe genetic *damage* was the wrong word, too. A genetic change! Plain Darwinian evolution. The things were changing from ape to human. How in the hell could that happen?

It took something of a struggle for Jason to face that question squarely. There was only one way it could have happened, absurd as it was . . . as incredibly far out and unbelievable as it was, that had to be it.

From the drawer he pulled out a Gideon Bible. Religious fanatics! They were everywhere. He had not looked in the Bible since he was a child, but after half an hour of searching, it was there in front of his eyes.

Yes! He knew what the things were! Jason knew exactly what he was chasing.

Jack Helder was alone in the Grizzly Bar, with the color television flickering lines across the screen. He had been counting receipts and sipping Scotch. Sip. Count. Sip. Count. He fell asleep with his head on the counter as the rising wind shuddered the lodge.

When he heard the crash of crockery from the kitchen, he awoke thinking it was morning and the cook had arrived to fix breakfast. Nice of him to get an early start.

Except it was three fifteen in the morning, according to the watch, which would not stay in focus.

The second crash was louder than the first and was accompanied by plaster tearing out of the wall and water gurgling onto the floor. It brought Helder to his feet, wide awake and hung over. He went into the lounge and listened.

The fire was low. Shadows consumed the corners, trying to possess the room as the flames dwindled. Feet shuffled around in the kitchen. Heavy, soft feet, as though someone were wearing rubber soles.

The third crash was the deep freeze being upended and spilling frozen meats. Helder shouted, "Hey!"

The sounds stopped. The intruder was listening.

Helder ran into his office, opened the standing gun cabinet, and took out his rifle. As he walked rapidly to the kitchen, he heard the service-entrance door screech from hinges which pinged onto the floor.

He banged open the swinging doors and beheld pure savagery. The wind whistled through the splintered doorway over a glutinous freezing mess of eggs, lettuce, milk, steaks, all the varied foods for varied appetites he had stocked for the week, scattered across the floor in an indescribable scramble. Steak blood was smeared across the walls. The sinks had been pulled from their pipes and water sloshed over congealing bread and salad dressing.

Helder ran to the doorway, slipping across the floor. He caught his balance against the jamb and cut on the parking-apron floodlights. No one—or nothing—was there.

"Hey, goddammit!" he screamed into the wind. "Come back here!"

A shadow lengthened from behind his car. Helder put a bullet through the windshield. He was hiding out there, him and his goddamned egg-sucking buddies.

A rock rebounded off the doorjamb, next to his fingers. Helder fired two shots in the direction from which it had come. "Come on, kids, out of there! I mean it!"

Another rock arced up to a floodlight on the east corner and exploded it. Helder fired again. One by one the lights in the parking lot were killed by rocks, plunging the area deeper and deeper into wind-blown darkness, in which he made out a scurrying form at each end of the lot.

He fired at the one headed down the road and ran out of bullets. There were only two of them, but that was more than enough. He turned to see people crowding into the kitchen, dressed in all manner of nightgowns and pajamas. They had been attracted by the shooting.

"Look at this! Just look what they did!" he screeched, kicking at a balled-up wad of hamburger. "That's a week's supply of food. They hit everything, the lockers, the cutting table, the stove . . . Look at this. Little bastards!"

Jason and Martha stepped through the service-entrance door. Jason held his revolver. He saw a rock lying in egg yolk and picked it up. "Did you see them, Mr. Helder?"

"Of course I saw them. They hid behind the cars out there."

"What did they look like?"

"How do I know what they looked like!" Helder shouted with immaculate illogic. He lifted a shoe and examined the muck mixed with eggshell. *What in hell was the man toting a pistol around for anyhow!* "It's . . . it's . . . just *barbaric!* Why would anybody do something like this, for Jesus—" He flushed red. He froze. His voice dropped. "Decoy. Diversion."

"What?" asked Martha.

"The bungalows! Was anybody robbed? Maybe it's a diversion."

Panic-stricken, the people pushed and shoved their way out of the kitchen, down the gallery hall toward the bungalows, leaving Jason and Martha alone.

Jason thoughtfully tossed the rock up and down in his hand. He was smiling. Martha was frightened. She searched out the sink-pipe water valve and shut it off.

"That answers our question," said Jason.

"Why would they do this?"

"Because they want the valley back. That means drive Helder out. They've been watching everything down here. I guess they figure if Helder goes, nobody will come back."

"I'm going to call Drake," said Martha. She ran out of the kitchen toward Helder's office. Jason was wiping the mess from his boots when she ran back in again, her somber eyes ignited with barely suppressed fear. "Raymond?"

"Yes?"

"The phones are dead."

Jason checked his watch. It was three thirty in the morning. Daylight would come in two hours. They could not check for any further damage until it was light. He decided he would stay awake until sunrise.

Morning dawned with Helder's lodge being pelted by flying branches, bark, and leaves blown from the woods by gale-force winds. Helder had not slept either. He remained in the bar, slowly sobering up and looking out the window as the morning light outlined the ruins of his ski trails.

By seven in the morning he had driven into Garrison and returned with three state policemen.

You found kids like that everywhere, Helder reflected bitterly as he stood by the ski-lift machinery, watching the wind scour the artificial snow into razor-sharp crests.

Helder's ski machinery had been ruined. Not just broken into or vandalized, but destroyed. The snow guns had been toppled from their supports; the chair cables were a broken jumble scattered down the slope; the shed had been cracked open, the wooden walls torn to pieces and the machinery inside rendered into an unsymmetric, overturned pile of cables, wires, toppled stanchions, and gear wheels.

One of the policemen came out, his gloves coated with grease. "What I don't understand is how they got up here, Mr. Helder." That was a neat trick all right. The slope had been plowed into a thirty-degree angle. Because of the wind and frozen fake snow, climbing it would have been quite an undertaking even for a mountain goat.

"What I don't understand is why," said Helder, looking up the slope to the mountain summit lost among trees bending under the wind.

The policeman was sympathetic. "I guess somebody just doesn't like you."

Fifteen of Helder's forty guests canceled immediately and arranged schedules with the van driver. Several of those who had driven themselves up—the weekenders, whose business Helder desperately wanted—also headed for home. The rest seemed undecided. They returned to their rooms or to the game room. Helder told Delbert to drive into Garrison that morning and return with a load of hamburger for the afternoon and tonight. What they would do about feeding people tomorrow, at the height of the storm, was something Helder could not face that morning.

12

Lit by bronzed fire reflected off the fireplace hearth, the huge lips moved. The Indian pressed his hands against them, trying to stop the word from creeping out between his child's fingers.

He tossed on the bungalow bed, trying not to wake up. He was ripsawed between his faith and the growing press of his grandfather speaking to him. He fervently wished the doctors were here with their calming needles. He tried to shut his mind to his grandfather's voice, lest he say something that would destroy him.

Someone rapped on the door. "Mr. Moon? Mr. Helder sent me. You're late."

The Indian groaned at the suffocating weight of reality. The wind blew fiercely, shrieking past roof eaves and through branches. The Indian's feet slid to the floor, and piece by piece he got himself to a standing position, from which he lurched across the room. "Yeah, I'm awake," he said, tugging the knob.

The pistol butt came straight for his forehead. The Indian's head turned an infinitesimal fraction of an inch, enough to divert the full force of it. He awoke fully on his way to the floor, blood flowing from his scalp. His eyes were closed, but his ears were attuned to the stranger stepping in and closing the door behind him. The Indian waited for his chance.

Jason had struck quickly but not accurately, and he hoped not too hard. The Indian's chest rose and fell in steady rhythm, his eyeballs rolled under his lids, but otherwise there was not a twitch from him.

The room stank of meat gone bad. Gun in hand, Jason kneeled beside the Indian and untied the medicine bundle. He opened the flap, and the stench poured forth in such waves that he gagged.

He overturned the bag. Out fell a clay pipe, a medal box, a billfold, a crucifix, and some dried corn. Whatever else was in there was stuck to the leather, as if hiding for a last few seconds. Jason shook the bag.

It tumbled onto the floor with a sticky plop. Jason recoiled with a sheet of cold zipping down his spine as though it were some kind of spider. But it was just a toe. The thing was unrecognizable but for the suppurated cuticle anchoring the huge brown nail. The flesh had drawn up from the severed bone, leaving it exposed. Hair clumped the top of it.

Jason grasped it between thumb and forefinger. Vertigo swirled through him, rushing out of his eyes to the toe like a drain for his emotions. After a second he calmed down. *What was the matter with him anyway?* He was at peace for the first time in weeks. Here was something for his efforts, at least. The end was in sight—the end of endless lonely exertions that had played havoc with his business and his life, the cauterizing climax of days of constant fear that he had lost the beast forever.

He turned it to the gray light from the window. It was big, at least the size of a silver dollar in breadth. In length it was well over an inch, jointed between two long bones as if Nature had designed it for a gorilla's clutching foot, then changed her mind at the last minute. Decay was advanced. The hair was loosening. He would have to get it into preservative quickly. There must be alcohol in the infirmary—

The Indian's hand caught him on the side of the neck. It hit like an ax blade, sending a bone vibration up the vertebrae to his skull, where darkness exploded in a black globe that drove light from his eyes.

He came to flat on his back with his own gun muzzle hovering like an evil eye between his nose and forehead. The Indian was seated on the bed, holding the pistol in both hands. The medicine bundle was tied fast to his waist.

"All right," said Jason. "I'm ready."

The Indian's body was relentlessly still. Only his hands moved, rotating the gun in small circles.

"Moon?" Jason said to break the silence. "I've seen it. I've seen your spirit."

The gun muzzle steadied on his forehead.

"I know what it is. It's not a spirit at all. Never was. Do you understand me?"

Moon's head vibrated in small negative shakes.

"He killed two men last summer. I was with them. Don't you remember that?"

"I never seen you before." His words were contemptuous, as though too precious to waste on a doomed man.

"In Canada, Moon. You hit me with a rifle. I had a beard then. Remember?" Jason tried to define a beard with one of his hands on his chin.

"No."

Jason raised himself on his elbows. Moon's foot pushed him down again. "Dammit, Moon, he tore off their heads!"

"I don't remember nothing past yesterday, no sir. My memory's gone."

Jason tried to sit up again.

"Stay put."

"Can't I have a last cigarette?"

The Indian nodded. Reluctantly.

Jason sat upright, tenderly rubbing his neck. The ache was a pole of agony that flared whenever he moved his neck. "Thanks for hitting me on the right side, Moon. It balances my left arm."

Moon was not amused in the slightest. This apparition had many words which he would use to shake his faith. "Just stay on the floor."

Very carefully Jason withdrew a cigarette from his pocket. "You really don't remember me, do you."

Moon shook his head.

"If I talk and you don't like what I'm going to say, are you going to shoot me?"

"I might."

Jason lit the cigarette with slow movements. He looked for some place to put the match. Seeing nothing, he slipped it into his pocket. "Have you seen your so-called spirit's face?"

" 'Course I have." It was a lie, but Moon did not want to be put on the defensive.

"Then you know it's deformed. But in a special way,

Moon. In a way that was familiar to humans thousands of years ago, when there were many more species of primate on the earth than there ever have been since. A genetic change hit a species of Bigfoot out here about two hundred years ago. It entered the bloodline of these creatures and has been making hash out of them."

"Shit on you."

"Let me finish. Kill me later. Okay?"

Moon gripped his pistol.

"This genetic change appeared to them as a disease. Every now and then an infant would be born strange and killed. But another would carry little or no visible evidence and pass it on to its own offspring. A biologist back in Kansas City set me up for this. He was right. But he thought it was a real disease, and it isn't. It's a human strain, Moon. One of your spirit's ancestors was a human being."

Not much of a revelation to Moon. He had considered similar thoughts himself.

"I call it a disease because that's exactly how it would appear to them. None of this shit about being touched by gods or anything like that. To them it would appear they were giving birth to monsters. Do you follow me?"

Jason was certain the Indian did not understand a word he said. He talked to keep the thumb away from the hammer of the pistol. Moon studied him as if he were a centipede that had invaded his room.

"There are human traits of your spirit, Moon, that simply do not fit primate behavior other than man. He travels alone, whereas apes live in bands. He has a very distinct chin, and no other nonhuman primate has that. I've seen him walk. Only humans walk upright for any length of time—other primates walk on their knuckles. He eats meat. He hunts heads—"

"No sir." The gun came up. "He don't do that."

"And he leaves footprints that are a total mix between human and ape. And there are other details, mostly in the thing's face. He has a long thin nose with a bridge and horns. Horns, Moon! Didn't you ever wonder why the devil had horns? This face that your spirit has goes back thousands of years and frightened people then. And why? It's not because they believed in an abstract devil, it's because there were enough creatures like this wandering around. It's in the Bible. It's in the Veda, Chinese legends, Scandinavian ones. People in ancient times were consistently warned not to sleep with giants. It used to happen more often than we can believe. Think of Polyphemus, the cyclops. Goliath. The Greek Titans. *They were outcasts from both species!* Just like your spirit!"

The gun continued circling. Jason babbled on, knowing he was getting too abstract for Moon but hoping his fervency would convince him.

"The original species was definitely humanoid. Very tall, very hairy, very strong. The other species are shy— you glimpse them in the woods for a few seconds at a time. But not yours. Yours is aggressive. And calculating. No ape could have dreamed up throwing a rattlesnake . . ."

In Moon's obsidian eyes, something splintered and fell away, blanking his gaze into a deadness that seemed to go through Jason. Something had happened.

"Moon? Moon?"

The giants.

His grandfather's mouth opened and the fearful word slipped out. *Natliskeliguten*, the fearful giants, and the old man had terrified the Indian with tales of their depredations. They had a powerful odor like burning horn, and they would walk up to tipis and look down the smokeholes. Sometimes they stole women.

Softly, softly, like a curtain shredding to golden threads,

then those threads to their constituent atoms, the Indian's memory unblocked and the old cracked voice returned to him. His grandfather spoke again in the grave, patient tones of his youth.

The giants were dead, John! Coyote the dancing dog, God who made the human race, killed them all and turned them into the black boulders of the Bitterroot valley. They were dead.

Weren't they? All of them? Could one have escaped? What did the giants look like, Grandfather?

Like . . . Like . . .

No!

This is it, thought Jason as the Indian bounded off the bed, thrust a hand into his jacket, and pulled him to his feet with a single yank. Jason protected his face until the gun barrel pushed into his stomach, almost to his spine.

The Indian hissed into his face, black eyes distilling fire, threads of saliva collecting in the deep clefts on the sides of his mouth. "He's a spirit! He *is!* I know what he is. And you're the devil, you bastard—" Moon babbled on, words spilling out of his mouth, juiced with a venomous hatred so potent they seemed to cling to the walls. He drenched Jason in obscenities, some common, some so bizarre they made absolutely no sense.

But he did not pull the trigger. Some uncertainty stilled his finger. Jason knew that if the right lever in Moon's psyche were touched, his own life would pour out, and he had not touched that lever. It was fear that really fueled the Indian's rage. Fear of Jason, fear sparked from some mysterious emotional terminals in his brain.

The Indian ran out of insults. He released his grip on Jason and stepped backward, his bony face a whitened mask of trapped anger.

"You were in the war, weren't you, Moon?"

Moon breathed harshly, the breath whistling through his nostrils. His forehead glistened.

"I'm very sorry," said Jason, straightening his coat.

He opened the door. Wind shrieked in, bearing twigs from the woods. There were no snowflakes yet, but there soon would be. The sun would darken and the sky grow fat with iron clouds that pressed tightly over the horizon. "I want my gun back, Moon. If you're not planning to shoot me, that is."

Moon threw the gun at him. It bounced off Jason's jacket to the floor. Had it been cocked, one of them would not be walking out of the room.

"Thank you," said Jason. He tucked it into his belt and bulled out into the wind.

Touching that toe had been a kind of addiction. He had to get back into the medicine bundle. Regardless of what the Indian did, Raymond Jason was determined to stick as close to John Moon as Moon had stuck to his spirit.

The late cousin Murphy used to say that Lester Cole was never on time anywhere. When relatives called Cole's trailer to find out how he could miss Murphy's funeral, an operator came on to say that the phone was out of order. He was not working at the lodge, where the phones were also down, so they became mildly alarmed and contacted the police.

A motorcycle cop braved the winds and drove up Hulcher Road to where Lester's trailer was parked deep in overhanging woods. Lester's truck was overturned, and the entire trailer was off its cinder-block mountings. The ground was littered with broken glass, furniture, and beer cans, thrown out the smashed doors and windows.

The cop took out his gun and shouldered his way inside. A rock lay on the floor. Blood was everywhere. A trail of thin blood led into the kitchen, to a great dried puddle of it soaking newspapers around the kitchen table. Lester had apparently been poaching deer. Everything else in the trailer was smashed.

The cop called headquarters, which in turn called the Forest Service. When Drake and his men arrived, the cop was poking through the woods, looking for Lester's body.

"Let's not fly off the handle yet," said Drake over the map spread out on the truck hood. He indicated a fanlike section of Colby's face with Lester's trailer as the base. Checking it out meant trudging uphill through tangled timbers and maintaining your balance by gripping bushes. "There isn't any reason for them to come all the way around the mountain. Oharaville's on the north side."

They climbed for an hour, searching the ground. After a hundred yards the blood gave out. Taylor was leaning against a tree, feet securely planted in the ground, cupping a match against the wind to light a cigarette, when he saw the shoe wedged in the exposed tree roots. It was a cheap loafer, the sole worn to paper-thinness. The heel was caught in the root.

Drake examined the shoe. Blood had dried on the instep. "It was upside down, so that means he was either walking backwards or he was dragged up and the heel caught in the roots. Let's look for clothing or something." They spread out, searching the underbrush and branch tips. Jones was standing next to Wallace when the wind shifted. "Listen!"

Wallace listened and heard nothing. "What?"

"It's gone now. Did you ever blow over the top of an open bottle and make this *whooo* noise? For just a minute there. . ."

Again the wind shifted and this time Wallace heard a lowing sound, like that of a distant cow, coming from a rock ledge above them. He and Jones scrambled up to it.

Brush was pushed tightly against the wall of rock. It did

not quiver as the wind crossed it. Jones grabbed a handful and pulled. The entire bush popped out like a cork from a small horizontal cave some four feet high and seven feet wide. The bush flew away in an ungainly ball from Jones's hand, hit a tree, and disintegrated.

They waited on the ledge for Taylor to puff back up the slope bearing a rope and lights. Drake tied the rope around his waist and flashed a light inside the cave. "Somebody make a note that Forest Rangers be equipped with gas masks next time."

"You don't need Rangers here," said Wallace. "You need a plumber."

Although the entrance was small, the cave itself was large. Stones had been piled against the floor, forming a sort of staircase. Drake saw stalactites hanging from the ceiling. The chart had said Colby was full of limestone. Under the action of water, limestone dissolved into caves.

"If I'm not back in five minutes, flush the thing," said Drake. Jones played out the rope as he slipped, rifle first, through the opening.

"It's like a church," said Drake, his voice booming. The interior was a good fifteen feet high. The walls were smooth and curved. On the opposite wall was a small opening leading to another tunnel. "It's clean except for the smell. It's dry, too."

Drake could not pin down any particular detail that told him the cave was used frequently, but that was what he sensed. Somewhere he had read that living things leave a memory of their presence behind, like a battery charge. It might have been technical nonsense, but he trusted his instincts.

"Everybody tie yourselves together and let's go in a little ways," said Drake. "Stay behind me."

The wind receded to a faint whistle as they followed Drake single-file into the tunnels. Unlike the mine, which was filled with the drip of water, the cave system was quiet. Dry and quiet. Silence was an unnatural state of nature, Jones thought. It meant you were being watched.

The tunnel branched, and they walked to the right. All of them smelled the smoke at once. "Taylor was right," said Jones. It was not thick or visible. It was an old odor, as if given off by a deposit of soot on the walls.

"Hickory smoke," whispered Wallace. "Now what in hell..."

Drake rounded a corner and aimed his light at the floor. Twenty feet ahead they saw the tattered remains of Lester Cole lying in a gush of dried blood.

Drake examined the body. "His head's gone," he said quietly. He flashed the light around, as if expecting to find it lying somewhere close by.

They carried Lester down the mountain in a tarpaulin and deposited him in the back of the truck. Drake called the state police. "We've found him. I want you to do something for me. I want you to take samples of all the blood in his trailer and find out what kind of an animal he was carving up in there, if that's really what he was doing. Okay? Ten four."

He stood outside the truck, breathing in great drafts of fresh cold air. He turned to Jones and said, "Now what, Jonesy?"

"I can't see them doing anything in the middle of a snowstorm."

"On the other hand," Drake drawled, "if they were going to do something nasty, a snowstorm is the perfect cover, isn't it? Anybody been up to the lodge over the weekend?"

Nobody had.

"I'll run up there myself. Helder won't be happy about being evacuated, so I guess it's only courteous for the boss to tell him."

Martha Lucas found herself standing next to John Moon as Helder called the guests together. Moon seemed so shrunken that his hair was the only substantial part of him. The rest was just a ghost.

As Drake stifled yawns of exhaustion, Jack Helder spoke tonelessly to his guests. "Ladies and gentlemen, we have been ordered by the Forest Service to evacuate Colby Lodge immediately for the duration of the storm. There is a very serious problem with bears at the moment—" A titter of laughter rippled through them. "Please! One of our kitchen workers was killed over the weekend. I'll ask you to have your bags packed and ready to go beginning at four this afternoon. Lodging will be furnished for you in Garrison. Thank you."

After that speech Helder entered his office, locked the door, and would not answer it.

Martha intercepted Drake at the parking lot. "It's them," he told her. "They got Lester Cole. I don't know why. Where's Mr. Jason?"

"I haven't seen him all day. He must be in his bungalow."

"As far as you two are concerned, it's still bears, understand? I want to see you both at the station tomorrow morning." He tipped his hat as he walked to his truck.

She found John Moon heading into the woods and called to him. "John? John?"

"Yes, ma'am." There was a dark-blue swelling ringed with little scabs on his hairline.

She faced him, trying to hold his eyes. "John, do you know who wrecked the ski lift?"

"How should I know, ma'am?"

"John, listen to me. It doesn't have anything to do with you personally. Have you ever, *ever* in your life come across any kind of"—she made movements with her hands —"gorillas in the woods?"

His gaze drew back and focused on her. "Why, no,

ma'am. That's silly. They ain't nothing like that in these woods."

"What about spirits? Have you ever seen any spirits?"

His eyes widened in pleasure. He smiled at some secret knowledge within himself. "Why, yes, ma'am. Why, a day don't hardly go by that I don't see spirits!"

He pushed out the door into the wind.

Over the next hours the van picked up people and luggage for the forty-five-minute drive to Garrison. The vehicle had room for only eight or nine people, and weather conditions were becoming so bad that the last ones would not be out until seven o'clock.

By four in the afternoon cold powdery flakes of snow were riding the wind. The day had darkened to dusk, and Jason had still not shown up. From Helder's office came the sound of loud, deep snoring. He was sacked out on his couch, probably next to a bottle, Martha decided.

For the third time, Martha pounded on Jason's bungalow door for a full minute. This time he answered.

"Where've you been!" she gasped.

Jason's eyes squinted in pain. His neck was stiff, and he rubbed it tenderly. "I've been sleeping off a headache."

"Sleeping!"

"That's right. I had a little argument with Moon this morning, and he won."

She told him about the evacuation order and the death of Lester Cole.

"Are you going?" he asked.

"We have to go! Everybody. Helder's putting us up in a motel."

Jason put his chin in his hands. "What about Moon?"

"He has to go, too."

"I bet he won't. And if he doesn't go, I don't either."

"We don't have any choice, Raymond."

"Neither do I." He told her what he had told Moon that morning. "The director of the Primate Center started me thinking about it. I guess it's been growing in me all along."

"But that's ridiculous!"

"Don't tell me—I know it's ridiculous!"

"Bestiality? I mean, it's inconceivable!"

"It happened all the time a million years ago. In fact, it happens on farms all the time today. Look at any police blotter or the records of any mental hospital if you want your eyes opened."

Wind trembled the little bungalow. Martha sat down well away from him. "How long ago did this . . . thing happen?"

"Kimberly—he's a biologist I know—figured two hundred years ago. After being dormant for a long time, the gene would gradually appear, causing them to change their behavior through the late nineteenth and twentieth century. Now that the whole species is in trouble, they're coming out of the woodwork."

"How many are there?"

"Not too many, I don't think. They're competing with two other species. No more than a dozen, I would guess, scattered from here to California. I think Roger Patterson got one on film."

"Who could have . . . done it, Raymond? Any Indian trying it would have been tortured to death or expelled from the tribe. Bestiality is as big a taboo as incest."

"I know. I've been thinking about that." He sank into self-absorption for a moment, then looked up laboriously as if surfacing from some great depth. "One, it's a psychotic act. There's no sensible motive of any kind for bestiality. Two, it wasn't a woman, for the same reason it couldn't have been an Indian. That leaves us with a psychotic white man. Most important of all is opportunity. Whoever did it not only had to be crazy but had to be out here years on end when their numbers were greater and was able to get close to them. Maybe he even lived with them. There's a type of man that fits the bill perfectly."

"Who?"

"What do you know about the mountain men?"

Images of fierce, bearded men with falcon eyes, dressed in animal skins, came to her. There were Charles Russell paintings all over the lodge, pen-and-ink sketches of hard-eyed men, drawn in such a texture that they were almost indistinguishable from the animals always portrayed with them.

Jason continued. "Forget Daniel Boone, Martha. They've been romanticized a lot, but a scruffier bunch never lived. They were trappers mostly, and all they wanted of civilization was a trading post to take their skins to once a year. Even the Indians thought they were strange. You had to be a little strange to want to live alone for all your life."

Martha looked involuntarily at the door. "They'll come for us, won't they?"

"They'll come for the lodge. When did Lester Cole die?"

"Friday night. I don't know the details, though. I think Drake must have told Helder everything."

Jason reached for his coat and checked the pistol in the pocket. "The question now isn't how ugly they may be but how different they are up here!" He tapped his temple. "So far all I know about the male is that he can throw rattlesnakes and stones and walk long distances. I'm wondering if they're capable of planning things. Coordinating things." He slipped on the coat and opened the door. "Maybe it's time I had a talk with Jack Helder."

They knocked on Moon's bungalow door. They peered in the window. The bed was messed up but empty. Snow was piling over the ground and banking up against the bungalows. The snowfall was so thick that it blanked out the world with a seamless whiteness.

Martha followed Jason into the woods where Moon had lost the dog. They heard that loud, lonely summoning whistle from the sea of white before them.

"That's what I figured!" Jason cried above the wind. "He's not going anywhere till that dog comes back. We better go back and get you on the van."

"Oh, that's okay," she said.

"Like hell! It's getting late!"

She scuffed at the snow and settled her head deeper into her fur collar. "I'll stick around. I am, after all, sort of an anthropologist."

"I see." Jason laughed. "Moon gets to you, doesn't he. Maybe I should forget Bigfoot and put *him* in a cage. It must be ten below with this wind, and I bet he isn't even wearing a coat."

Helder's door was still firmly locked. There were several people waiting apprehensively for the van to return. The loading entrance was propped open, and a huge fire thundered in the hearth.

A man with wiry red hair and a bulky build sprawled in one of the stuffed chairs. "He's locked himself away real good," he said to them. "I nearly knocked the door down trying to get in. What's the matter with the phones around here anyhow?"

"They don't work," Jason responded, pounding loudly on Helder's door.

The red-haired man leafed through a *Sports Illustrated* and grinned. He held the magazine up to Martha. It was a photograph of himself decked out in a football uniform. The caption stated that Duane Woodard of the Dallas Cowboys had broken some yardage records that fall. "I figured I'd take a couple days off up here," he said to Martha.

"I'd still rather stay. I don't know why everybody's so afraid of a little old storm."

"It's not the storm, it's the bears," said Jason. He sat in a chair, impatiently cracking his knuckles.

"Naw, it ain't bears," said Woodard. "I've hunted bears. They don't tear up ski lifts."

"What do you think it is, then?"

"It's people. Has to be. How would a bear know how a ski lift works?"

The van wheezed up and creaked to a stop at the loading entrance. The tires were clogged with slush and the fenders rimmed with muddy ice. Delbert helped lash the luggage to the roof.

The door to Helder's office popped open and the lodge owner swayed there, reeking of good Scotch. His natty coat was crumpled and his cuffs were open, splaying over the sleeves of his sport jacket. He lurched out to say farewell to the guests.

"Thank you so much for, *hic,* coming. See you next year. So sorry about this nonsense . . . Marvelous . . . We'll be open by the end of the week."

"Last chance," said Jason to Martha.

She might have gone had Moon not walked into the lounge just then. His hair streamed with melting ice, and his clothes were stiff. He walked to the fire, oblivious to his surroundings, and warmed his palms.

"I'm staying," she said to Jason, her eyes on the Indian.

The van pumped clouds of bluish exhaust, which were torn away by the storm. Delbert leaned out the window and shouted to Jack Helder, "We got most of them into the Pines Motel and some others into Howard Johnson's down in Clayton."

"Excellent," hiccupped Jack Helder. "Fine people. Give them my best."

"When are you coming down, Mr. Helder? The road's getting bad."

"In my own good time, Delbert, my boy. It's my home, and no Bigfoot is going to chase me out."

"No *what?*" Delbert cupped an ear.

"Never mind, Delbert. It's all a crock of shit." Helder started back to the door. "A . . . crock . . . of . . . shit! Don't worry, I'll have more fun than a barrelful of boa constrictors. Drive safely, my boy." Helder blew a wet kiss at the sour faces packed against the windows. "Good-bye, my lovelies."

He waved as the van backed around, facing the road, then churned away through the wind-lashed night until the red taillights disappeared. He waved again as he tottered through the door and closed it behind him.

Martha Lucas, Raymond Jason, and John Moon were waiting for him when he stepped into the lounge.

Helder looked at each one of them. "Moon!" he roared.

"Yes, sir?" Moon replied quietly.

Helder pointed a wavering finger at the door. "You missed the van!"

Moon did not deign to answer. He put his back to the fire and watched Jason.

"Didn't you hear the orders of the big bad Forest Service?"

"I'm staying," said Moon with icy finality. "Until my dog comes back."

"Martha!" Helder roared.

"Yes, Jack?"

"What's going on around here!"

"Well, Mr. Jason is staying because Moon is. And I guess I don't have anyplace to go either. I never liked motels. Besides, I've got to think of my reputation, haven't I?"

Helder had the disjointed feeling that he had walked into a room he had lived in all his life and did not recognize it. "But . . . but . . . Oh, the hell with it. Glad for the company. We can all go to Mexico together."

"Mexico?" Jason inquired.

"Yup. Mexico is where we'll wind up if this wind doesn't let up." He sniffed the air. The lodge trembled under a gust of wind. It was still settling its joints. "My little baby," Helder murmured in a loving voice.

Then to the others he said, "Listen to this. You will never guess what Mr. Drake told me this afternoon."

"I can guess," said Jason. "The Bigfeet are restless."

"Is that a crock or isn't it?" Jack Helder slumped onto a footstool before the fire.

At mention of the word *Bigfeet,* John Moon turned toward Helder. What did white men know about spirits? His spirit had returned for him at last.

He looked back at Jason, his hand resting on his belt midway between his medicine bundle and the knife.

13

Duane Woodard was stuffed against the rear door of the van with his legs crowded up by the luggage piled in the center. The van was being boxed violently around the road by wind bursts. He could barely see through the little wedges carved out of lashing snow by the windshield wipers. Delbert was hunched over the wheel, trying to see the road through this cauldron of ice.

This whole thing is arranged exactly bass ackward, Woodard thought in disgust. *The bears aren't half as dangerous as this storm.* The van lurched, and his overnight bag fell from the top of the pile to his feet.

How they got down the road without tumbling end over end was something Duane Woodard would never understand. The road leveled out, and presently he glimpsed the two red bridge reflectors.

Now that bridge is covered with ice. It's like a skating rink on top there. He wondered if he should close his eyes, as some of the other passengers were doing, but decided he might need to see what was happening.

All the passengers had slipped on their overcoats. Duane pulled his pile jacket from the luggage and angled one arm into it. He was straining for room to get the other arm in when he saw something dark, lit for a fraction of a second by the brake lights, scurry past the rear window.

A man, he thought in amazement. *There's a man out there!*

The reflectors slid to both sides of the van and they were on the bridge. Duane zipped his coat up.

The windshield cracked into thousands of starred frosty fragments held together by safety gum. Delbert touched the glass. The ventilator window by his head exploded inward, and a rock hit his skull.

Delbert slumped over the wheel, throwing the passengers out of their seats and sending luggage tumbling in every direction. Duane Woodard grabbed the door handle and pushed it down. He opened the door, letting in wind and snow and the rumble of the river far below.

In the red glare of the taillights he saw a long crack break the mantle of ice and snow on the surface. *The bridge is going,* Duane thought dully. *Goddamned bridges, nobody knows how to build them any more.* The van hit the railing, tumbling the passengers to the floor as they tried to climb out the door. Duane Woodard popped out to the ground with a heavy impact that knocked the wind out of him.

The rest happened so fast that Woodard was unable to reconstruct the events in order. The rear wheels were churning fountains of snow on him as he crawled past the widening crack in the road. The railing crumpled like tinfoil, its stanchions breaking loose. The van flipped over the side; the wheels, deprived of traction, screamed for a second in mechanical agony; then there was a metallic splash, followed by the drumming of metal struts, concrete blocks, and railings falling into the river.

Duane scrabbled, like an ant trapped in an ant lions' collapsing cone, to the highway as the serrated crack became a chasm in the center of the bridge. Under the twin forces of wind and swollen, rushing river water, it crumpled in on itself and flew to pieces. It was not until Woodard had caught his breath and turned around, expecting to see more escapees climbing to their feet, that he realized he was the only one to get out.

The speed of the catastrophe benumbed him. He looked down at his feet, his torn jacket and ungloved hands turning into frigid lumps of marble in the cold.

A final hunk of concrete gave way and tumbled down into the gorge. The bridge was not just weak. The bridge had been sabotaged.

Being a hopeless optimist, Duane was certain that somebody must have gotten out through a window after the van hit the water. He tramped around the ground, looking for a path leading into the gorge.

With a furious yapping, a ball of snow-fuzzed canine fury surged out of the wind.

"Hey, boy," said Duane Woodard, kneeling down and coaxing the dog. "Who do you belong to?"

Feet crunched through snow off to his side. A black cloud burst out of the storm, a boulder held high above its head. Woodard did not have time to wonder why it looked like a bear or smelled so ghastly as the rock slammed down. Adrenaline triggered by the ferocity of the attack impelled him to jump sideways as the boulder socked into the snow. The figure closed long fingers over its rough edges and picked it up again.

The dog lunged at him, and Duane kicked the beast onto its back. He scrambled to his feet with a rock of his own and flung it at the thing, affecting its aim as it threw the boulder a second time. It landed clear, and Duane put away all thoughts of rescuing passengers. He ran for the road.

Another rock hit his thickly padded shoulder, and he slipped over the tarmac. The snow was up to his knees, slowing down his movements.

He heard snow crunching off the road to his left. The thing was pacing him. Thing? Why did he think that? It was some psycho local boy who liked auto accidents, wasn't it? Big, though. Farm guy.

Duane instinctively stopped and jumped backward. Another rock made a hole in the air where his head had just been.

He was good with those rocks. He was better than Duane with a football. He had a fur coat, didn't he? Had to. Arms and legs and everything.

Duane broke into a run, chewed up a few yards of road, and stopped to listen again. The psycho made a growling sound. *Ahead of him!* He had run clean past Duane and headed him off. Duane cut off the road into the crumpled, ridged meadow, where dead trees swayed and branches covered with snow humped the ground. He heard the guy coming after him.

A tree branch propellered through the air against the wind and clawed up the ground, entangling his feet and tripping him. Duane rolled over as whoever or whatever it was bounded up. He jumped to his feet and ducked past a mountain of fur and gristle back toward the road.

That was not a man!

Fear rose like smoke from Duane's vitals up through his chest and permeated his head. He zigzagged his way back to the highway through clumps of buried grass and weed as the snow whirled around him. The ground formed ripple-shaped hummocks, their lee sides banked with deep, soft snow. That was when Duane had his idea. It was not a good idea, but ideas of any kind were hard to come by in this particular situation. That thing was a living snowplow, as unheeding of lumpy ground as a locomotive was of stopping. Duane turned back off the road, doubled around a few times, and managed to put some more yards between himself and the thing. He turned off the road one final time and body-flopped deep into a snowbank slanting up the side of a hummock.

With luck the storm would cover up his traces in seconds. He would be buried completely. If not that, at least his form would be indistinguishable from any of the branches lying around the meadow.

He felt the growing weight of snow on his back. He breathed shallowly, so as not to crack the precious mantle as it built up. Driven by the wind, the snow piled against every crevice of his body, the separation of arm and legs, the gentle rise of his back, past his ears and over his head, sending his consciousness into a limbo of unearthly frozen quiet.

It was not a bear, he thought. He wished it were a bear, so it would kill him quickly. More wind. More wind, more snow, let the storm burst open, let the heavens fall.

A foot sank down into the snow six inches in front of his head.

Jason put his fingertips together and said, "Moon? I will make you an offer. I will give you ten thousand dollars cash for the toe in your medicine bundle."

"Sir," Moon answered. "If you come near to me, I will cut your guts out and string them over that fireplace there."

Helder wheeled around in his chair, a Scotch glass in his hand. "None of that, you two. Be nice. Be nice." He sipped his Scotch, then said, "I say. What toe?"

"Moon's got a Bigfoot toe in his medicine bundle."

That detonated in Helder's booze-fogged brain like a slow-burning phosphorus grenade, growing hotter and hotter until its heat broke through his drunkenness. "That leather thing?" He looked at the Indian, mouth open. "Moon, is that true?"

Moon's jaw muscles bunched up. If looks were daggers, Jason would have been sliced to pieces.

Here we go, Martha groaned inwardly as the Indian slipped out his knife. He advanced toward Jason, flipped the knife, and caught it by the tip. Flipping it again, he pointed the blade at him. He smiled so broadly that his face cracked into hundreds of wrinkles, into which his eyes disappeared. "You're making a mistake, mister."

"I don't think so," Jason said, slipping out his pistol and holding it loosely in his hands.

"Yeah, you are. You know why? 'Cause he's *your* spirit, too."

"How do you figure that?"

" 'Cause you're following him, just like I am."

"Hardly for the same reason, Moon!"

Moon shook his head, the smile stamped on his face. "It don't matter shit what your reasons are. Everybody's got different reasons. Every day I said to myself, that's it. I've had it. One more day and if he don't give me my name I'll quit. But you never quit. You just keep after him, and you find out one day he's taken over your whole life." He pointed the knife again. "That's what a spirit does to you. That's what he done to you and me."

"He's got you there," said Martha, wanting to defuse the tension.

"Bull," said Jason.

"It's no more incredible than what you suggested."

"I am following a flesh-and-blood creature, Martha. Not a ghost. That's all."

"But that's just what spirits are to the Indians, Raymond," said Martha, walking over to the fire. "They were alive. They ate and slept and hunted and made fools of themselves. They were so real you couldn't tell them from animals. Maybe there never was that much difference."

Moon was wary of her. She was leading off into tracks of her own. "There were differences, ma'am."

"Yes, but how could you tell a bad one from a good one?"

"You were taught."

"But didn't they sometimes work the way the devil did? The Christian devil? Didn't the bad ones ever convince you they were really good and get you into a situation where you were trapped and didn't know it till too late? That's how the devil works, you know. He comes on like a saint. Or like a poor, misguided, pitiable little bird that everybody feels sorry for. Treachery, John! Didn't the Indian spirits know treachery? Did they betray humans?"

The Indian studied Martha with profound interest as firelight flickered off his knife blade.

"Moon, did you know there's another of your so-called spirits up here?"

Something thumped at the door of the Grizzly Bar. A slow, measured scratching grated, then stopped. "That's probably my dog," said Moon, walking into the bar.

He stopped as the scratching began again from close to the floor. "No," he said slowly. "That's not him."

Jason rose from his chair, cocking his pistol. "Hold it, Moon. Helder, do you have that rifle handy?"

"It's in my office." Helder sidled away and returned with the rifle.

"There's no need of that, sir," said Moon. "He won't hurt nobody." He yanked open the door.

A thousand pythons of wind and snow gibbered in blowing chairs off tables, toppling liquor bottles from shelves and swirling snow into every corner.

Jason crouched behind the bar with his gun.

Nothing there?

No. A hand lay just inside the threshold. Moon grasped it and pulled the body inside, shouldering the door shut. The man's face was scratched by branches, his red hair was clogged with congealing snow, and his skin was pale white, setting off blue lips. His mouth stretched in a smile.

"Hi," said Duane Woodard. "Hot out there."

Woodard sat before the fire, tented in a blanket Helder kept in his office. His clothes steamed on the hearth. He cupped a brandy glass, which looked ridiculously small in his huge hand, and shivered. "Bigfoot!" he exclaimed to Jason. "Ain't that something? I thought they weren't supposed to hurt people." He looked at the Grizzly Bar, struggling to digest this revelation. "He just stood there in front of me for five minutes, then let out a howl that would have broken glass a mile away. I was sure you'd heard it."

"It actually attacked the van?"

"You better believe it. And sabotaged the bridge. I'd put money on it. I never knew they were supposed to be so damn clever." Woodard swallowed the rest of the brandy and lowered his head into his hands as the enormity of it all seemed to hit him in a delayed reaction.

Jason noticed that Martha Lucas had gone white. His quarry had a shape now, a shape, form, and malevolent personality. It was human, *too* human, in fact, nothing like the other two species of Sasquatch. Those mountain men, those pioneers who had been idolized by generations, had inadvertently created a monster.

He came out of his thoughts. "They're sealing the valley off," said Jason. "The only other road goes back through Oharaville, and I bet they've been there, too."

Helder's arms dangled limply over the arms of his chair. He seemed to have shrunk a little. "Mr. Woodard, you don't recall how many people there were on the van, do you?"

"Eight. Nine." Duane shrugged, his head still in his hands.

"Is there the slightest chance anybody else could have gotten away?"

"Not with that thing running around down there."

"But he wasn't down there, was he?" Jason cleared his throat. "He was chasing you. Or at least one of them was chasing you. If somebody got out of the bus to the meadow . . ." He swallowed and his voice died. The silence weighed down the room. Even the fire seemed subdued.

"You said there were two of them, Raymond," Martha murmured. "One to chase Duane Woodard, the other to get whoever got out of the van."

"No," said Jason. "The other one would have gone after Woodard too. The other one must be up in the mine or something. At any rate, somebody's going to have to check out the van. Right now."

"Christ," said Helder.

"There's five of us . . ."

"And only two guns. Yours and mine," Helder said.

"Besides, a man on a snowmobile is a sitting duck," said Woodard. "So it's ridiculous. He could pick you off before you got to the river."

"Two snowmobiles isn't ridiculous," said Jason. "Two men backing each other up. We can leave the rifle here and I'll take the pistol."

"Very well," said Helder, hiccuping as he climbed to his feet.

"Helder, you're so drunk you can't see what you're doing," said Jason.

"The blizzard will sober me up."

"I have a better idea. Moon?"

The Indian had been leaning by the fireplace, well away from them. If Woodard's story had made any impact at all, it was not visible on his face.

"Can you drive a snowmobile?"

An almost imperceptible nod.

"That gives us three weapons. Two guns and Moon with a bow and arrow. Okay with you, Moon?"

The Indian looked away from them. Martha thought for a moment that he was contemplating the stuffed grizzly by the bar, but his eyes were turned inward. His fingers played with the tasseled flap of the medicine bundle. "I will come."

They stacked two snowmobiles with blankets, brandy, bandages, and heavy coats. Jason and Moon wore fleece-lined nylon riding suits with helmets and faceguards. Jason slipped his pistol into a zippered pocket. Moon tied a quiver of aluminum arrows to his back and slid the bow around his chest. Heavy flashlights completed their gear.

Helder shouted through chattering teeth over the wind that rattled the snowmobile shed, "I'll try to raise Drake on the radio. Maybe he can meet you down there."

"Okay." Jason pulled on his helmet and motioned Moon to precede him.

"You first," said the Indian. "I don't want you behind me." He wore his medicine bundle under his coveralls. Tonight he would need it.

Helder slid open the doors of the shed. Jason tested the accelerator on the handlebar, inched forward a few feet, then got the feel of the overloaded machine. Cautiously, adjusting for wind, he drove steadily out to the parking lot and entered the road. Moon followed behind him, guided by Jason's taillight.

When Helder returned to the lodge he found Duane Woodard slipping into his partially dried clothes. Martha sat in the bar, discreetly averting her face.

"I could use about six steaks, Helder," Woodard said.

"Don't you want any sleep?" asked Helder in awe. Physical people tended to intimidate him. After Woodard's experience, he would have taken to his bed with enough aspirin for three days.

"Hell no. I feel great. Little brandy. Little food . . . Ain't you got *anything* to eat?"

Helder took him into the shop, where Duane Woodard gobbled down six Hershey bars. One two three. Pause. Four five six. He licked chocolate from his fingers. "That's a start," he said, fingering a bag of potato chips.

To Martha's disgust, Jack Helder helped himself to a full glass of undiluted Scotch. If this was the way he reacted to emergencies . . .

"Woodard, maybe you can help me with the radio. I've got to call the Ranger station."

The radio was in a small pine cabinet adjacent to the gun rack. Drake had given him an emergency frequency when he began construction, and he rifled the desk, looking for it.

Duane Woodard switched on the radio, filling the office with a skull-piercing static that seemed to drive nails through their ears. He dampened the volume, but even at low level the fuzzy whine was uncomfortable.

Helder handed him the band number and Woodard set the tuner directly over it. He gave the microphone to Helder. "Here you go. Press the button to talk, release to listen."

"Hello, Augusta Station. Anybody there? This is Jack Helder . . ."

When he released the button, Drake was shouting at him: ". . . you to get the shit out of there, Helder! What's going on! Over."

"The bridge is out."

"What!"

"The van fell—" The radio cut off, dead.

Overhead the lights flickered. They blinked in the lounge, too.

"Is something happening?" asked Helder.

Martha ran into the office, her face slate-white, and pointed at the Grizzly Bar. Duane Woodard ran past her, grabbing the rifle from the sofa, to the window. He raised the glass and pushed open the shutters.

The power line ran from a light pole at the edge of the parking apron to the corner of the building. A Bigfoot was pushing the pole out of the concrete, with hollow popping sounds.

"Got him, got him, got him," Duane said to himself.

Sparks of released current shorted by snowflakes burst from the wires as they tore loose. One by one the lights blinked out in the lodge.

Duane slipped the rifle out the window and fired. He was certain he hit it. The ponderous head looked in surprise at him. The body quivered. But it turned and ran around the corner, out of range.

The pole descended in a tangle of wires to the eaves. The top crosspiece punched through the shingled roof in the lounge, sending down wooden bracing blocks, nails, and shingles that nearly hit Martha.

The fire was the only light in the lounge now. It illuminated Jack Helder's sodden figure in the doorway, with the microphone still clutched in his hand. Woodard closed the shutters and lowered the window.

"What is going on here?" said Helder.

"Sssh!" Martha hissed at him. They could hear feet thumping outside. Past the chimney. More slowly toward the leading-entrance door.

"I will not be silent in my own lodge—"

Duane Woodard raised his rifle at Helder. That silenced him for a moment. They waited, barely breathing, as a log settled into the fire, flaring in a bright glow that receded immediately.

"I think I hit him," Duane whispered in the lowest of tones to Martha.

"It might be a her . . ." she began.

"What are you whispering about!" Helder blared.

"Will you please shut up, Mr. Helder, it will hear us," she said. Her voice was still low, but the tone was deafening.

Helder lurched across the floor, tripping over a shingle. "Oopsy," he mumbled with a smirk. They formed a tight protective circle, with Helder as the swaying weak link.

Silence.

"I think it's gone," said Helder.

"I wouldn't bet on it."

"Young man, if you dig that rifle into me once more . . ." Woodard clapped his hand over Helder's mouth and shook his head. Helder straightened his tie and sighed with a guttural burp.

They waited some more. The quiet still held. Jack Helder became impatient again. "Is it the one without the toe?" he whispered.

Martha impatiently shrugged.

" 'Cause if it is, it's in no shape to do anything." Helder put a finger to his lips and started tiptoeing toward the door.

"Get back here," whispered Woodard.

"I just want a little peeky." Helder grinned. "Especially if it's going to put me out of business."

"Helder . . ." Duane Woodard's voice rose.

"It's all a crock of . . . shit." Helder pulled open the leading door. Nothing happened. He grinned at them and stuck his head outside.

In the black square of the door where the firelight did not penetrate, Martha saw an arm, large and bristly as a tree trunk, batter down in a single movement. The sound of Helder's skull cracking merged with the rifle crack slashing around the confined room.

Helder collapsed to the floor. Hands clasped his ankles and pulled his body out the door. Duane Woodard rained shots around the door frame that sent splinters flying. The Bigfoot howled.

Duane waited, wary of rocks. After a moment he heard a thump, and Jack Helder's head bounced through the open door like a basketball. Bile formed a nauseating soup in his stomach. On the sofa, Martha screamed as he kicked the head out and slammed the door.

"Shut up, shut up!" Woodard shouted into her face. He shook her shoulders, waggling her head back and forth like a rubber doll's. "We got to listen for it."

"You've got to get a doctor," she babbled.

"He's dead, so stop thinking about it."

"He's not dead!" She tried to squirm free, but Woodard slapped her into the sofa, where she curled up, a half-conscious ball of heaving delirium.

Duane Woodard ran into the office and returned with the box of shells. He shoved cartridges into the bolt and slammed them home. "You know what this is, lady? This is *psychological warfare*, that's what this is! That's how they win if they scare you. I read about that."

The crosspiece vibrated in the hole, sending more debris clattering to the floor. The pole bounced against the eaves. The giant was ascending the pole to the roof.

"Just like a monkey," said Woodard. "Monkeys are stupid. I read about monkeys." Before Martha could scream at him, he was across the room and out the door.

The wind made his eyes water. He pulled his feet through snow around the corner and looked up to the chimney. He could make that out but not much else. Snow trickled in a continuous powdery stream from the roof.

It was not on the pole. Already the thing was on the

roof. Duane could see firelight where the flames in the lounge filtered through the cracks of the roof.

The cold paralyzed every cell in his body. It covered him like a painful liquid that would not dry off. He raised his rifle toward the roof and found his hands shaking so badly he could not aim.

That was the ball game. He did not fancy wasting ammunition. Regretfully he shambled back to the door and latched it.

"Are there any lanterns in this place?"

"Yes. In the shop."

"How about getting five or six of them?"

The gallery was dark. She looked at it and climbed to her feet. "I don't want to go in there alone."

"I don't blame you," said Woodard. "I'll be right behind."

They collected lanterns and filled them with kerosene while feet thumped against the roof. Duane Woodard pumped pressure into them and lit them one by one. They gave out a hard white glow that softened farther out from the filament. Duane placed them on tables and the floor so as to fill the lounge with some kind of light.

The chimney stones creaked. Some hit the roof and rolled down to the ground. Snow gushed down the chimney, dousing the fire into steaming odorous coals. After a second, chimney rocks tumbled down on top of them.

14

The Indian's snowmobile bounced in swishing heaves, like a boat fighting waves. He felt himself to be on a planet that hated him, an insane world rippled with bone-shattering ridges of ground. The storm tried to entomb him into a block of ice as an oyster coats an irritant with the smooth glossy shell of pearl. The physical anchors of the engine's heat, the pull of the handlebars, and the red glint of Jason's taillight kept him oriented.

His faith was all but smashed to pieces. It had survived Jason's assaults in the bungalow this morning, but the girl's casual remarks had pried it a bit looser. The most savage blow had come from the words of the red-haired man minutes before. His spirit did not kill people! Jason would turn and ambush him at any moment. This was all an accident. His spirit had mistakenly led him into a place where devils dwelled. The cold, the storm, the night ride over this spine-compressing land was all a trap. The vanful of passengers was safe in town.

Yet the strongest assault came from his grandfather's words. His faith could not sustain a betrayal. He would not believe that his "spirit" was a *natliskeliguten*—a devil. Everything—his life, his soul, his sanity—depended on what they found at the river.

They crossed the road well back from the bridge and headed down the lip of the gorge. Jason switched on his spotlight and swept it from side to side.

They stopped at the edge of the black river. Jason's light found a brassiere swept up against a jutting rock. They forged up the shoreline into the gorge, the lights picking out pants, shirts, underwear, sweatshirts with Colby emblems, spilled toilet cases and flight bags mixed with toothpaste and ski poles.

A girl's body undulated half in the water, half on shore, her arm wedged between rocks. The van lay on its back in the middle of the river, square columns of water gushing through the punched-out windows. Some bodies were still wedged in them; others lay against the rocks in the water as though being scrubbed clean for their final journey.

Jason dismounted and walked up to the concrete pillars in which bridge supports had been sunk. The base surfaces had been chipped away. Some holes were gouges, some mere pits, but Jason now knew what Lester's apparition had been doing down here that night.

He ran his light over the concrete. Pointed tools had been used. This was the result of many patient hours of night work.

They used tools. Jason's imagination again reeled with horror. Iron tools, probably, maybe even pickaxes left behind in the Limerick. Perhaps through the years they had glimpsed men chopping wood or digging in the ground and in their huge dim brains the human spark had connected that activity to this bridge.

Jason ran his light over a man lying splayed against the rocks of the opposite shore. The passengers were scattered among the luggage like thrown rags. Faces, some mangled, some peaceful, swam down the beam of his flashlight. Over all was the foaming rumble of the river.

Abruptly Jason could stomach no more. He walked back to Moon, who was kneeling beside the girl, face stony-blank, his thumb rolling back an eyelid.

"Moon, forget it!" he shouted. "They're all dead. Let's get out of here."

The Indian moved his hand from the girl's eye to her wrist, feeling for a pulse. Jason shook his shoulder.

"You hear me? We'll call the Rangers from the lodge." The Indian lowered the girl's arm. He stared motionlessly into the river, with such concentration that Jason involuntarily looked to see if anything was there.

Then the Indian stood up with a slow movement, like a fish laboriously surfacing. He opened his coveralls and untied his medicine bundle.

He took out the toe and handed it to Jason. Without a word, he walked down the embankment to the snowmobiles.

"Moon? Moon?" Jason examined the precious toe in the light. "What's going on?"

The Indian climbed onto his snowmobile and pointed it up the slope. Jason stumbled down the gorge after him.

"Wait a minute, Moon! Why are you giving up your talisman? Answer me, will you?"

Moon roared up the slope toward the road, leaving Jason alone.

With trembling fingers, Jason slipped the toe into a zippered pocket next to his gun and climbed onto his own machine. He shouted at Moon as he drove up, but the wind and the sound of his motor whipped away his voice.

The Indian set a tremendous pace into the wind, but Jason did not mind. All his aches and pains—his sore neck, his injured arm—left him as though exorcised by the toe in his pocket. The greatest of anesthetics is elation, Jason decided. Next to tension, of course. The Indian had given him the toe. It was his.

Those bodies must have jolted the Indian out of his haze. Perhaps they reminded him of Vietnam, a lethal dose of reality if ever there was one. Moon had lost his spirit but gained back his sanity. Not to mention ten thousand tax-free dollars. Jason was euphoric with gratitude. Moon wasn't such a bad sort—a little confused, but he had many fine qualities. Jason would set the Indian up for life. He would give him a job with his company, a good one, if he wanted it.

They were ascending the road, almost halfway to the lodge, with the Indian still far ahead, when Jason was attacked.

A rock popped out his headlight. Jason decelerated and crouched over his handlebars. He pulled out his pistol and fired into the air to signal Moon.

He swerved into the meadow. The snowmobile jounced off the road and snagged a branch with the front ski, raising a curtain of snow that blinded Jason. The snowmobile hit a sharp hummock, knocking the handlebars into Jason's chin. He toppled off the seat. Riderless, the machine careened crazily around the meadow and stalled.

Plastered with snow, his head swimming from the blow of the handlebars, Jason got to his hands and knees clutching the pistol in his right hand.

The dog! Watch out for the dog! Woodard had warned him that the dog was like a pilot fish for a shark. His appearance always preceded the beast.

From out of the wind came the pup, its fur stiffened by cold, dodging and retreating from Jason. A rock caught Jason full in the chest and knocked him down. He fired at the dog. The animal yelped and bounded off into the wind.

Jason climbed to his feet and ran toward his snowmobile in a crouching stoop. In the Army they had taught him that constant motion was the key to survival.

Behind him! Jason whirled around. The dog was returning. It turned around again when Jason saw it. Jason aimed and fired with both hands.

With a strangled cough, the dog went a full four feet into the air and came down in two bloody pieces.

Jason slowly turned around, praying that his helmet was strong. In the distance he heard the buzz-saw of Moon's snowmobile finally coming to his aid.

The Bigfoot materialized behind his snowmobile. Jason aimed with both hands and fired again. The bullet whanged off the metal.

The giant picked up the snowmobile and threw it at Jason. It bounced over the snow and stopped upside down. Jason crouched behind it as light from Moon's machine spread a pale-yellow glow over the snowy field.

Jason saw clouds of steam from the thing's breath as it shielded its face from the light. It was the same horned beast both of them had followed for so long. Jason steadied his pistol on one of the snowmobile's treads.

The beast jumped out of the light. Jason fired into the storm, the gunflash lighting up ice crystals, but it was gone. Like a spirit.

Moon halted his snowmobile at the edge of the road. He slipped the bow from his chest and took an arrow from his quiver. Then he noticed the shattered remains of the dog.

"That was him, Moon. I think he's headed for the mountain."

Moon slipped off his helmet and flung it into the snow. The wind made tentacles of his long black hair that grabbed and caressed his lean face.

"Moon, I want to pay you for the toe. Really, I mean it. A deal is a deal. I'll get a money order soon as we get back to the lodge."

The Indian kicked at the dog's remains. Then he walked past Jason, following the fast-filling prints of the giant.

"Moon?" Jason called out uncertainly. "You won't find him in this storm."

When the night swallowed him up, Jason saw Moon fitting the arrow to the bow.

"Moon?" Jason called out again. The wind answered.

No, he would not come back. Might as well try to stop the wind. There had been murder in the Indian's eyes. His spirit had betrayed him. His spirit and that ridiculous hound had been his whole life. His existence was thin ice through which he had finally plunged into empty cold darkness. The bottom was gone, the foundations smashed utterly and finally. Jason knew that feeling. He had barely survived it himself. He did not think the Indian could.

He slipped the gun into his pocket. And then horror chilled him to his very marrow. The toe was gone. It had flipped out when he took out the gun.

Jason went completely to pieces. He clawed through the snow on his hands and knees. He had been *here* when attacked . . . no, no, he had opened the pocket *here!* He traced the marks left by the snowmobile, his fingers turning over every toe-sized clump of earth they found. Every few seconds his hands scratched at his coveralls, searching for the telltale lump that would signify that he had only overlooked it, long after reason told him it was gone for good.

The scanning traffic monitored by the radio at Ranger headquarters was concerned mostly with highway-patrol dispatches closing off roads with storm warnings or spotting fallen phone lines. These were normal occurrences for a blizzard. For that reason, Drake was unable to make up his mind whether the interrupted broadcast from Colby signaled a disaster or just more of Jack Helder's poor luck.

Drake had asked the cops to test the tower on Mount Crane to see if the lines were down up there. When the calls came through perfectly, he knew the trouble was at the lodge itself.

Helder had solemnly sworn to have all the guests in a Garrison motel by eight o'clock. Drake had called them, and they said they had expected another group of passengers momentarily. Momentarily stretched into half an hour, and the van still did not show up.

At eight fifteen he received a call from the hospital in Garrison. "It's about that blood?"

"What blood?" Drake asked. "Oh. That blood."

"Right. We classified Mr. Cole's from the body you brought in. We've been trying to get a line on the other stuff."

"Okay. Fine. What is it?"

The doctor paused. "Well, that answers my question. I was about to ask you."

"Uh-huh."

"I believe you said it was a bear."

"Did I?"

"Somebody said it was a bear. We checked that. It's not a bear. It's not a deer, either. Did Lester keep hogs or chickens or anything?"

"Try human." After hanging up, Drake shouted, "Tony?" Jones looked in the door. "I hate to do this, but take Wallace and run up to Colby Lodge."

"You mean now?"

"Yeah. You'll have to go through Oharaville. Helder said the bridge was out. Take some extra lights and a tow truck. And all the firepower you want, short of flame throwers."

"If I see one of those things, boss, I'll kill it."

"You do that. Just don't shoot somebody in a fur coat."

Drake poured coffee into a cup and stirred slowly. Wouldn't you think Helder had batteries for that radio? Maybe he didn't know where to put them. Drake would like to tell Helder where to stick his batteries.

Wallace and Jones dressed in quilted jackets next to the tow truck in the garage. Both carried heavy .30.30 deer rifles with starlight scopes for night shooting.

Wallace took down two snowmobile helmets and handed one to Jones.

"You're kidding," said Jones.

"I'm not kidding. They throw rocks, remember? That's what Lester said the first time he saw one."

Jones sighed and took the helmet. They climbed into the truck cab and started the heater. As they drove out, Wallace lowered his window a bit and put out the gun muzzle. He was ready for anything. Jones hoped the grease in the rifle didn't freeze up just when they needed it.

15

They barricaded the lounge as best they could.

Duane reinforced the Grizzly Bar windows with chairs and propped tables, the loading entrance with a sofa, which he wedged against the corner, and the sliding wooden doors connecting the lounge to the gallery with coffee tables. The service-entrance door to the kitchen was off its hinges, but there was nothing he could do about it.

Shortly after the fire was doused, the cold began sucking heat from the room. The lantern metal gave off warmth, so Martha kept her hands close to one.

From the parking lot came the steady squeak of springs being compressed. The squeaking continued for a minute, getting louder and louder; then the wall of the shop split and burst inward.

Blankets, paintings, archery equipment, sunglasses— all the paraphernalia in the shop tumbled off the walls. Duane Woodard opened the sliding lounge doors an inch or so and looked at the shop. He was just able to see the wall, which was seamed with cracks and bulged inward. Martha Lucas's Volkswagen had been overturned and pushed against it.

The car was pulled upright. Then it crunched against the wall again, knocking down wooden slats and buckling the ceiling.

When the car was pulled back a second time, there was a hole in the wall through which snow blew. Duane aimed the rifle, expecting the beast.

He kept waiting. He was at the door as a rock smashed against the metal sun-deck shutters behind him. The glass collapsed in tinkling sheets, and a pimple of aluminum protruded inward. More rocks hit the shutters, tattooing their way down toward the shuttered dining-room windows.

"It's trying to draw fire," Duane whispered to Martha. "Keep me pinned down with this hole and raise hell everywhere else." Smart son of a bitch. The open hole was a breach in their defenses which they could not cover yet could not leave. One of them always had to keep an eye on it.

Again there came that tearing stillness, that violent silence that weighed more heavily than the bluntest attack. This time it dragged out into five full minutes. "Listen, do you think Helder kept batteries for the radio in his office?"

"He's very disorganized. If he does, I don't know where they are." She still spoke of him in the present tense, as though he were alive.

"If you can find them, I can fix the radio and we'll have some Rangers up here in five minutes. Check his office, and take a light with you." Woodard edged back to the center of the lounge, where he could watch the shop and her in the office simultaneously.

She went through his desk. No wonder he couldn't find anything—his food bills were in the folder with heat and electricity, a bill for a cord of wood was stuffed back in a drawer. No batteries. They probably moldered in a box down in the basement somewhere.

Alone for the first time all night, she tried to collect her thoughts. This thing was pure concentrated hatred. It or they were not merely wrecking the lodge, but trying to get at them. This was not patience living on a hill watching humans scurry about, this was a primal rage that broke all restraints, including that of self-preservation. Martha sensed that some particular incident must have caused it. Maybe the male's return. Maybe. Though the attacks hadn't started until the incident with Lester Cole. Perhaps there was some connection.

Glass tinkled from a bungalow down in the woods.

"Duane!" she called softly. "It's down at the bungalows."

"What's it doing down there?"

"Maybe it's going away." She put her ear to the shuttered window to listen.

The shutters exploded on both sides of her. Two arms preceded by serpentine fingers broke through and closed around her chest like a vise, hugging her to the wall. "Duane—" she said weakly.

The beast had thrown the rocks to the bungalows to lure her to the wall. The pressure around her chest was beyond belief. Her breath squeezed out, and a groan was all she managed before blacking out in a dim haze shot with blood.

Duane Woodard smashed at those arms with his rifle. He pried at them with the muzzle and nearly sobbed in frustration as they crushed her with her feet off the floor like a bug banded against the wall with metal staples. There seemed nothing left of her body between breasts and hips.

He shoved the rifle muzzle through a crack between Martha's body and the arm and felt it hit flesh. He pulled the trigger. The hands unclasped, the arms snaked out of the wall, and Martha slid to the floor, a small trail of blood trickling from a corner of her mouth.

He frantically searched out a pulse as the feet chuffed down the sun deck and around the corner, headed for the shop wall. Her pulse was strong and regular and her breathing deep although ragged. She had probably broken several ribs.

He ran into the lounge as the beast crashed through

the wall of the shop and into the gallery. He fired toward the partially open sliding doors. The Bigfoot paused, then pushed hard, scattering the furniture like toy boxes. It ducked back as he fired again.

The door shuddered, then split, and the sliding rail tore loose from the ceiling. The doors fell inward with a final grunt of effort and seesawed over the piled furniture. Duane aimed and fired. He hit it. The thing howled. It picked up a sofa and threw it as Duane fired a third time and found himself out of ammunition.

It was a female. The chest rippled with soft breast flesh, and it was smaller and lighter than the beast that had chased him across the meadow.

He threw the puny rifle at her, and she caught it. She broke it in half and came for him, arms reaching out, the hands passing in and out of shadows from the feeble lantern light. The other one had walked fifty miles without a toe. Her fur was thick, her body massive and quick. She seemed almost unhampered by her wound.

Duane backed up and stumbled over a sofa. She tried to close with him. He ducked away, nearly fainting from the musky stench, and grabbed a poker. He faked a move toward the gallery, trying to keep her away from Helder's office. She moved to block him, and he jabbed her with the poker. He was rewarded with a screech that impelled him to try again. She flicked a huge arm, and he ducked and jabbed hard. This time the tip came back coated with blood.

As they circled each other, Duane deliberately avoided looking at her face. Those hands that opened and closed spasmodically, those fingers—they were the real danger.

Duane grabbed a lantern and flung it to the floor. It exploded in a sloppy pressurized burst of kerosene that flooded the floor and drizzled in rivulets on the walls. So much for animals being frightened by fire. She stepped, fur-armored and untouched, right through the stuff and kept coming. He swung the poker at her head, felt it graze the thick skull. She grabbed the poker out of his hands and tossed into the fireplace.

Her breath floated out in a steamy cloud, forming ice crystals over the fur on her chest and face. He heard a snowmobile buzz on the road.

Abruptly, she rushed him. He swung his hand edge outward like an ax, but missed completely, for she bashed the furniture and went full length through the plate-glass window of the shop. From the shop she ran through the hole to confront the returning snowmobile.

In that moment of stalemate Duane managed to beat the fire out with a rug. He ran into the office to find Martha Lucas sitting up on the floor, her hand holding her chest.

The lodge had disappeared. The lights were out. Jason crested the drive to the parking apron before realizing that the building was almost in front of him. He saw a burst of flame through chinks in the Grizzly Bar window, then furniture thumping around.

He took out his pistol again as the female burst from the shop wall in a flying edge of broken planking and dashed down the parking lot. He gave chase, narrowly avoiding braining himself on the fallen power pole, swerving between Helder's Cadillac and the overturned Volkswagen, but she was well into the woods behind the bungalows when he reached the corner.

His pistol was empty, anyway. He crouched against the wall and reloaded it. He fired into the woods to light up the trees. Nothing moved. Nothing lived. But she was there.

Jason stood guard at the little blood spot where Helder's head had lain as Duane Woodard moved Martha Lucas into the lounge and laid her on the sofa.

Jack Helder.

A house whose owner has died is the loneliest place in the world. The lodge seemed permanently weakened by his absence, a sort of orphan without whose loving parents the walls would collapse as surely as a house of cards under the slightest pressure.

It was not entirely a delusion. The lounge, kitchen, dining room, everything at ground level was hopelessly vulnerable. It was punctured by weak points which could no longer sustain any attack. The metal shutters would fall if Jason fired.

"Raymond, where's Moon?" asked Martha.

"He went after the male."

"Why?"

Jason knew he could not limn in words the details that would describe Moon's change after seeing the bodies. "Let's just say he saw the light."

"Why didn't you stop him?"

"I couldn't. He walked right past me. He gave me the toe, you see? And I lost it."

"That's why you took your time coming back," said Woodard.

"I'm sorry. How could I know you two were alone? Look, this is no good. She could knock on doors and draw fire until we run out of bullets. Is there one solid room in this place?"

"Maybe downstairs. The game room." Martha coughed at the acrid smoke hanging in the air.

"What's it like?"

"It's part of the foundation. The only way through is oak doors. There's a corridor going in front of it to the furnace and generator room. Jack had to dynamite it out of rock."

Jason helped her sit up. Something was wrong with her ribs all right. She was in intense pain, both psychic and physical, and trying hard not to show it. Jason found himself admiring her a bit more than objectively.

Something rattled the shutters, freezing them into statues before they realized it was a branch. "We better do *something*," said Duane Woodard. "We're all going to go nuts if we don't do *something*."

"Martha, did Helder have a flare gun?"

"No."

"What about those ski torches they use in the show? Where did he keep those?"

"In the snowmobile shed. He was afraid of spontaneous combustion."

Jason kicked at a footstool. "Terrific! She's boxed us up like a present. We can't shoot flares, we can't call anybody on the radio, we can't do anything. All right. Load up, Woodard. Let's take a look at the game room."

Cozy was the ideal Helder had aimed for with the game room. A quiet, secure place where people could wait out blizzards at pinball machines, card tables, and televisions, or lounge in artfully arranged corners filled with over-stuffed furniture. It was a miniature of the lounge upstairs, less spacious, with a smaller fireplace, but a compact little standing bar, low ceiling, and exposed beams. Since they were below ground level, there were no windows. Jason lit the candleholders embedded in the beams and spaced the lanterns around.

They moved pinball machines and sofas to the door. They lifted the machines off their casters. They were heavier than any furniture.

The storm was muted by the plaster-and-stone wall to a distant roar. If she gets us in here, Jason thought, she'll have earned her heads.

Somewhere on a great golden plaque outlining the sins

of Man, stupidity was underlined with heavenly forceful-
ness. Poor, poor humans. They should not depend on their
gods so much, because their gods were too much like
them. Well, his grandfather had warned him of that, too.

The Indian ran over the snow, following the footprints
of the giant, deliberately not using the word *betrayal* in his
thoughts, for he would fall down and cry. All that was left
was a chance to redeem himself, some tiny sliver of pride
to polish as a shield against the monstrous humiliation he
felt.

Under the Indian's running feet, the ground began a
slow steady rise up a slope. The Indian paused only long
enough to empty his medicine bundle of the accumulated garbage it contained—chicken foot, corn kernels,
clay pipe, the worthless crucifix, even the medal—while
following the plowed-up snowdrifts the running giant had
left. From time to time the wind shifted, bringing down
the thing's smell. It was frightened. Good.

He lost the trail in the sparse, tangled trees and rocky
ledges of the higher slope. He leaned against one of the
pines pushing up through the tangle of broken rock
terraces to catch his breath and plan his next move. The
driving wind made his eyes water, and he rubbed away
tears until the flesh was sore.

Smoke.

The Indian sniffed the freezing wind. Again he smelled
the lightest delicate touch of wood smoke, coloring the
blizzard as gossamer-pink colors the air. There were no
houses up here.

The smell led him to a cave higher up on the slope. It was
like a mouth concealed under shelves of rock. Mixed with
it was the odor of the giant. The Indian pulled himself
up to the entrance and strung an arrow onto the bow. He
stepped just inside the cave, out of the wind, and listened.

He was in a narrow passageway connecting to a mine

shaft. Light shone in a faint smoky glow down this tunnel. The miners had broken into this cave.

The Indian crept forward to the shaft entrance and looked down it. The light came from rudimentary candles made of animal fat poured into rock depressions on the walls. The wicks were pieces of brush that sputtered and hissed. These smoky flickering lights lined the walls all the way down to a corner. Mixed with the acrid smoke and giant smell was the overpowering one of spoiled meat.

Lying by the opening between cave and tunnel was a neatly stacked, roughly human-shaped pile of rocks. The smell came from it. The grave was surrounded by a circle of carefully arranged acorns. It was a small grave, signifying the death of a child.

The spirits went when the world changed. The white man brought his own spirits. Let his spirits protect you, John, otherwise you're as naked as a child.

Don't think about it. The Indian skirted the grave and stepped into the tunnel. In doing so, he walked into a horror that nearly made him faint.

Several cubicles had been blasted out of the rock by miners and used for storage areas. Some were still in use. There was an ancient pile of pickaxes, pitons, and old candlelamp hats stacked in one, along with a fiberglass helmet stamped with the name Jameson. Some of the cubicles had also been used as graves, but of a different type from the one on the floor. Here the bodies had lain exposed. All that was left were bones, complete skeletons like none the Indian had ever seen in his life.

The bones belonged to infants so deformed that they could not have survived a single hour after birth. He turned up one tiny skull with a single eyehole set on one side, a misaligned jaw with huge incisors and a thinned layer of bone where the other eye should be. He found spines looped in circles, legs that articulated backward, doglike crouching demons with little human heads, and one skull fused tightly to a breastbone without a neck. They were tiny, pitiable bones.

His spirit was a monster. The white man had been right. The Indian had seen deformities before, mostly misbred dogs and horses, weak and sickly and crippled. Those were one-shot accidents. This nightmare had taken generations to produce.

The smoke thickened against the ceiling, flowing its silent way upward. There were cracks in the roof, through which it disappeared. The tunnel had careful, constant ventilation. The Indian followed the lights. He passed a cubicle whose roof had been chipped to a cone with a smoke hole in the center. Hickory branches smoldered on a rock shelf. Sides of meat—deer, bear, squirrel, even fish—were stacked and hung from branch crosspieces.

Around a corner was a vaulted room with a light that painted the opposite room. Upon this wall the Indian saw the shadow of the giant, elongated and wavering with each flicker of flame. He drew back his arrow and stepped in front of the entrance.

The giant was standing by a large candle. He had been waiting for the Indian.

A small niche had been carved into the wall at floor level. Surrounding it was a pile of acorns. Within the niche was a human skull propped on a metal miner's spike that had been rammed into the rock.

For a moment the only sound was the crackle of the burning hickory branches and the beating of their own hearts. The Indian looked squarely into the giant's face.

"*Natliskeliguten,*" said the Indian.

The red eyes went down to the bow and arrow. His breath wheezed out of the thin nostrils. Then the horned face looked up at the Indian again, and the mouth split in a grin revealing large yellowed molars.

"You betrayed me," the Indian said. "You kill people. You're no spirit. You can't give me a name."

The face contorted into something resembling hatred. The head swirled with greasy smoke from the candle.

The Indian stepped warily back, planning to sink the arrow in its chest in one quick movement.

The giant flicked out his arm with the speed of a striking cobra. He splashed out the candle in a sizzle of hot fat as the Indian loosed his arrow and heard it clatter along the floor.

The Indian stepped down the tunnel and kneeled on the floor, covering the doorway. The giant walked out. The Indian fired an arrow into its leg.

The giant walked away from him up the tunnel, the arrow bouncing like a poorly attached pin. His hand grasped it, pulled it free, and threw it away. The next arrow sank into his shoulder. He pulled out that one and crumpled it.

The Indian drew a third arrow and walked up the tunnel too. Blood glittered on the floor. The giant did not try to run. He did not turn to attack. He merely walked steadily up past the smokeroom as the Indian coughed his way along behind.

The giant paused at the small grave and looked down at it. Then he doused one of the candles, cutting the light severely. Then he entered one of the cubicles, and the Indian heard him moving equipment.

The Indian waited with growing puzzlement, with the string pulled back till it bisected his nose. The giant backed slowly out of the cubicle carrying a wooden box.

"Look at me," said the Indian.

The giant looked at him. Through the peepsight of the bow, he saw the fading, flecked paint on the box reading

DYNAMITE. The giant raised the box high over his head, ready to smash it to the ground.

He was killing himself! Next to the grave of the child. The last *natliskeliguten,* the one that Coyote missed, was ending his own life without the Indian's help.

The Indian released the arrow and dropped to the floor without seeing where it went. He heard the box smash on the rocks, then the soft plop of an explosion that blew dynamite tubes over the floor. These exploded on impact with lazy, weakened detonations that pulled the walls and ceiling down around the giant.

When the Indian looked up he saw a groaning mass of rock blocking off the tunnel. One last light wavered on the shaft. Guttural rumbles sounded from deep within the walls.

The Indian leaped up and ran down the tunnel as the collapsing ceiling sent a plug of concussed air down the shaft, dousing the lights.

He snatched a handful of smoldering hickory sticks from the smokeroom, their weak light the only illumination to be found in the mine. He was running down the shaft, deeper into the mountain, holding the sticks aloft like flags, when thousands of tons of granite, limestone, slate, and lastly that vein of copper ore for which those rabid miners had searched in vain, came down in a long, trembling, settling, endless crunch like jaws grinding together.

Jones and Wallace were cranking gears up the back road into Oharaville when they heard the rocks coming down. They knew immediately that Colby was collapsing, fatally weakened by the shafts inside her.

Wallace grabbed the microphone and cried, "Avalanche! The mountain's coming down!"

"Ten four," Drake answered in a calm voice. "Take care of yourselves."

Wallace whined into Oharaville and turned hard left up Bullion Avenue. The rockslide piled down over the mine entrance and the mass following propelled stones and trees into the air which rained down on the buildings. The truck windshield splintered, and rocks drummed on the roof. The buildings swayed and creaked under the onslaught of stone and storm. The SALOON sign flipped to the ground like a playing card as the roof was holed through, over and over. To Jones it sounded as if a hundred men were clearing the town away with axes.

The rain of rocks ceased, leaving a smell of mud which dispersed before the wind. Wallace knew that where the shaft entrance had been was now a featureless mass of muddy rubble whose edges encroached on Bullion Avenue. With a final crack, the church steeple disintegrated over the roof.

They listened to the slide continuing over the rest of the mountain. Jones called up Drake on the radio. "We're in Oharaville, and that's as far as we're going tonight. The lodge road is totaled over."

"Was there a slide on the east face, too?"

"Do fish live in the sea?" retorted Jones. "That lodge doesn't stand a chance. It's not so bad in Oharaville, because we're high up. I bet it's taken out most of Hulcher Road on the south, too."

"Ten four. Wait till things settle down, then try to get to the lodge on foot. It looks like we'll have to mount a rescue."

The mountain's thunderstorm belches faded away by degrees. They would rig lines, bosun's chairs, and a temporary bridge to traverse the gorge, Wallace reflected. Then they would rush to the lodge to find it gone. If they were lucky they would find bodies, too, but he would not bet a hog's wart on that.

16

The avalanche hit the lodge like a gigantic ax, chopping away the roof and sun-deck timbers and burying them on their way down the east face. Dust materialized out of the walls in a shroud that fuzzed the candlelight. The ceiling split over the door, disgorging plaster, asbestos insulation rolls, and electrical wiring. The rest of it shivered under the hammer of rocks. Cracks appeared and raced out to link up with each other. Duane Woodard scrambled under a table with Jason when his section of ceiling split and dumped muddy snow and the crumpled fender of Helder's Cadillac on his table.

The avalanche muted to a sibilant hiss of smaller stones and straggler trees. Sheet ice from snow melted by friction and refrozen by the storm oozed through the ceiling gaps. The groans faded, and the walls of the game room held.

Duane Woodard and Jason moved the billiard table and pinball machine from the door. They opened it slowly, ducking debris cascading in. The corridor was now a parallelepiped, with angles of ceiling and wall bent toward the east. It was clogged with rocks, plywood, more insulation, and mud. The stairs led upward to nothing; the ground floor was a mass of rubble.

"Everybody all right?" asked Jason. "Martha?"

"Fine," she answered in a tired voice. "What happened?"

"A mountain fell down on top of us. That's what happened, lady," grunted Woodard. He joined Jason by the rubble and looked at the stairs leading nowhere. "Half a mountain, anyhow. I bet that Indian had something to do with this."

"No takers," commented Jason. "Drake said that mine

was full of old dynamite. Maybe he lit a stick and threw it at the thing." He looked back at Martha Lucas. "Or something like that."

She remembered Moon's dark, fathomless face as he had looked at the leering grizzly earlier that night. A stuffed grizzly. A skin full of cotton. A spirit that wasn't a spirit. When the gods died, so did the worshippers.

The furnace door was jammed open by a crushed door frame. Jason said, "Do you smell something?"

Woodard wiped his nose on his sleeve and sniffed. "Fuel oil, ain't it? The tank must have busted."

"Martha, what's in there?"

"Generators," she whispered. "Water tanks. Stuff like that. There's a door leading—"

Jason hissed and held out his hand for quiet. A small, liquid tap came from the door. A splashy tap. It was followed by another, and mad joy seized Jason like a drug rush that overwhelmed his tension. "It's her," he whispered. "She must have got in before the avalanche hit."

Jason found his gun on the floor. He slipped on his jacket and put the extra box of shells in the pocket. Then he grasped Martha's arm and pulled her to her feet. "Upstairs. You and Woodard. Get going!"

"Leave her alone, Jason," said Woodard in a cool, low voice.

"No way. You hear me, Woodard?" Jason's eyes were wild.

Woodard peered down the hall at the furnace room. "I don't know about that. Somebody ought to back you up . . ."

"I don't need anybody's help."

Woodard glanced at Martha and scratched unhappily at his chin, wondering how to handle the situation. "Mr. Jason, I know I hit her a couple of times with the twenty-two."

"Spitballs, Woodard! Twenty-two-caliber spitballs!" He held up his .38. "Couple of these. That's what it takes."

"Then let the Rangers do it," pleaded Martha. "Forget it, Raymond, you've gone far enough with this."

"She killed Helder, didn't she?" said Jason, stung by her tone. "And you. She nearly got you—"

"What do you care!" Martha cried. "I mean, what the hell do you care about me or Helder or Moon or anybody but yourself?"

"Keep your voice down!"

"You've been shooting them, you've been stalking them, you've been setting traps for them ..." Her voice rose. "It's your fault they're killing people, Raymond, it's not them, it's you! Moon was right, you're just like him! *What do you want from them!* You're—"

Jason slapped her.

"None of that, Jason!" said Duane Woodard, picking up a broken chair.

Jason made a motion with the gun. "Everybody calm down. You stay put, Woodard. She's hysterical. Look at her! Take her upstairs."

Martha walked past Jason to the corridor. Woodard tossed away the chair with a grimace. "It's okay by me. Hell, you want a Bigfoot rug that bad—"

"I do. I'll be up with one in ten minutes."

"Yeah." Woodard sounded unconvinced.

Another small tap from the furnace room. She was still there.

He found a flashlight in one of the drawers. The cold had numbed his fingers, and he had to exercise them to get the circulation going. Firing a handgun was a matter of wrist control. Dozens of tiny interlocking muscles determined whether a shot went true.

Jason breathed deeply in anticipation. He was in control

now. After tonight he would relax completely. Nothing could possibly go wrong now. The bullets were notched and would mushroom on impact. That female was dead.

His search was over.

He loosened the flashlight lens to throw as wide a beam as possible. He tiptoed over the rubble to the furnace door. He could feel the gigantic presence inside as palpably as his nose smelled the fuel oil.

He kneeled before the doorway, flashlight in one hand, gun in the other. From the furnace room came the wet clink of something hitting a pipe. He clicked on the light.

And cried out in shock. She was six feet in front of him, a rock clutched in a raised arm, eyes flashing green from the light.

Jason rolled aside from the doorway. The rock did not fly out. Rather, she moved into the deeper recesses of the furnace room, her feet making sticky sounds in the black layer of fuel oil that coated the entire floor.

She had a horned face, just like the male, with that fixed thin smile. Jason thought he glimpsed a bloody hole on her shoulder, with tangled fur.

Inside a rock clanged against a pipe.

What was she doing?

Jason jumped in the doorway, squatting, light flashing around. The room was full of humps of machinery and heavy pipes. One of the humps scuttled behind another one, and again he heard a rock click against metal.

A huge, long-fingered hand poked out from behind the furnace and snatched a rock. She rapped it against a pipe, causing a spark. Flint against metal. She struck it against another rock. Flint against stone. She was making fire. She was going to reduce the wreck of the lodge to ashes. Scatter the ashes on the wind and clean the wind with incantations.

Jason cocked the pistol. He moved sideways, trying to

slip behind her. His feet made wet sounds on the fuel oil. He cut off the light and got behind a pipe as she struck at another rock. This time she got a sizable spark, which pinpointed her position for Jason.

He fired. The bullet struck the concrete floor, ricocheting to the ceiling, striking a spark of its own that ignited the fuel oil. Fire fluffed gently up, covering her escape as she crashed out the door leading outside. It scurried like a hungry ripple into every hiding place, every corner formed by floor, wall, and machinery.

Dammit! Jason felt the fire's heat on his legs as he scrambled to the door and fired at the huge figure running into the trees. Snow spouted from the bullet at the edge of the woods. Stunned and shattered by missing her again, Jason stood just outside the lodge as the flames poured gritty smoke around him.

"Come on, Mr. Jason." Woodard and Martha each grabbed an elbow and sleepwalked Jason to a safer part of ground. The storm had lessened, as though its energy had been mysteriously used up by the avalanche. The fire ate away at the timbers of the gallery like a parasite, determined to chew at its host despite the wind.

The ski chairs had been carried down the slope by the rockslide. They moved to the parking apron as sparks rode the wind down the road. From there they could see well into the woods, which were illuminated by the flames.

Stupid, stupid, stupid. "She got away," mumbled Jason.

"Yeah, that was a real neat stunt, Jason," said Woodard. "You with a gun in the same room with her and she gets away. You just ain't cut out to be a hunter, Jason."

"She was wounded," he said dully. "She can't get much further."

"Raymond, put the gun away. The Rangers are coming." The snow had cleared sufficiently for them to see a line of snowmobile lights far down in the valley. Someone had crossed the bridge already and was on the way up.

Drake, probably, coming up for an explanation. *Have we been shooting at Bigfoots again, Mr. Jason? I see. And how many people are dead in the van? I see. And Mr. Helder, too?*

"It's not my fault," Jason said clearly. The floor of the lodge caved into the fire, sending up a cataract of sparks. The heat warmed the surface of Jason's coveralls. "They're half people. That's why they're killers."

"Raymond, put the gun away," said Martha Lucas again through clenched teeth. "Who gives a damn what they are?"

"The male is dead. She's the last one." Jason made a move for the woods. Martha grabbed his sleeve.

"You don't know that! She could be waiting in there to ambush you. Maybe the male's alive, maybe the avalanche didn't have anything to do with Moon—"

Jason twisted free of her hands. He could hear the noise of the snowmobiles already. *Maybe she was watching the fire. Maybe she was just inside the trees right now, just a few yards away. This time! This time!* He felt better now with every step he took. "I'll be back with a body in an hour," he called cheerfully back to Martha Lucas.

"Raymond, you'll never get them!"

She was a nice girl but she was a mystical Cassandra, which was an attitude he had never sympathized with. Not that he did not admire her still for her fortitude, but his admiration curdled a bit. He disliked being lectured.

Raymond Jason scrambled over the rocks and shattered, tumbled trees well past the fire. On a birch trunk he found a splash of blood thickened by snowflakes, and another one farther on. She had left a trail that all but glowed in the dark.

He slipped the hood over his head and followed the blood into the timbers.

*

The Indian ran through the bowels of the night, guiding the way with the feeble light from the smoldering branches. He did not run to escape to earth again; he ran because he would go insane in this tomb if he paused to think. He was a rat in a maze of stone, a piece of flesh who would thrash away down here, screaming away his mind, running forever into the depths of hell itself without his spirit, without a faith. His flesh-and-blood body would starve in darkness, sealed away forever from light and life.

Sometimes he ran full tilt into rockfalls. Sometimes he nearly broke his ankles over fallen beams. Once he nearly pitched headlong into a pit, which was actually another tunnel opening beneath him.

The tunnels held in the center of the mountain. Here the rock was so deep that surface water did not weaken it. But the collapse had filled them all with a fine soft dust, which grated the nose and lungs.

The hickory shafts smoldered ever smaller, and he stopped blowing on them in order to conserve light a little longer. When they were ashes, he decided, he would dash his head against a boulder and die quickly. He had already tried carving a piece of timber from a beam cut for a torch, but the wood was too hard to catch fire.

Sometimes he tried to pray to his grandfather for help, but he barely remembered the old man. Under the irresistible weight of his predicament, his mind was unfastening the latches to reality which the doctors in the Army had tried so hard to repair. Sometimes he thought he was back in the jungle, but more often he thought he was dead already. Perhaps he had died in Vietnam and this was where he had gone.

He thought about why the giant had killed himself. It had looked at the child's grave before pulling out the dynamite. The last one was dead, the future was dead for its kind. Some kind of grief had consumed it. The great dim brain had concluded that life was not worth living any more. The Indian was now experiencing that kind of despair.

He was in a high-ceilinged tunnel, running up a slight incline. The hickory sticks flared, then faded.

What was that?

The Indian halted and looked at the hickory coals. The sticks had burned down almost to his wrist. They glowed again. This time he felt the caress of cold, fresh air coming from ahead of him.

He walked slowly, holding the light high. He passed a pile of rubble on the floor.

The sticks glowed again. This time the air touched his back.

Oh God, not a trick! Not a playful wind spirit running around him.

He backtracked to the pile of rubble and touched the rocks. There was a layer of melted snow on them. Snow touched the top of his head. He looked up.

The ceiling was some eleven feet high, supported by rocky, irregular walls. In the center of it, several feet from the junctures between walls and ceiling, was a three-foot hole.

The Indian thanked the Black Robes of the mission school. God was good, or at least encouraging. Now the only problem was to get up there. He could not exactly levitate straight up.

He found a fallen tunnel beam down the tunnel. Moving it would have been sheerest agony under any other circumstances, but hope gave him strength. He rolled it down to beneath the hole and, with an effort that should have broken his back, propped it against the wall. It was separated from the ceiling by a good six feet.

He wrestled another beam down and propped it next

to the first. Then, carefully, nearly crushing his fingers in the process, the Indian moved it on top of the first. Wood against wood was slippery, and the walls were soft and gravelly. Using the first beam as a ramp for the second, the Indian braced his feet on the floor and slid the second beam's blunt wooden end against the soft rock.

The wall crumbled out a steady stream of muck and gravel. Then bits of the ceiling fell, widening the hole until finally it touched the wall.

The Indian shimmied up the beam and found a weak foothold in the wall. With his aluminum bow he dug away at the rock, forming more weak niches to serve as handholds. Then he clutched at these irregularities like a fly ascending a wall. His fingers poked through the hole, touched squishy mud and grass, and he pulled himself up and out of the earth like a man rising from the dead.

He was in a ghost town, dead center in a main street that petered out to rocky bluffs preceding more woods, everlastingly damned, lonesome woods. It was bitterly cold, although the snowfall had almost stopped and the wind had died. There were other sinkholes pocking the street, closer to Colby's slopes, all but obscured by tons of rubble.

The Indian crept through the dead town on delicate feet, careful not to force another sinkhole. Not until he was in the woods again, hemmed in by the whispering pines, did he really believe he had escaped.

He prepared himself to die. Better to die on the earth than go mad beneath it. It would be a satisfactory death, if not a noble one. Killing that *natliskeliguten* was a barren honor, for it had done much murder before he even realized what it was. He had even helped it by sending it food, by keeping it alive.

His spirit. His protector.

He would have to die nameless.

The Indian sat in the snow, feeling the cold. It would be

a painless death, something like falling asleep, an endless, dreamless sleep. They would find him frozen, his face expressing no anguish.

He closed his eyes and waited for death.

The cold sank into his bones, but death did not come.

Something irritated his mind, standing between him and death. A thought of some kind. Now that was interesting! A thought was trying to protect him from death.

His protector.

Somebody had protected him like a spirit all this time!

Then, piece by piece, memories surged up from the well of his consciousness like a movie film of an exploding castle run backward, so that it re-formed itself into a fortress. It glittered and shone with the pure fire of truth.

The Indian opened his eyes. He knew what his spirit was!

He covered his face and wept. He was still weeping as the storm passed on to ravage other mountains and the sun slowly rose over the diminished broken hulk of Mount Colby.

THE SPIRIT

17

Drake had expected to find Jason within minutes after arriving at the glowing pile of embers that had once been Colby Lodge. He dispatched Taylor into the woods after him with instructions to bring him back, spitting and hissing if necessary. "Mr. Jason's going to need himself a lawyer for this one." Then to Martha he said, "Why in hell didn't you tell me about this Indian!"

"I was going to. We were going to. We thought he'd leave—"

"Where is he now!"

She pointed up the mountain. "Jason thinks he went up there after the Bigfoot."

"To the mine!"

At which point Martha broke down into tears at the transformation of Drake from a Ranger into a very bad-tempered policeman. Drake informed the state police by radio that a fugitive from Canada was missing and presumed dead. "Unless he's a mole," Drake snarled. "It'll save us all the trouble of burying him." He passed out hot rolls and coffee and arranged to have Martha trucked to the Garrison hospital, where her injuries could be repaired.

After half an hour, Taylor and Wallace came out of the woods, followed by the others. "We lost the trail after about a hundred yards and didn't find it again. Do you want to start a real search?"

"Damned right," Drake replied. He called the state police back and told them a man was lost in the area around Colby. Last seen heading north over the slide area, wearing an orange snowmobile suit and carrying a gun and flashlight.

By the end of the following day the countywide alert for Raymond Jason had become a statewide one. Drake spent a fruitless hour circling Mount Colby in a helicopter while several men poked around mine tunnels for some sign of John Moon. They found nothing. "There's a lot of sinkholes, though," said Taylor. "He might have been lucky. He might still be in there somewhere."

They would spend days at the mine, clearing away tunnels, tapping on walls, calling out Moon's name. Perhaps they would hear rocks tapping in answer. Or perhaps they might find something else down there. But Drake did not think so. John Moon was gone.

At four in the afternoon, he was sitting in his truck, watching the men clear debris away from the mine entrance, when the radio beeped. The hospital had called back about the blood. "Drake, it's human all right, but we don't know what type. I'm going to put it down as unclassified."

Lester Cole might have been a creep, but he was not the type to carve up people on his kitchen table. Whatever he had had in that trailer did not look human to him. Yet blood will tell. Drake had had enough of this business. It was time to consider a little bit of burying in the files. If there were other Bigfoots, leave them be. Leave the whole thing be.

At five o'clock, a car bounced down the Oharaville road. Martha Lucus stepped out, walking carefully to avoid disturbing her taped ribs. Drake was eating cottage cheese from a cup. He rolled down his window.

"Am I under arrest?"

He chewed reflectively looking over her pale, wan face and shabby clothes. They had retrieved some of her luggage from the ruins of the lodge. "There'll be an inquiry, so I wouldn't go anywhere for a couple days. But you aren't under arrest or anything like that." He opened the door to the truck and let her inside. "You better get into bed or something before you catch pneumonia. Where's Woodard?"

"I saw him jogging past the motel. He says it calms him down."

Drake was scraping the last of the cottage cheese from the bottom of his cup. "This Indian might have come out okay if he'd turned himself in. You and Woodard could have backed him up. I don't know about Jason, though. I don't know." He crumpled up the cottage-cheese container and dropped it in the litter bag. "What does he want with these things, anyway?"

She remembered Jason's tight face, his self-absorption, his congenital unease. "A trophy, I suppose. If anybody can get that female, he can. Have you found any sign of her at all?"

"Nope," said Drake. "Which doesn't surprise me in the least. She's real good at staying hidden. There's been people who've hunted these things for years and never found a sign of one."

"Not like these. These are smarter."

Drake let it drop.

"Do you think you'll find Jason?" she asked after a moment.

"Oh sure, we'll find Jason."

"How long do these searches take?"

"For a normal person, about four or five days. For a dead one, just a couple. But for Mr. Jason. Well, now, he could hide in those woods forever. Or he could head on south till he hits California, living off the land like that Indian. And he could walk into a phone booth and call us up and say the hell with it, I'm tired of following this thing. Pick me up. Does that sound like Jason?"

"No," she replied. "He'll never give up."

"That's what I mean. We'll find Mr. Jason when he wants us to find him." He leaned forward to watch the helicopter that still circled Mount Colby. "I wouldn't spread this around, you know. I'd hate the taxpayers to think we were wasting their money looking for somebody who's not going to be found."

All this for an animal that nobody ever heard of. Drake snorted in the truck cab. The whole bunch of them were made for each other.

Raymond Jason leaned over the bank and looked into the mountain stream. A wild animal looked back at him, a forest creature, bearded, with fierce eyes. He sloshed cold water around in his mouth, then spat it out.

He was on a little peninsula of sand jutting into a stream, a good twenty or thirty miles south of Colby, or so he calculated. The female was still on the run. He could not believe her stamina. He expected to find her body under every bush, but so far that had not happened. It was a spotty trail, but he knew where to look—hard ground, spongy grass, surfaces that did not retain prints—and always he found blood. She could not have that much blood left. Even elephants did not have that much blood.

He placed another branch on his fire. It was banked and low so she could not see it. He polished his pistol. He did that a lot when he rested. Just sat on the ground and polished the gun with a carefully cleaned cloth. Minutes before he had shot a bird for dinner. He dropped the empty cartridge on the ground and replaced it with a good one.

Yesterday he had almost been sighted by a helicopter.

They were still looking for him. Let them look! He would return with a body or he would not return at all.

Not return?

He stopped polishing. Why did he say that?

Not without a body, that's what he said. He resumed polishing.

He might have been wrong about her being the last one. She could be leading him to others somewhere. If so, Raymond Jason might find himself in a nasty predicament. They were good at ambushes, as he recalled from the male's activity at the lake. And the bus. And the crash in Canada. All of them ambushes. They could lure you on . . .

He should call for help. He should get to a phone and contact the Rangers.

Except what if they took so long the trail got cold?

Forget it.

He didn't want to face Drake. Fat Drake. The bile churned in Jason's stomach at the memory of that fat, stolid face. He would like to put a fist through that face. The same held for the others, Martha of the gray eminent face, a mole living in papers, and Woodard. Even Kimberly played by the ridiculous rules. Christ! The dregs. Only a carcass of something incredible would shield him from their scoffing, their papers and depositions, their stupid questions. *Look what I found! You did not believe in such things until I showed you!*

Jason stirred the fire. He was getting good in the woods. Tracking came naturally to him now. Once he had been a Boy Scout and liked it. They had taught him how to carve an *atlatl*, an Indian spear thrower. He should think about that; his ammo would not last forever. A man could do anything if he set his mind to it. Maybe he'd make a bow and arrow like that Indian . . .

That Indian.

What was his name again?

Jason crushed his temples with his fists. Wait a minute here, calm down, it'll come back. You've had your mind on this thing too much. You talked to that Indian only . . . when?

Christ Jesus. How many days had he been doing this?

One day. Two days. No, more, many more than that. When had he seen the helicopter? Yesterday. No. Not yesterday, longer. Much longer . . .

Raymond Jason was scared. This was going too far now. Time to call it quits. Get to a phone and call somebody. Go on back to Kansas City. "Damn right," he said out loud to the fire, slapping his hands on his knees. "To hell with her. To hell with the whole thing."

Suddenly she was with him.

She had materialized from the forest, as massive as a mountain and light as a wraith. She stood on the peninsula between the fire and the trees, breathing with a slight wheeze, the flames congealed into two green stars where her eyes would be. He could not tell if she carried rocks or not.

She did not know he had seen her. His fingers tightened on the pistol. He raised it to chest level.

And then, as silently as she had arrived, she was gone. She made no sound on the gravel. No thrash of trees marked her movement. She was absorbed into the timbers as though she had never quite left them.

With a curse Jason kicked out the fire. His exhaustion was dissolved, his hunger diminished, his fears gone. He sprang into the trees after her, hard on the trail once again, every nerve in his body tingling for conquest.

Much later the Indian found the campfire.

The ashes of the fire were scattered across the little sand

spit. He noted with some relief that the bootprints led south. It was warmer that way.

The Indian's moccasined feet padded around the sand, his eyes raking it for a sign. Finally he found one. A shell casing from a .38-caliber revolver.

Gently the Indian picked it up, wiping off the sand. The smell of powder was cold. It had not been fired in hours.

It was his talisman. The Indian smiled in satisfaction as he dropped it into the medicine bundle.

He wept no longer about his own foolishness and the way he had treated Raymond Jason. He accounted himself luckier than most men. He had destroyed a devil and found his spirit. He knew it was a spirit, for it belonged to a mortal whom he had killed with a rifle butt in Canada. His memory had returned.

Painted in hard pastel outlines in the center of his memory was a helicopter spinning downward in a swirl of lights to a shattering crash in the forest. Next to that memory was another one of a surprised white face looking up from behind a rifle as spruce branches were swept away, the mouth open in surprise just before the rifle butt hit.

Sometimes the Indian wondered what the man was going to say just before dying. Beware of the giant. You are betrayed. Something on that order. And though the flesh had died, the ghost had dogged his footsteps. He had tried to kill the devil for him in a river. He had tried to make him remember him at the archery field. And he had spoken the truth on the floor of that little hut as the Indian debated whether to shoot him.

Strange thought. You could not kill a ghost.

Over and over the ghost had warned him about the giant and the Indian had not listened. His protector. His spirit.

The Indian plunged his hands into the ashes of the

campfire. The bottom was warm. The fire was about twelve hours old. He looked over at the woods, half hoping the apparition in the orange suit would appear to give him his name, but he knew it was not there. It was farther south. It was running, though he did not know why. One never knew why spirits did anything.

When he met him, he would apologize to him. Perhaps they would apologize to each other. Both had much to forgive. They might meet tonight. If not, then tomorrow. Or the day after, whenever the spirit was ready.

The Indian splashed cold water on his face and dried it with his sleeve. Night was falling again, and he should get moving, for that was when the spirit walked. Lovingly, patiently, and loyally, the Indian followed the bootprints into the woods, on the trail of the spirit of a mortal who had once been called Raymond Jason.

HUNGRY FOR MORE?

Learn about the Twisted History of '70s and '80s Horror Fiction

by Grady Hendrix

"Pure, demented delight."
—The New York Times Book Review

Take a tour through the horror paperback novels of two iconic decades . . . if you dare. Page through dozens and dozens of amazing book covers featuring well-dressed skeletons, evil dolls, and knife-wielding killer crabs! Read shocking plot summaries that invoke devil worship, satanic children, and haunted real estate! Horror author and vintage paperback book collector Grady Hendrix offers killer commentary and witty insight on these trashy thrillers that tried so hard to be the next *Exorcist* or *Rosemary's Baby*.

- -

AVAILABLE WHEREVER BOOKS ARE SOLD.

Visit QuirkBooks.com for more information about this book and other titles by Grady Hendrix.

QUIRK
BOOKS

Made in United States
North Haven, CT
20 June 2024